Lucy Robertson was bo[rn] [in]
Harambee school in Ken[ya] [and]
London University. She h[as]
Panama. She obtained a [_____] [Gla]sgow
University and is currently working as a research parasitologist
in Scotland. Lucy Robertson's first novel, *Zig Zag*, is also
published by Black Swan.

Author photograph by A. T. Campbell

Also by Lucy Robertson

ZIG ZAG

and published by Black Swan

SUFFER THE LITTLE CHILDREN

Lucy Robertson

BLACK SWAN

SUFFER THE LITTLE CHILDREN
A BLACK SWAN BOOK : 0 552 99551 7

Published simultaneously in hardcover by Doubleday,
a division of Transworld Publishers Ltd

PRINTING HISTORY
Black Swan edition published 1993

This book is set in 11/12pt Melior by
County Typesetters, Margate, Kent

Black Swan Books are published by Transworld Publishers Ltd,
61–63 Uxbridge Road, Ealing, London W5 5SA,
in Australia by Transworld Publishers (Australia) Pty Ltd,
15–25 Helles Avenue, Moorebank, NSW 2170,
and in New Zealand by Transworld Publishers (NZ) Ltd,
3 William Pickering Drive, Albany, Auckland.

Made and printed in Great Britain by
Cox & Wyman, Reading, Berks.

For my sisters,
Jill and Clare

SONNET 60

Like as the waves make towards the pebbled shore,
So do our minutes hasten to their end;
Each changing place with that which goes before,
In sequent toil all forwards do contend.
Nativity, once in the main of light,
Crawls to maturity, wherewith being crown'd,
Crooked eclipses 'gainst his glory fight,
And Time that gave doth now his gift confound.
Time doth transfix the flourish set on youth
And delves the parallels in beauty's brow,
Feeds on the rarities of nature's truth,
And nothing stands but for his scythe to mow:
    And yet to times in hope my verse shall stand,
    Praising thy worth, despite his cruel hand.

William Shakespeare

Chapter One

I travelled with Amelia to the funeral, all the way from London to Stonehaven by train. It was a long journey and was made longer by the main east-coast line being off for some reason: a signals problem at Doncaster, I think. Amelia sniffed crossly and, with the lenses of her half-moon spectacles glinting fiercely, she gouged holes in the face of the British Rail ticket man at Euston with the frost-sharp daggers of her eyes. At least, she tried to do so, but the ticket man, a West Indian with chewed nails and a slovenly, dribbly waistcoat, was imperturbable. He dug in his black whorly ear with his little finger and looked casually away from Amelia's angry face. Amelia walked away with short fast steps, her heels clicking crossly on the grubby floor of the station concourse, and I followed her, reckless and clumsy with the luggage trolley. We caught a train which went up the other side of Britain instead.

It was, as I said, a long journey. Amelia had two novels, Czech or Hungarian authors, three newspapers, *The Times,* the *Telegraph* and the *Independent*, and a bag of mauve fluffy knitting with a complicated pattern. I wrote a dull letter to Billy, my son in New Zealand, and looked out of the window at the chugging grey-green countryside, the towns of red brick terracing and quiet chimneypots, and fell asleep. When I woke up again we were somewhere in northern England, stopped at a drab station with an unmemorable name beginning with W. It was dirty and ugly and tired, just as I'd always imagined this part of Britain would be, and there was a crumbling warehouse with a stark black and white sign on it:

Uncle Freddie's Mint Balls. It seemed appropriate and I giggled softly and looked guiltily across at Amelia, but she was asleep now. Or at least, she had her eyes closed. You could never be too sure with Amelia.

In Glasgow we not only had to change trains, we had to change stations.

'Ridiculous!' snapped Amelia, and frowned at the weary-eyed man at the information desk. Again her heels clicked sharply across the station concourse. The scabby-toed pigeons scattered in short bursts of flight before her.

We took a taxi between the stations, Central Station to Queen Street, even though we were assured that it wasn't far to walk and that our connection didn't leave for another two hours. It was windy and drizzling and half-past five in Glasgow. The pavements were crowded with black umbrellas and there were crisp packets floating forlornly in the puddles in the gutter. The taxi driver was squat and solid. He had a fat black moustache like a sleek caterpillar, and a flat cap. He hunched over the steering wheel and jumped three sets of traffic lights on our short journey. He was chewing gum with a rhythmic viciousness and listening to a football match on the radio. I thought that Amelia might command him to turn off the radio, but she didn't.

'Queen Street,' she said to him imperiously and, pursing her lips, perhaps at the fuddled blare from the radio or perhaps simply because she was in Glasgow, she leaned back in her seat and closed her eyes. I always felt absurdly pleased to meet somebody who appeared to be acting a caricature of themselves and I gave the driver a smiling 'thank you' as we left the cab at Queen Street; I knew that Amelia wouldn't tip him.

We had coffee in an expensive-looking hotel in a square near the station while we waited for our connecting train. The hotel had a glass-fronted terrace with little round coffee tables with pink linen table-cloths and white wickerwork chairs. We sat at one of these tables and gazed out at the rainy street. Everyone outside looked cold and angry. They were walking fast with their heads down and their shoulders butting forward aggressively. I marvelled that there were no collisions, for nobody seemed to be paying attention to where they were going. Although it was only just November there were Christmas decorations already up in the square: a carelessly-pricey municipal effort with lights in all the stunted trees and flashing bells between the lamp posts. Their reflections danced dizzyingly up from the wet pavements.

A smiling girl with dimples in her cheeks and elbows brought us our coffee. A small bitter cup of espresso for Amelia and a cappuccino for me. The waitress gave Amelia the bill and I wondered how it was that people could tell, with barely a glance at us, that it would be Amelia who would pay.

'Horrible night,' volunteered the waitress, but Amelia ignored her. We sipped our coffee and looked out at the damp, black curtains of the evening.

'I hope it doesn't rain tomorrow,' said Amelia suddenly. 'William wouldn't want us to get wet, would he?' I thought, as I glanced at her smeary reflection in the window, that I saw her thin shoulders shudder, ageing her and making her vulnerable. I looked around at Amelia quickly, but she seemed quite composed and there was no indication that she was any older than her fifty-three years. I paused and thought before replying to her remark.

'I'm not sure,' I said.

The train journey from Glasgow to Stonehaven was full of rattles and jerks and long unexplained waits in bleak places with the rain splattering dismally down the grimy windows of the train. The train itself was almost empty of passengers and smelt tired and stale. I looked out of the window, but all I could see was the rain and the mocking reflection of myself, grey-haired and round-shouldered, and across the table, Amelia with her eyes closed. Perhaps she was sleeping.

In the whole of that long journey, William had only been mentioned once. Just that once by Amelia in the glass-fronted hotel in Glasgow while I watched the passers-by and the sad, silly, Christmas decorations flashing in the drizzle. But I thought about William a lot, especially on the last section of the journey from Glasgow to Stonehaven through the night rain. It was because of William that we were making this journey, from the comfortable regularity of our lives in London to the unknown chill of Stonehaven. We were going to Stonehaven for William's funeral.

Chapter Two

Amelia was three years older than me. She was three when I was born, six when I was three, nine when I was six and so on and so on. The gap between us never appeared to narrow, as it so often seems to between other people. In our case, with each passing year it appeared to widen; an increasingly unbridgeable chasm between us.

We lived, Amelia and Mother and me, in a semi-detached house off Tredannick Close in a poky and unfashionable corner of Truro. No grand sweeps of Lemon-Street-style Queen Anne façades here, just a jumbled clutter of small houses and walls of crumbling red brick and corner shops and the dank, dripping shadow of the viaduct. From the top corner of the bathroom window (you had to kneel on the cold polished-slate top of the washstand) you could see the cathedral, just a corner of it, but that was enough. It dominated the whole town, glowering over it like a huge brooding toad. I hated its dark coldness and its looming immensity. I hated the way it refused to let anyone in Truro forget about mortality and morality and God.

Then, in the hot, humid June of 1950 when I was eight years old and Amelia was eleven, William McCullen and his mother moved into the house across the street. William McCullen was nine and a half, and therefore fell exactly between myself and Amelia. He had freckles and red hair and raw elbows and knees. He grinned and picked his nose and read daunting books with long difficult words in them and no pictures, with every appearance of interest. He did

13

the washing-up and climbed trees and was said, by the adults who drifted amongst us in their incomprehensible way, to be very clever.

Us and them, us Wests and them McCullens were linked from the moment the blue Albion removal van rattled the McCullens up the tarmac and cobblestone patchwork road of Tredannick Close, and emptied them out into the threadbare house across the street. Not only did William plop exactly midway between Amelia and me in age, but also we were both families without fathers. We just had to be friends.

My father, Ross West, had died shortly after I was born. I couldn't remember him at all, and I always wished that I had known him. It was not enough to be familiar with his small granite tombstone and the smell of cut grass and wilting daffodils. Amelia, clever, quick, bright as a dewdrop, sharp as a glass splinter, was like Mother. Everybody said so. Surely then, I, the antithesis of Amelia, must be like Father.

Father, barred from active service in the war by colour-blindness and flat feet, had died in a clumsy, foolish manner with neither dignity nor grandeur before I reached my first birthday. A bit of masonry, a gargoyle in fact, had fallen off the cathedral just as he was walking past on his flat feet carrying a pound of sausages and three lamb kidneys back home from Mr Edwards, the butcher. He died on the spot, then and there in High Cross. At least it was quick. The sausages and the kidneys, the family's meat ration, had been taken away by a scavenging dog. It was another reason, I suppose, for hating the cathedral.

'So how did your father die?' Amelia asked William. 'Was it the war?'

We were sitting, the three of us, on the low brick wall that separated the scrubby front garden of our house from the road. William sat between Amelia and me. Amelia had her hair pinched and pulled into tight, uncomfortable plaits that stuck out from the side of her head and made her face look more bright and birdlike

14

than ever. Her eyes, rather small and close together, and the same muddy grey colour as my own, peered curiously out at the world – and in particular at this moment at William McCullen – from behind ugly wire-framed spectacles. Amelia was either long-sighted or short-sighted, I could never remember which.

William was wearing shorts and wellingtons. Between the bagging hems of his shorts and the wide tops of his boots, his legs looked thin and pale and ill. There were scabs on his knees and one had been picked and was bleeding in a bitty sort of way. We had been teasing out snails from the cracks in the wall and throwing them on to the road, making them spin and their thin shells break. It had been William's idea. Amelia had been introducing us, the Wests, to William.

'I am Amelia West and I'm eleven years old and I've won a scholarship to the girls' high school. I'll start there in September. This is Caroline West and she's my sister. She is eight years old and goes to the vocational school on the other side of Truro. She hasn't even learned to read or write yet. And the lady who is helping your mother is our mother and she teaches French and needlework in the grammar school, which isn't as good as the high school.' And then Amelia explained about Father. Amelia was always forthright and brisk and unembarrassed, and I kicked at the wall and looked the other way when she mentioned my illiteracy.

'How do you know that my father's dead?' William answered Amelia's question, jutting his chin out at her. He had a bossy little chin, much like Amelia's. Amelia hated being answered back and she scowled at William while I snickered softly and picked at the grey-green moss in the cracks on the wall.

'What are you laughing at?' William rounded on me. I blubbered my lower lip and wondered whether I might cry. I didn't like this ugly, clever boy. He had a

15

strange rasping accent and his vowels made a hard noise like rusty nails.

'Aw, don't be silly,' said William and pushed me with his hand. It was not a hard push, but his hand felt hard all the same and I decided not to cry. Then he frowned.

'Anyway, my da's not dead,' he said. 'He's in Stonehaven. That's where we're from. Stonehaven. We've left him, me and Ma.' He frowned again and ricocheted two snails off the road and didn't look at us. I could see that his own eyes looked teary-bright and I felt that we had been mean and unwelcoming. But Amelia was not soft like me. She was bright and persistent.

'Why?' asked Amelia. 'Why did you leave him?'

William turned angrily to Amelia and I could see that two of his tears, one from each of his pinkish-blue eyes, had spilled over and left glistening trails, like snail slime, on his cheeks. But he was angry rather than sad.

'Nosy parker! Nosy parker!' he jeered at Amelia. Then, more quietly, he added, 'He wanted to be in the army still. He didn't want to come home to us. He got drunk every Friday and Saturday night and hit us.'

He jumped off the wall, his feet making a hollow glumphing noise in his boots, and stumped defiantly across the street, crunching the snails beneath his furious strides.

'Nosy parker! Nosy parker!' he called back again from the sagging gate of his own new home. He went up the three grubby steps into the house and the door banged angrily shut behind him.

'I hate him!' I said tearfully to Amelia. What I really meant was that I hated fights and tears and hard words.

'Do you?' asked Amelia, looking at me curiously from behind her spectacles with those bright, clever eyes. 'How silly you are, Caroline, we hardly know him.' She shrugged her shoulders and looked down at the squashed bodies of the snails on the road.

'Come on,' she said to me, 'let's go inside and look up where Stonehaven is in the atlas.'

I lingered behind her for a few minutes, gathering up the snails who had had the good fortune to evade William's stamping wellingtons. I rolled them gently into the long grass behind the garden wall.

Chapter Three

Amelia was lying on her stomach on the battered rug in the living-room when I went inside. She had her pointed chin cupped in her hands and she was looking intently at the big atlas which lay open on the floor in front of her.

'Do you want to see where William comes from?' she asked me without looking up as I came into the room.

'No,' I said, but I went over and knelt beside her on the rug.

'Here,' she said, pointing to some place on the atlas. 'Stonehaven.'

She had to point out Truro too, down on the spindly, claw-toed leg of Cornwall, before I could properly comprehend that William and his mother had, more or less, traversed the length of Britain to live in that small dark house across the road. It seemed an awful long distance. Especially to me who had never been further than Launceston; never even crossed the Tamar into Devon.

'No wonder he speaks so strangely,' I said wonderingly. I was almost surprised that he spoke English at all.

'Scottish,' said Amelia disparagingly and sniffed. Amelia sniffed a lot; she was allergic to house dust and pollen and cat fur, and our house was full of all three of these. But Amelia's sniffs were often a comment more eloquent than words.

'Scottish,' I repeated and stared wonderingly at the map. 'Scotland.' Even the sea on the map around that small point that Amelia's finger had indicated as Stonehaven looked grey and cold. Scotland was snow and mountains and tartan bagpipers slaying each other in strange, rocky valleys called glens next to rushing waterfalls. We'd had a tin of crumbling shortbread triangles called petticoat tails from Mother's brother, Uncle Tommy, one Christmas. There was a picture of Edinburgh Castle and a deer with multi-pronged antlers on the lid. Now Mother kept the bobbins for the sewing machine in the tin. My knowledge of Scotland was, I realized, rather limited.

'Scotland,' I said again. 'Do you think that they have polar bears there?'

'Oh Caroline!' said Amelia in her exasperated, don't-be-so-silly voice, and scrambled to her feet, closing the atlas with a bang. That was a pity; I'd always longed to meet someone who had actually seen a polar bear.

Mother brought William McCullen and his mother home for tea that evening. She bustled them into our house, chattering all the while and apologizing for the mess, although there wasn't really any mess at all.

'Seeing as you've barely unpacked . . .' she kept saying. Amelia filled the kettle and I carried the willow-patterned plates from the dresser to the kitchen table and looked fearfully up at Mrs McCullen. William's mother was tall and thin and dark. She had short black hair, bushy eyebrows and a mole on her left cheek. There was the shadow of a moustache on her upper lip and her face was thin and pinched. She took her cup of tea from Mother and drank it quickly in noisy gulps.

Apart from her air of worn scrawniness, Mrs McCullen looked nothing like William, and I was secretly pleased. William was like me. He surely resembled his absent father. But William's father was not dead. He lived in cold, distant Stonehaven and hit his wife and son.

'Stop staring, Caroline dear,' said Mother, and I jumped guiltily and dropped a saucer. It broke neatly in half on the kitchen floor.

*   *   *

Mother ladled out soup and there was bread and margarine and two sorts of jam. I was snivelling a little because of the broken saucer and I didn't say anything, but then I never did say much. Amelia was always the one who did all the talking; she was like Mother and longed to chatter. William didn't say very much either, at least not on that first evening. He ate hungrily, stuffing the bread into his mouth with greedy, tearing noises. His bright eyes glanced around the room, his gaze bouncing off the walls, the furniture, his mother's face and the faces of his new neighbours, us, the Wests.

Mrs McCullen spoke like her son, her accent hard and flinty and her Rs rolling and grumbling like waves on a shingle beach. I looked up at Mother to see if I could tell what she was thinking, but her face, bright and pointed like Amelia's, never gave anything away unless she chose to let it.

'Eat up now, Caroline,' said Mother, 'Mrs McCullen and William will be tired.'

'Can I ask a question?' asked Amelia, her voice high and piping. 'Why have you come all the way from Stonehaven to Truro?'

'Oh Amelia!' sighed Mother, and I wondered if she knew about Mr McCullen beating Mrs McCullen and William. I could visualize him so clearly myself: huge and ruddy, freckled and red-haired like William, but with brawny arms and broad shoulders. I could picture his fists, big knobbled hams, slamming into Mrs McCullen's moustache line. I could hear William's squeals as his ears were twisted between his father's massive finger and thumb. I shuddered. Surely it was obvious that they had travelled all this way to put as much distance as possible between themselves and this drunken ogre?

But Mrs McCullen, sighing a little, and turning her empty teacup in nervous circles on the saucer, talked about other reasons: childhood memories, friends, recommendations, distant relatives. No mention of Mr McCullen's fists at all.

'Thank you, Mrs McCullen,' said Amelia clearly, 'we do hope that you'll settle into Truro well.' I could see Mrs McCullen thinking, 'what a polite, intelligent girl,' but Mother only sniffed. Like Amelia, Mother's sniffs were a language unto themselves.

Mrs McCullen already had a job lined up for herself in Truro. She was going to serve behind the haberdashery counter in Hurlinghams, the department store in Victoria Square. She told us that a friend of a friend, or an aunt of a cousin, or a friend of an aunt's cousin, or some other suchlike tenuous connection was married to the manager of Hurlinghams and had pulled strings on her account. I could imagine Mrs McCullen counting out the buttons with her long thin fingers, and measuring out the bias binding into foot lengths. It seemed to me that it would suit her. William kicked me under the table and looked bored and querulous. There was not a crumb left on his plate.

'Mother keeps her bobbins in a biscuit tin,' I said to William, 'with a picture of Edinburgh Castle and a red deer stag on the lid. Would you like to see it?'

Amelia, William and I went through into the living-room, leaving Mother and Mrs McCullen to have a last cup of tea over the debris of our meal.

'Look!' I said to William and showed him the tin with the antler-heavy deer and the cold grey castle on a hill.

'Oh yes,' said William, 'Edinburgh. All the rich people live there and the English. My da hates people from Edinburgh. Especially the English.'

I saw again the rough ham fists and I quickly put the tin back in the drawer below Mother's Singer sewing machine.

'But we're English,' said Amelia, 'and we don't care if your da likes us or not.'

Amelia showed William the atlas and all the miles of safety that lay between him and Stonehaven and the English-hating fists. I crept back to the kitchen door and heard Mrs McCullen saying, 'What a polite, intelligent child Amelia is.' I nodded knowingly.

'Hmmm.' Mother's voice, like Amelia's, was clear and high and carried like a bell in frosty morning air. 'Intelligent, yes. Almost too bright really. She has won a scholarship to the girls' high school. She's not like Caroline at all. Caroline's a strange girl: clumsy, slow. A slow learner. I sometimes worry that she might be simple. She can't even read yet although, God knows, I've tried to teach her. She goes to the vocational school, you know, where even if they can't teach her to read and write, they'll make sure she knows how to turn a hem. And she means well. She really thought that William might like to see my old biscuit tin.'

I crept away from the kitchen door then, brushing away the hot, hateful tears. I'd heard these things so many times before, it was, perhaps, surprising that I still reacted in this way. I listened, as I'd always listened, from behind doors, from under tables, from concealed places that adults never thought might hold a pair of listening ears, and I heard Mother discussing her children with other adults. Amelia was bright and intelligent; she asked questions and she won scholarships and she knew how to seem polite. I was slow and clumsy; I couldn't read or write and I dropped saucers and thought that other people would be interested in the same things as myself. It wasn't fair, and although, deep, deep down inside I was sure that I didn't care, it still brought tears of shame to my eyes.

We went to the front door to say goodbye to the McCullens. We went to watch them cross the road, still spattered with the crushed shells and oozing bodies of the trampled snails, to the gate of their own home.

'Oh!' exclaimed Mrs McCullen on our doorstep. 'Sunday tomorrow. Perhaps, if you didn't mind, you could take us along to church with you. Do you attend in the morning or the afternoon?'

I blushed and looked at the ground and even brazen Amelia picked at her nails. But Mother only smiled.

'I'm afraid that we don't go to church, Mrs Mc-Cullen,' she replied without flinching. 'I am an atheist, as was my husband, and we decided not to inflict religious worship upon our children. When they are adults they can decide for themselves whether God exists.'

'Quite!' said Mrs McCullen and she took William's hand firmly in hers. 'Well, thank you for your hospitality, anyway.'

Scarcely had she finished speaking than our guests were across the road and their own front door had clicked shut behind them. Mother smiled dreamily at her own private joke.

'Bedtime, Caroline,' she said. I could hear Amelia saying something under her breath.

'Ignorant Christians!' she muttered. 'Ignorant Christians!'

Chapter Four

On all the mornings of the endless, drip-dropping Sundays that fell through the weeks and months ahead, Amelia would take up a position by the living-room window. Although she was huddled up in Mother's cushions of patchwork hexagons, and although her hands were busy with stroking the silky fur of the nape of Mother's tortoiseshell cat, a good mouser named Hilary, and although she seemed to be engrossed in yet another tedious book, and although between her and the windowpane was a straggle of dusty, etiolated spider plants, Amelia never failed to notice William and Mrs McCullen setting off for church. Perhaps she heard the sighing creak of their gate or the clickety-click of Mrs McCullen's boots of Sunday shine on the pavement. Whatever it was, Amelia was constant in her observations.

'Caroline!' she would call. 'Do you want to see William and Mrs McCullen setting off for church?'

'No,' I would reply, and if Mother was in the room she might murmur, 'Oh Amelia!' in a weary sort of way, but I always joined Amelia at the windowsill and peered out at William and Mrs McCullen walking briskly down the street.

As well as her shining black boots Mrs McCullen wore a narrow and severe dress, also black, and a black hat was perched up on her head with a sombre, purple-dyed feather, curling backwards, held against it by a satin-sheened black ribbon above the brim. All this fuliginous severity made Mrs McCullen's thin face seem sad and jaundiced, and her yellowed skin clashed unpleasantly with William's red hair. This was smarmed down on his head and plastered damply across his forehead; his face had a scrubbed and raw look. Like his mother, William was also dressed in his Sunday best. William, to Amelia's scornful amusement, wore a kilt of dark green tartan with a red belt and a foolish little leather bag with fluffy tassels swinging from it, a sporran, dangled in front. The sporran was secured to his belt by thin leather straps and it bounced a little forward, and then slapped back against his kilted thighs, with every step.

'I bet that's where he keeps his collection money,' said Amelia that first Sunday as we watched them both stepping out to church.

'And maybe a clean handkerchief too,' I added with awe in my voice, for I'd never seen a boy dressed up in a skirt before. As well as admiring his brazenness, I actually thought that it was quite a jaunty little outfit.

'Perhaps,' conceded Amelia.

We watched them, the thin black shadow of Mrs McCullen and the scrubbed and kilted William, until they turned the corner by the postbox and were out of sight.

'Ignorant Christians,' muttered Amelia beside me. 'Ignorant Christians!' She was to mutter that every Sunday morning as she watched them turn the corner, and never once did either mother or son so much as glance towards our window or even towards our house. Their eyes looked straight ahead and seemed to me to be observing something far away.

William and Mrs McCullen attended the local Protestant church of St Michael. Unlike the cathedral that I so despised and feared, I had a secret fondness for this ugly building with its dumpy tower and rusting iron railings that local dogs pissed and shat against with no fear of divine retribution. It seemed a friendly, homely place and once, at Eastertime, when I had peeked inside, I had been struck by the comforting smell of polish and the sunlight streaming through the windows on to bunches of spring flowers. No huge pillars leading ever upward to a distant vaulted roof and the dark chill of enormity here, but fat wooden beams across the white-painted ceiling and a pair of chubby-cheeked cherubs grinning out from the carvings on the pulpit stairs.

I'd stood in the doorway of the church of St Michael, unwilling to cross the threshold, not in fear of the wrath of a deific being, but because I knew that if Amelia should chance upon me there, the scorn that she would level at me would make me run home crying, my hands clamped across my ears in an effort to keep out her taunts. But Amelia was, on this occasion, safely at home with Mother who was giving her a little private tutorage in French. When I heard footsteps crunching up the gravel path behind me I turned and saw a stoutish man with big hairy ears and a dumpling nose. He wore a stiff white collar that looked most uncomfortable, above which his Adam's apple bulged and trembled nervously. Even I, one of that atheist West family, was able to recognize the Reverend Peploe, vicar of the church of St Michael.

The Rev. Peploe smelt of wet dogs and decay, but his brown eyes were kind and hesitant, and I'd accepted the proffered peppermint from him before I realized what I was doing. Rev. Peploe invited me into the church and offered to show me the ancient font and the brass by the altar, but Amelia's derision drummed about me and I, at the time seven years old, could only shake my head. Still shaking my head, I slipped past the Rev. Peploe's wet-dog bulk, down the gravel path and away back to Tredannick Close and home, spitting out the sucked smooth lozenge of the peppermint by the garden wall so that there would be no awkward questions about its origins from Mother or Amelia. I knew what Amelia, and, I suppose, Mother, would think of the Rev. Peploe. 'Ignorant Christian,' they would think. 'Ignorant Christian.'

Despite this fundamental difference in religious views between us Wests and them McCullens, the

26

friendship between the two families, destined by our ages and our absence of fathers, blossomed. When the summer holidays began, no more than a month after the McCullens had arrived in Truro, William seemed to spend nearly every waking hour, bar Sundays, with Amelia and Mother and me. Although term had ended for us school-goers, pupils and teachers alike, there were no school holidays for Mrs McCullen in the shadowed recesses of the haberdashery counter in Hurlinghams. Gradually, like a piece of furniture, or an ache, or a colour, William became incorporated into our lives until I could no longer remember what it was like without his teasing and his kindness and his endless circular arguments with Amelia. I could no longer remember what life itself was like without William.

It was Tuesday, the day Mother always went shopping. Amelia and William and I went up to the meadows, as we so often did on Tuesdays, and looked down on the world. Directly below us was the railway line, stretching, true as a song, westward towards Redruth behind us, and ahead of us, slicing through the hills northward towards St Austell, Lostwithiel, Bodmin, all safe familiar names, and on again to bleak and friendless places, London, Newcastle, Stonehaven. The little branch line, southward towards Falmouth, was immediately lost in a valley of green. Below the railway lay the town, a huddle of grey and red roofs and the squat, brooding menace of the cathedral. Not far from there the river Fal made its presence felt, glinting fat and glaucous through its swathe of mist and smelling chokingly of decay when the tide was low. Somewhere down there amongst that muddle of streets and people, Mother, pert and organized, bustled about the shops, her mind orderly and her step and voice sharp. Somewhere down there, Mrs McCullen, tall and thin and dark, stood behind the glass-fronted haberdashery counter in Hurlinghams and measured out lengths of braid and counted out press studs, hooks and eyes, reels of thread and packets of multi-sized needles from the rows of fascinating, fussy little drawers behind her.

But we three, Amelia, William and I, lay in the meadows above all this and the world smelt deliciously of sunlit hedgerows and long grass. I lay back and looked at the blue sky and wondered if perhaps, as William had told me, sheep really did turn to clouds when they died. I didn't think so, but, oh, how nice it would be, for sheep, for clouds, for me, if they did. But William and Amelia were arguing again, this time about religion. They squabbled on and on, and round and round went their voices, piercing, defiant and self-righteous, competing with the look-at-me shrillness of the summer grasshoppers, until their words became no more than a muddled jumble and I could close my eyes with a happy smile.

Then suddenly my dreams were interrupted by William, his ugly little face only inches from mine and his hard little hands pushing my wrists back into the ground.

'But Caroline believes in God, don't you? Don't you?' he crowed, forcing me down with wiry strength, telling me to rebel against my mother's words. 'Say yes,' he squealed at me, 'or I'll poke my tongue into your ear.'

'No,' I gasped, but it was more in protest to his threat than in answer to his question. 'No.'

I felt his tongue in my right ear like a hot, wriggling fish. I turned my head away sharply and his tongue was in my left ear.

'No! No! No! I don't know!' I shrieked, rolling and shaking and flattening down the grass about us as I tried to get rid of this hard-handed, clinging creature with his slithering tongue in my ears. But William was satisfied, and he sat back from me, grinning triumphantly.

'See!' he crowed. 'She says that she doesn't know.

28

She's just been bullied into a godless existence by you keeping on at her.'

'And wasn't trying to stick your tongue down Caroline's ear also bullying?' rejoined Amelia dryly.

I sat up, rubbing my ears with the backs of my hands and wishing that they would stop conducting their arguments through me. I hated arguments and hard words with winners and losers and tears. I wanted to watch the clouds and smell the rich, earthy, summer smells. But I had found out that two people can argue so much better, so much more sharply, fiercely, if they can manage to involve a third person. Amelia and William loved to argue, and that third person, the audience to be convinced and persuaded, was nearly always me.

'Stop it! Stop it!' I cried out to William and Amelia, my thoughts of sheep and clouds destroyed by their cross, clever faces and voices. They looked at me then and their eyes went wide with surprise, so I rubbed the grass between my fingers and added, because I felt I should say something else, 'Let's go and see Father's grave.' Amelia sighed and grunted, but I knew that she wouldn't refuse.

'Come on,' she said to William, and climbed to her feet, brushing down her skirt and picking bits of dried grass from her hair.

The three of us wandered westward through the meadows towards the road that led down into the valley away from Truro. It would take us to where Father's grave lay in the cool shadow of a beech tree. Amelia and William were silent, their argument, for a while at least, forgotten.

Chapter Five

Father's grave was in a walled grey-green cemetery
with ash and elm trees and the muffled, forever sound
of a nearby brook. He had been buried here, Mother
had been at pains to point out to her children, and now
Amelia lost no time in pointing out to William, not
because of any affiliation with the attendant grey
church across the road whose shadow fell across a
corner of the graveyard in the afternoon, but because it
was pretty and peaceful, and, after all, he had to be
buried somewhere.

There was a lych gate into the graveyard with
church announcements pinned on notice boards. I
couldn't read them, of course, but I could imagine
what they said: times for choir practice, I guessed, and
perhaps rotas for taking the collection. Between the
notice boards was the long narrow granite table on
which the coffin always rested for a while before
burial. William lay down upon it and closed his eyes
and crossed his hands on his chest.

'Get up! Get up!' snapped Amelia. 'That's not funny!
Our father was once lying there.'

William stood up and rubbed at his bony buttocks.
'Cold and hard,' he muttered to me. 'I hope your da
had some insulated padding wrapped around him.'

I didn't say anything. I wanted to lie on the cold,
hard granite table too and see if I could imagine what
my father must have felt. But I didn't want Amelia to
start nagging at me.

'Let's go and see Mr Ambrose before we see Father's
grave,' I suggested and we went back out of the lych
gate, first me, then William, and behind him, Amelia,

who had been trying to ignore us. She pointedly trailed behind, lingering over the church notices.

Beside the lych gate, to the left and set back a little from the grey sunlit wall which surrounded the cemetery, was a small whitewashed cottage with square winking windows, leaded into tiny diamond panes. There was a minuscule patch of garden in front of the cottage with rows of lettuces and radishes and borders of marigolds and wallflowers and sweet williams. The eaves of the cottage drooped low over the walls so that it seemed as though it might be frowning, belying its orderly garden and twinkling windows and belying its front door which was nearly always ajar and painted hectic red. Beside the low garden gate stood a motorbike, all gleaming black paint and glittering chrome.

'Wow!' murmured William. 'A Triumph Tiger!' But neither I nor Amelia had any interest in, or time for, motorbikes. We pushed open the gate and went up to the front door.

Inside this cottage lived Mr Alfred Ambrose, owner of the motorbike and sexton of the churchyard, and his sister, Dorothea Ambrose. Dorothea Ambrose was less than five feet tall and had a simple, open, flaccid face and a most grotesquely hunched back. Ever since I could remember, which was presumably since my father's death and subsequent burial in a grave dug by Mr Alfred Ambrose, both he and his hunchbacked midget of a sister had been our friends. We frequently went into their tiny, tidy cottage, past Mr Ambrose's gleaming motorbike and through his immaculate garden, for mugs of milk and slices of bread and honey. Alfred Ambrose, it was always he who poured the milk and cut the bread and spread the honey, would rub his knees with his soil-stained knobbly hands and ask how we were keeping. Sometimes he would play us tunes on his harmonica that lived in a neat wooden box like a coffin, painted green, and Dorothea Ambrose would clap her hands and smile up

31

at us from her seat, her pale blue eyes shining and her ugly, downy face transformed by her pleasure. People in Truro said that Dorothea Ambrose was not quite right in the head. 'Slow,' they said, 'clumsy, simple, handicapped.' 'Dotty Ambrose' they called her and winked at each other, nudging their elbows and tapping their temples with their forefingers. But who was I to care? People called me slow and clumsy and simple too. Even people like Mother.

Mr Ambrose came to the front door to greet us. His shirtsleeves were rolled up to his elbows and his sagging trousers were held up by a pair of green and white braces.

'Look who it isn't!' he exclaimed to us as he always did, chucking me under the chin with his gnarled forefinger and winking knowingly at Amelia and William.

'Mr Ambrose, this is William McCullen,' said Amelia in her best grown-up voice. 'William, Mr Ambrose. Mr Ambrose is the sexton. William comes from Stonehaven but he lives across the road from us now in Truro.'

'Stonehaven,' said Alfred Ambrose thoughtfully, stroking the uneven grey bristles on his chin. 'That's a fair and mighty way off isn't it, son?' and he winked again at William and invited us all inside, leading me by the hand as was the ritual.

Dorothea Ambrose sat in her chair by the fireplace as she always did, although, of course, on this sunny summer's day there was no fire burning in the grate. Their cat sat purring on her knee as her pudsy, freckled fingers ran repeatedly through the fur on its chest. That cat, Claudia they called her, was the fattest, greediest feline that I've ever come across. Spoiled, petulant, indolent, it used to sprawl on the sun-warmed wall of the graveyard in the long, stretching fingers of summer evenings and blink its tawny eyes at the birds, fat thrushes, blackbirds, and the bobbing pied wagtails from the stream, that fluttered and hopped carelessly

32

close. It was the mother of my mother's own cat, Hilary, but Hilary must surely have inherited his lithe, mouse-catching skills from his unknown paternal ancestry.

'William, this is Dorothea Ambrose, Mr Ambrose's sister,' Amelia continued with her introductions. 'Miss Ambrose, please let me introduce you to our friend William.' William smiled and scratched his elbow and muttered a shy and inarticulate greeting, but Dorothea Ambrose didn't even look up. Her fat fingers continued to stroke Claudia's silky fur rhythmically and there was a bubble of spittle on her lower lip. Her short plump legs in twisted stockings dangled from the chair, her toes, in black sturdy shoes with laces, just within tapping distance of the floor. With every stroke of the cat, Dorothea's hump rose and fell grotesquely as though it were a living creature.

Amelia and I were used to Dorothea, and of course her brother was too, but William had never met her before and I could see the words drying and dying in his throat as he looked from her to Amelia, back to Dorothea and then to her brother who was coming into the room carrying a tray. It was the same wooden tray as always, with curly handles and a plain linen cloth. On it stood three mugs of milk and three fat doorsteps of brown bread smeared with honey. The whole of Mr Ambrose's face beamed and his eyes, beneath thick, scrubbing-brush eyebrows, twinkled with merriment.

William and Amelia sat on the sagging settee with Claudia's clawmarks on its round wooden legs and I sat, as I always sat, on Mr Ambrose's comforting but uncomfortable lap.

'Well now?' murmured Mr Ambrose, but it wasn't really a question at all, and while he watched us and Dorothea continued to stroke the cat we ate and drank in a warm sweet silence. Then Mr Ambrose stood me down and we took our leave; no tunes on the harmonica this time nor hectic clapping from

Dorothea, just milk and bread and honey and the lumpy warmth of Alfred Ambrose's knees beneath my thin summer skirt.

We went back through the lych gate into the graveyard, William, Amelia and I.

'You're too big to sit on Mr Ambrose's knee now, Caroline,' said Amelia reprovingly. But I shrugged and turned away. I didn't think that I could ever become too big and grown-up to sit there, safe and warm, with a mug of milk and a slice of bread and honey.

'I wanted to ask him about his motorbike,' muttered William.

'Then why didn't you?' snapped Amelia. This time it was William who turned silently away and ran his hand along the top of the cold stone table where my father's coffin had once paused.

The graveyard always seemed to me to be full of sunlit warmth, birdsong and the muffled, ever-constant, ever-capricious singing of the nearby stream. I suppose that I never visited it on rain-soaked days. The grass was short and neatly clipped about the tombstones by Alfred Ambrose and even the oldest, most neglected graves had an air of care, almost a feeling of prosperity, about them. I loved the feeling of peace that seemed to envelop us as we entered the graveyard, and I felt certain that neither William nor Amelia would be able to raise their voices into querulous argument within these grey and gentle walls.

Father's grave was towards the back of the cemetery: a small granite stone and a raised grassy mound. I couldn't read the words on the stone, of course, but I knew by heart what they said. His name, naturally, and dates, and then at the bottom of the stone in inverted commas and a neat italic script,

'My heart has left its dwelling place and can return no more.'

William read the line out slowly, seeming to taste each word with his tongue and lips.

'That's not from the bible,' Amelia said quickly as he finished speaking. 'It's poetry.'

'I know, I know,' replied William crossly, but it sounded to me almost like an automatic response. His voice was more distant than usual and his gaze was fixed on something far away.

I said nothing. The inscription on my father's headstone seemed the most beautiful thing in the world to me. Although I could only grieve for the absence of my father, denied, by my lack of knowledge of him, the grief of loss, that simple snippet of poetry could still bring hot prickles of tears to my eyes and faint flutters of impossible sorrow to my throat.

'What epitaph would you choose to have on your gravestone?' Amelia asked William. He seemed to have to make an effort to force his mind back from some far-off place to consider his reply, and he sighed from deep down inside.

'William McCullen,' he intoned at last in a sombre voice. 'Born in Stonehaven; lived in truth; died in innocence.' He coughed a little self-consciously. 'Then the dates,' he added.

'Why?' asked Amelia with curiosity sharpening her voice, her birdlike head cocked to one side. 'Why do you want that silly little ditty?'

'Oh, why not?' answered William, his voice seeming weary rather than exasperated. 'I just thought of it. I'd like to live truthfully and die innocent. Why not?'

Amelia sniffed disparagingly, and that brisk intake of breath through her nostrils seemed to snap William back to the present. His voice rose sharply with irritation.

'So what would Miss Amelia West choose to have on her gravestone?' he demanded. 'What witticism or sophisticated line of poetry would suit your decaying remains?'

Amelia sniffed again and looked away from Father's grave.

'Oh,' she said smugly, 'I wouldn't want anything. It's

all a lot of silly religious nonsense if you ask me. Just a cremation and my ashes scattered to the four winds would suit me fine. Once you're dead, it can't matter what they do to you anyway.'

Amelia smiled triumphantly and looked at William, but he was frowning and staring hard at my father's small grey tombstone as though trying to memorize it. I fancied that he didn't see the stone in front of him at all, but something quite different.

'And what about you, Caroline?' continued Amelia, after a short pause in which the echoes of their bickering voices died away and were replaced by trembling birdsong, the singing brook and the honeyed quiet of the sunlit churchyard.

'I don't know,' I replied, kicking with my awkward feet at a dandelion plant that had escaped Alfred Ambrose's attentions. 'I don't want to die at all.'

I hated and feared the idea of the quarrel mounting between Amelia and William to shatter the peace once more. I tugged at my sister's hand.

'Let's go and pick flowers for Father's grave,' I urged her, 'and then we'll have to go home.'

There was a place to cross the wall not far from my father's grave. Glinting blocks of granite jutting out stepwise led you up out of the churchyard and then brought you down beside the brook. Amelia climbed over first and I followed. Behind me William, still unusually quiet and subdued, was dawdling a little and hanging back.

All was green and lush beside the stream, and the earth smelt damp and mossy. The brook itself was narrow and chortling and overhung with leggy sycamore branches. Curling ferns reached out across it from the steep-sided banks and on the surface of the water, now smooth and black and deep, now burbling and broken into brown and white shining flashes by stones, fallen leaves floated past, rotating serenely with up-pointed stems.

I thought to myself that I wouldn't mind being buried here, beyond the insulating walls of the cemetery and beside the dance and glitter of the brook. Rather than a stone, inscribed with words that I couldn't read, I thought that I would prefer an acorn to be planted. The oak tree which would surely grow in this dark, fertile soil would mark my passing and my resting point. Its roots would thread their secretive way through the harp strings of my ribcage and in the winter its leaves would fall and decay beside me. The picture that my demise painted in my imagination brought a sudden, unexpected rush of tears to my eyes, but I brushed them away quickly, unwilling to share my thoughts with William and Amelia; it seemed a too beautiful and private dream to be spoilt by clumsy words.

On a sunny embankment beside the brook, William sat down and gnawed absent-mindedly on a stalk of hard-headed timothy grass while Amelia and I gathered armfuls of wild flowers. There were the creamy-green clouds of cow parsley, bright flowers of pink campion on tough, velvet-furred stems and the more delicately-petalled flowers and intricate leaves of herb Robert. There were also magenta and soft pink dog roses, heavy-headed and drooping fragrantly in an adjacent hedgerow, surrounded by the indolent buzz of summertime bees. But they dropped their petals at the most careful handling and so we left them untouched in the sunshine. With armfuls of wild summer flowers we climbed back over the wall, and left our offerings in a festive but disorderly heap to wilt and fade on Father's grave until Alfred Ambrose removed them.

Close by the lych gate was the most beautifully kept and tended grave of all, a small oblong of pansies and violets and a knee-high headstone of white marble with only the faintest tracery of coppery green veins. There were neither dates nor names on the stone, but a raised motif of flowers and leaves and angels, and a few words.

'Suffer the little children to come unto me,' read William, pausing beside the grave on our way out of the cemetery. Amelia couldn't restrain her sniff at the words, but I knew by her eyes, bright and gleaming behind the lenses of her spectacles, that she was eager to tell William whose grave it was.

'That's where Baby Ambrose is buried,' she informed him. 'Mr Ambrose tends it most carefully. He comes every day to check that no weeds have dared to show themselves.'

'Baby Ambrose?' William was curious despite himself and although I knew the story and although it sent cold, damp fingers of fear slithering down my neck and back, I also paused beside the tiny grave to listen to Amelia.

'Oh yes,' Amelia's voice swept on enthusiastically, 'I don't suppose you know. Dorothea Ambrose had a baby. It was years and years ago, before Caroline was born even. Nobody knew who the father was, and even if Dotty knew, then she wouldn't tell. But the baby only survived a few days. It was just like Dotty, you see: hunchbacked and deformed and handicapped. Some people said that Alfred Ambrose himself killed it, but they couldn't prove it of course. But I don't think so. Mr Ambrose doesn't even kill wasps. He catches them in a teacup and puts them out of the window. The baby probably just died, especially being so handicapped as well.'

Amelia finished with a bright grin and marched onward towards the lych gate, but William remained on the mossy path beside Baby Ambrose's grave. His eyes were inward-looking and he stood on one leg, scratching his thin shin with his foot.

'I don't think,' William said at last, looking downward at Baby Ambrose's headstone, 'that it would have been wrong if Mr Ambrose had killed his sister's baby. It can't be fair to keep people like that alive.'

I gasped a little and imagined all too clearly Mr

Ambrose, his kindly eyes twinkling, bringing down a pillow on the face of an ugly hunchbacked baby, while his sister cooed and giggled aimlessly and stroked the cat. I shook off this horrific picture with a shudder and looked up to see if Amelia had heard what William had said, for his voice had been quiet and subdued. Amelia was standing by the lych gate. From her pursed lips and tilted head I could tell that she was considering William's words, and I waited for the sharp condemnation in her reply. But it never came.

'Do you know,' she said slowly, almost shyly, as though making a confession, 'I think, William, that you might be right.'

They talked about death and dying, murder and mercy killing and manslaughter, all the way back to Truro, did William and Amelia. Their voices were bright and alive and bubbling in the afternoon sun, but I hung back, kicking at stones and weaving green-fronded tiaras from ferns as I walked. Although I was glad that, for a change at least, Amelia and William were in agreement rather than squabbling, I didn't want to hear or partake in their eager chatter. It made me feel cold and dark and ashamed, and I wished that we had not been to see Father's grave and Alfred and Dorothea Ambrose at all.

'Come on, Caroline! Hurry up!' shrilled Amelia from the top of the hill, before the steep descent into Truro. I looked up to where William and Amelia impatiently waited for me, their faces pink and happy. I kicked again at the stones and threw my fern tiara in the buttercup-studded grassy verge.

'What's wrong with you?' Amelia asked irritably as I lumbered up to where they stood together. I was panting slightly from the steepness of the hill. I could feel that my face was red and that my lower lip was trembling. I paused for breath, ready to shrug and shake my head.

'Well?' said Amelia, and the sharpness of her voice

goaded me, usually so slow and passive, into a tumultuous response.

'You said that Dorothea Ambrose should be killed!' I shouted accusingly, tears welling up from nowhere and spilling down my cheeks in two streams of burning rage and indictment. 'You want to kill Dorothea Ambrose, and her baby if he wasn't dead already, and all the other people in the world who aren't as clever and horrid as you are! You're no better than Hitler and you even want to kill me!'

My voice ended on a shrill shriek of despair, and I turned away from the pair of would-be murderers and started running towards Truro, tears blurring my sight and my breath coming in pounding, snuffling snorts.

William and Amelia caught up with me easily. William held me securely by the wrists while Amelia applied two brisk slaps to each of my cheeks. At first my tears flowed faster and I struggled to escape from William's grip, then, as Amelia slapped me again, the hysterical weeping slowed to a controlled and regular sobbing. Amelia kissed my nose and sat me down and held my hands with a sororial affection that I had never seen in her before. Her face was white and her lips a thin dry line. I suppose, in retrospect, that my outburst must have frightened her.

'We don't want to kill you or Dotty or anyone,' Amelia explained after I had wiped my eyes on a corner of grubby rag from William's pocket that he claimed was his handkerchief. 'We just thought, or think, that if a baby is ever so handicapped it might be better off dead than alive.' Her voice, usually so sharp, was soft and persuasive, almost gentle.

I gulped down a threatening sob and, rejecting William's proffered rag-handkerchief, wiped my nose on the back of my hand.

'Oh!' I said. I couldn't think of anything else to say that might not spark off another burst of tears. Being dead was surely the end, the absolute ultimate; how could that ever be better than being alive? But it didn't sound so bad the way Amelia had put it.

'How would you like it,' William took over from Amelia, putting his thin arm around my still-heaving shoulders, 'if you were like Miss Ambrose? How would you like it if you were so physically or mentally handicapped that you couldn't do anything yourself?'

I shook my head forlornly. I couldn't even begin to imagine being in such a condition. Or perhaps I could, but I shied away from such a vision and pretended that it didn't exist.

'I'd sooner be dead!' interjected Amelia, her voice regaining its customary bite. 'And so would William.'

'Would you?' I asked, staring wide-eyed at William, overawed by his bravery. 'Would you?' I asked, swivelling my gaze towards Amelia's face. They nodded silently.

'Oh!' I still couldn't imagine actually wanting to be dead.

'So,' continued William, 'we thought that since that is what we would wish, if we came across a newly-born baby in such a condition then it would only be right and fair to . . . well . . . to kill it. It would have to be a baby though; once it's grown up a bit it's too late.'

'Oh!' There seemed nothing more to say to this serious, grubby boy and this bright, quick-tongued girl whom I once thought that I knew as my sister. They seemed to have grown up, up, up and away from me, within a matter of hours. I sat thinking for a few minutes. I had stopped crying now, and the tears were drying on my cheeks. With the anguish no longer pounding in my brain I felt as though I could think more clearly.

'I thought that Christians didn't kill people,' I said at last. Amelia snorted and followed this with one of her most derisive sniffs, but William looked thoughtful.

'I would pray for forgiveness,' he said quietly.

There was one last thing that I had to ask them before we set off home. I looked down at the ground between my feet and focused my gaze on a small cinnamon-coloured ant scaling a long thin blade of grass.

'If you'd known me,' I began, and then I paused awkwardly. Surely they, so clever, so certain, so arrogant, must be able to anticipate my question? But they couldn't; glancing up briefly I saw their gazes of curiosity fixed on me.

'Yes?' prompted William.

'If you'd seen me as a baby, would you have killed me?' The question was out now, in a flurried rush of words that started off another uncalled-for explosion of tears in my eyes.

'You!' they exclaimed simultaneously. 'Why?' Their gazes and voices were round gasps of foolish amazement.

'I'm backward and slow,' I mumbled, losing my ant in the blur of my tears. 'So slow that you might even call me simple. Why, I can't even read yet.'

'Oh Caroline, don't be so silly,' said Amelia, her voice a mixture of incomprehension, laughter and irritation. But William had stood up from where he squatted beside me on the grass verge.

'Come on,' he said, tugging at my wrists with his hard-palmed hands, 'climb up on me and I'll give you a piggyback and when we get home, I'll teach you to read.'

Chapter Six

William's reading lessons didn't begin, as he had promised me that they would, that evening. Thin, shadowy Mrs McCullen had a migraine. I saw her as she stood on the doorstep of our home waiting for us to return. Her complexion was more yellowed than ever, like chamois leather gone hard and wrinkled with age, and that fascinating mole on her left cheek seemed to have outgrown her gaunt face. Her eyes were lost beneath those bushy eyebrows, drowning in purpled vampire wells.

It fell to William, under Mother's instruction, to draw the curtains in Mrs McCullen's bedroom, to plump up the pillows on her bed, and to leave her there in the dim quietness with just a glass of soda water within easy reach.

'Poor Mrs McCullen,' said my mother pityingly as she handed over the bottle of soda water to William. 'She doesn't have much luck.'

But she sniffed in a disparaging sort of way after she had closed the front door. My mother never had headaches nor fevers; she was never sickly nor tired; she never even caught colds. Although she had not said so, I felt that she regarded illness in others as some sort of sign, an emphasis if you like, of her own superiority. I could almost hear her thinking it in her sniff.

Amelia, apart from her allergies to fur and dust, was like Mother. Unlike myself, she had never missed a day of school from illness and she was proud of this feat. She also sniffed as William brought back the empty soda-water bottle.

'Is your mother often ill?' she enquired of him curiously. But William evaded Amelia's question and looked away from her tilted, watching face.

'I have to get back home,' he muttered and stumped quickly out of our house, banging the door behind him.

Mrs McCullen seemed to have recovered by the next day, for Amelia and I watched her from the living-room window heading off down the street of early-morning light towards her dark corner behind the haberdashery counter. We couldn't see her face from that distance to check whether her eyes were still buried in those violet sockets or whether they had emerged, cautiously, to face the day. Nor could we judge the yellowness of her face or the darkness of her moustache shadow, lurking like an unsavoury question on her upper lip, but she walked briskly and her head was held upright. From a distance, at least, she seemed just as healthy as usual.

'She can't have been very ill,' sniffed Amelia. 'Do you think that she was perhaps malingering?'

But Mother, who had joined us briefly at the window to watch Mrs McCullen's receding back, was more sympathetic.

'She looks quite worn out,' she said chidingly to Amelia. 'She needs a holiday, or at the very least a break. Next month we'll make sure she gets a couple of days off and we'll all go down to the Pollards' farm.'

'And William too?' I asked anxiously, suddenly seeing the possibility of another break in my bumbling progress towards literacy.

'Oh Caroline!' laughed Mother, stroking my hair briefly. 'Of course William too. Do you think we'd leave him?'

The 'couple of days at the Pollards' farm' had been an annual event in my life for as long as I could remember. Annie Pollard, almost as capable and certainly as brisk-tongued as Mother, but much rounder, plumper and fairer, had been Mother's best

44

friend at school all those unimaginable years ago, although of course she hadn't been called Pollard then, any more than Mother had been called West. Annie had been the only daughter of a slater who had built up, by a mixture of hard work and determination, a prosperous business for himself. I always thought that her plumpness and her fairness must be some sort of reflection of her father's wealth. On the exact same day that Mother had married my father, Annie had married Diggory Pollard.

Diggory Pollard was small and dark and dreaming, with purple-blue Celtic eyes set rather close together in a heart-shaped face. Amelia had once told me, very privately, that Diggory was really a pixie king and that at midnight, when the moon was full, he would sprout gossamer wings from his thin shoulder blades and fly off to fairyland for a magical party. It had seemed such a beautiful, probable idea that I had quite believed Amelia's tales, whispered to me in the semi-dark across the bedroom, and I looked for hours for fairy footprints beside the chicken run where Amelia said that I might find them. I cried for hours too, bitterly and inconsolably, when Mother shattered my illusions after I had asked her to help me in my search. My eyes had burned with the misery of irreplaceable loss.

The Pollards' farm lay just to the north and east of Gwithian village on the north coast of Cornwall. It lay amongst low green hills, but with the heathery cliffs still in sight. On stormy days the sound of the surf crashing against the rocks on the shore throbbed amongst the muddle of barns and outhouses like the beat of a distant, uneasy drum, making the cows roll their mad brown eyes and jostle nervously together. It was just the place, I was sure, for some elfin royalty to choose to inhabit, with the huge sands of Godrevy beach and the blueness of the sea just visible from the topmost windows of the farmhouse. If I had been disappointed in Diggory Pollard's origins, I had never been disappointed in his home.

But we weren't to visit the Pollards' farm for another month, and in that month, I resolved as we watched the thin black line of Mrs McCullen disappear around the corner by the postbox, I would learn to read.

It was strange for me, usually so timid and hesitant, to feel such a strong surge of conviction and determination. But perhaps stranger still was that when I mentioned my plan to Amelia, after Mother had returned to the kitchen, she, who always made all the plans herself and was ever scathing of my foolish hopes, endorsed my idea so wholeheartedly that I could only sit back and gaze at her with surprise.

'Stop gawping at me, Caroline,' snapped Amelia. 'It makes you look like a fish.' But she continued with the eagerness surmounting the irritation in her voice. 'We won't tell Mother at all,' she said with her face glowing with delight, 'and then, one day while we're at the Pollards' farm, we'll get you to read something to her and won't she be surprised!'

There was excitement shining in Amelia's eyes at this vision of her achievement, and she clasped her thin knees to her chest.

'I can hardly wait,' she said. 'Let's go and get William and then we can start straightaway.' She hugged me briefly and was out of the house and across the road, bouncing up the steps to the McCullens' front door, before I could really comprehend her words.

So this was the way it was going to be. I would be presented to Mother like a performing bear that has been taught a new dance. And the claps and the cheers and the rounds of amused applause might go to the dumb, foolish bear, but surely it was the trainer, bowing and smiling and handing around his cap, who received the real credit. And yet I didn't care. Really and truly, I didn't mind at all. To be able to read, and perhaps later to write, seemed a big enough reward to me, and I uncurled myself from the squidgy, dusty warmth of the sofa and followed Amelia across the street to the McCullens' house.

The reading lessons, such as they were, took place in the meadows looking down on Truro. At least, on sunny days they did. On the days of swirling mists that punctuate the Cornish summers like nostalgic memories, we had to stay inside. To avoid Mother and keep our secret safe, we could not stay at home, but had to content ourselves with the damp, fusty clutter of Mrs McCullen's kitchen.

Amelia sniffed with disapproval as she looked around. Her unforgiving gaze darted from the row of chipped plain white mugs to the forlorn droop of pale-leaved geraniums on the windowsill, and then to the scratches and stains on the surface of the kitchen table.

'Was your home in Stonehaven like ... like this?' she asked William, waving her arms around as though trying to embrace the whole feeling of chilly neglect.

'No,' replied William shortly. 'Of course not.' And Amelia didn't push him any further. There was work to be done, after all.

It wasn't the conventional method for teaching the skills of literacy, of that I'm sure, for I'd stumbled unsuccessfully around those hoops of learning with Mother and with teachers already. William was quite surprisingly gentle with me; endlessly tolerant and forgiving of my repeated mistakes as I toiled over some book of poetry or prose, quite inappropriate for learners, that smelt of powdery age. Amelia, however, was less patient with me.

'We've got plenty of time,' William would say consolingly as I tripped and fumbled around those harsh, spiky letters yet again. Amelia bunched her fists so tightly in irritation and frustration that the taut skin around her knuckles glistened a sickly yellowish-white, reminding me of poor Mrs McCullen.

'There's no need to fret,' William soothed as Amelia stood up and stamped her little feet on the ground, sending up clouds of pollen from the grass in the

47

meadows, or mouldering dust from the floor in Mrs McCullen's kitchen.

'How can you be so useless, Caroline?' Amelia would sigh with exasperation, her words hissing out between gritted teeth. 'Yesterday you almost knew that and now you don't seem to have a clue. You'll never, ever learn at this rate. And certainly not before we go down to the Pollards' farm.'

The Pollards' farm shone before me like a guiding star. I felt that its very existence depended upon me. If I didn't learn to read before the appointed hour, then I was certain that something terrible and irrevocable would happen to it. The farmhouse would crack along its warm, ancient walls and it would crumble into dust. All that would be left of Annie and Diggory Pollard would be their pale bones; across their skulls would be stamped mocking, accusatory grins.

I trembled at the very thought of my possible failure to learn, and yet, despite Amelia's furious despair, I was quietly confident of success. I battled on without ever once succumbing entirely to the tears that so often rose to my eyes, blurring the barbs of black letters into unintelligible smudges.

And I did, under the dual prompts of William's gentle encouragement and Amelia's sarcastic goading, make progress. Gradually I learned to spell out words, letter by clumsy letter, until I could grasp at some sort of meaning. William would smile his kind smile and Amelia would screw up her face as though the slow words that I produced caused her acute pain.

'But that's not reading, Caroline,' Amelia said. 'That's . . . I don't know what it is, but it's certainly not real reading.'

Her face would become pinched with frustration and her voice was alternately petulant or disappointed.

'And next week,' she added, 'Mother's arranged our visit to the Pollards' farm. You'll never have learned to read properly by then.'

But Amelia, who was always right, was wrong this

time. Two nights before the planned trip to the Pollards' farm I had a dream; such a very brief dream that it was really more of a tableau than a dream of actions or events. But it was a dream, nevertheless, of such vividness that even now, after so many nights and years of dreaming, I can recall it without any of the shadows of passing time.

I dreamed that we three, Amelia, William and I, were climbing a steep headland. The sun was warm on our backs and the heather beneath our feet was a purple-green carpet of gnarled springiness, throbbing with the hum of summer bees. William and Amelia reached the crest of the headland a little ahead of me, and they turned and reached down to pull me up to join them. But I ignored their hands and ran up to them with easy strides. From the top of the headland, standing beside Amelia and William, I could look down upon the sea on the other side: a sea of a blue so dark and deep that it was like the night. This sparkling sea was ruffled with crisp waves. Five boats with sails as brightly white as the foam on the waves sailed briskly past, and I felt that I could stretch out my hand and touch them.

It was, I suppose, a dream of happy freedom and success, and when I woke to the pale, misty July morning, the first tendrils of light filtering through the curtains and falling in arrow-bright splashes on to Amelia's still sleeping back, I just knew that this had to be the day of the miracle.

The miracle, and even now it still seems to me to be a miracle, happened in the meadows looking down on the railway track, which before the end of the week would bear us westward towards the Pollards' farm. How well I remember those first words that seemed to jiggle their spiky, spiteful letters before my eyes and shout out together one coherent meaning. It was a Shakespearean sonnet, number sixty.

The words came out, slowly and a little shakily at first, and then faster and more firmly with increasing confidence, until I felt that I was stronger and louder than any other force in the whole world. William and Amelia, the one leaning back on his hands and smiling, the other crouched eagerly forward following every movement of my lips, watched me with shining eyes. The look on my face, reflected in their eyes, matched their delighted expressions and united us. Although I understood nothing of the meaning of that Shakespearean sonnet, numbered sixty, I thought that words, written words, had never sounded so much like glorious and stirring music.

We took the train, us Wests and them McCullens, from the flower-tubbed tidy station in Truro with all the buttons shining brightly on the porters' uniforms and the hands on the station clock, black as letters printed on a white page, correct to the very second, to the rather less neat, rather less shining and pristine station at Hayle.

It was the first time that either William or his mother had been beyond Truro. Mrs McCullen sat bolt upright on the slithery train seat, a long black coat buttoned severely from her stringy yellow throat down to below her knees, keeping a watchful eye upon their luggage, crammed into a pair of dilapidated Gladstones in the luggage rack above our heads. William knelt on the seat and looked out through the smeary window at the folds of green-gold countryside outside. Although William was not in his kilt, he was as scrubbed and neat as though he were heading off to church on a Sunday morning, and his hair was smarmed wetly down across his forehead. William nodded and smiled as Amelia and I pointed out sights through the train window as though they belonged to us personally. Gradually his hair dried and resumed its usual tousled appearance, and his clean handkerchief was used to try and clear the grime from the window to improve the view.

Here a handful of brown-grey rabbits, skittering

away lopsidedly from the rhythmic rumbling of the passing train. There a motionless cock pheasant, its long russet tail sweeping the ground and its small, silly head cocked sideways as though listening. Here flashing glimpses of the sea, and there the gaunt grey tower of an abandoned engine house. I, still drunk on the heady miracle of my literacy, thought that the world had never looked more wonderful, bursting and alive.

'Look! Look! Look!' I wanted to shout, but it was not customary for me to be the extrovert chatterer, and so I left it mostly to Amelia to tug repeatedly on the sleeve of William's slightly too-small jacket and point out the world to him in a voice high with enthusiasm, as though he could not see these things for himself.

'Shush now, Amelia,' Mother said occasionally. But it was obvious from the smile in her voice that she didn't mind our exuberance at all. Once or twice she even leaned forward as though to catch a glimpse of whatever we were pointing out and exclaiming over now. Perhaps two heavy carthorses with shaggy tangled manes and huge thumping hooves frisking together in a field dappled with the shadows of tall elm trees. Perhaps two small boys and a little girl in a faded blue cotton dress, with blackcurrant stains on their hands and faces, waving at the unknown strangers in the train. We waved back, of course, but Mother didn't and Mrs McCullen gave a weary sigh.

At Camborne, a tired, efficient town, two portly ladies with fat uncomfortable ankles and gaudy scarves around their throats scrambled into our compartment with ungainly haste and much panting and wheezing. They had pink wobbling cheeks and turnip noses and they smelt of an oppressive but comforting mixture of cheap violet scent and sweat. They were laden with baskets and bags and as they forced their fat thighs down on to the seats between their piles of chattels, their floral dresses stretched tightly across their heaving chests and they smiled in a cheerful, apologetic way at Mother and Mrs McCullen.

'Perhaps we'd better put the baskets in the luggage rack, Jess,' said one of the pair, the older lady with streaks of grey in her hair. I could tell by her comfortable, slightly bossy voice, blurred beneath its broad Cornish accent, rather than by their similar appearances, that they must be sisters. Jess, her hair still a ripe and glossy brown, squeezed herself out of her seat again, her smile intact and without a word or sigh of complaint. Her dress stayed rucked up around her thighs and her sister leaned forward and twitched it down sharply with a quick tut-tutting noise.

The train started with a rumble and a jerk, and Jess swayed around the cramped compartment like a tall-masted ship in full sail in a tiny and overcrowded harbour.

'Oh William! Do give the ladies a hand now,' murmured Mrs McCullen. William tore himself from his window on the passing world and, as Jess settled gratefully back into her seat, he started heaving the baskets, one by one, up on to the luggage rack.

'Watch that one now,' said Jess's older sister to William as he stretched out to lift the final basket, a plump and smiling wicker bulb with a lid held down across its mouth by two broad leather brass-buckled straps. 'There's a fat goose in that one, there is,' said Jess's sister, and, as though on cue, a querulous hiss was heard through the wickerwork. Just visible through the gap between the lid and the basket was a malevolently glistening black and beady eye.

We left Jess and her sister and their goose, still hissing irregularly in a grumpily insistent manner from its basket, at Hayle, for they were travelling on further west and south to Penzance. We unloaded our belongings into an untidy heap in the middle of the platform. Jess, under her sister's instruction, tried to help us, but she only succeeded in getting in the way and once sat suddenly and rather heavily down on top of one of Mrs McCullen's Gladstone bags. When we were all out, Jess handed us very dark and sticky toffees of irregular shape and size from a torn paper bag, through the train door. We, Amelia and William and I, all took one eagerly but Mother smiled and shook her head and Mrs McCullen pretended not to notice the proffered bag.

As we stood amongst our bags on the bustling platform, which always had the faint smell of fish and decaying seaweed drifting over it from the estuary, we sucked uncertainly on our toffees and the train snorted out of the station. My thoughts still could not keep very far away from the marvel of my own ability to read and I couldn't help asking, mumbling a little through my toffee, 'But do you think that *they* could read?'

William and Amelia shot me angry looks, somewhat marred by the toffee bulges in their cheeks, as though I was purposely spoiling their secret. But Mother only laughed, giving me a curious, distracted look, and straightened my collar.

'Really Caroline! I haven't got the least idea. Certainly their goose couldn't read anyway.'

Amelia sidled up to me as Mother's attention was quickly diverted to the more pressing concern of luggage trolleys. She had spat her toffee out on to the railway line and her mouth was pressed into a thin angry line.

'If you're not careful, you're going to give everything away, Caroline you silly,' she whispered and her eyes, which seemed to glitter behind her spectacles, and her hissing voice reminded me of the goose in the wicker basket. The twisting pinch she gave me on my bare forearm was sharp and quick, just as a goose peck would be.

But as I flinched away from Amelia's jabbing fingers and William's cross blue glare, gagging uncomfortably on the sweetness of my toffee and worried that the day which had been so beautiful was going to be quite spoiled, Mother gave an enthusiastic cry.

'Annie!' she called, 'Annie!' She had spotted her friend on the other side of the station and she hurried across to her, pulling Mrs McCullen behind her like a thin black shadow.

Chapter Seven

The Pollards' farm was situated, as I have already said,
to the north and east of Gwithian village. Gwithian lay
hunched behind Godrevy beach and the sand dunes,
shimmering with sunlight and marram grass. The road
twisted upwards beyond the village, towards the cliff
tops and the smell of salty heather breezes. The road
forked, and the narrower branch, a singing green
tunnel between high leafy hedges, took us briefly away
from the sea, across a humpbacked bridge over a
shallow, pebble-happy river to the ridge of hills and
the muddy yard of the Pollards' farm.

The yard around the farm always seemed to be
cluttered with intriguing farm implements, spiked and
pronged like instruments of torture. Also it was
invariably covered in a layer of greenish-brown mud,
thick and glutinous, and there were rich cowpats
scattered about that steamed gently and smelt of straw.

'Watch where you're walking,' Annie called back
cheerfully from the front door. Mother laughed and
skipped lightly across the yard with a bag in each
hand, but Mrs McCullen gave a little sigh and pulled
her coat even tighter around herself.

'William, would you bring in the bags please dear?'
she asked.

But after a cup of tea in the kitchen – it so often
seemed to be time for a cup of tea in the farm kitchen,
with greedy fat mugs and flour-dusted scones
smothered in a thick jam made of redcurrants and Victoria plums, and spoonfuls of yellow-crusted clotted
cream – even Mrs McCullen seemed to relax. With her
coat banished to the cupboard under the stairs to hang

with all the other coats amongst the smell of leather boots, damp wool socks and coal dust, she seemed to become less long and grim and yellow. And, as she accepted another cup of tea from Annie and watched William stretching out his scrawny hand for another scone, there was a warmth glowing in her brooding eyes which I was sure that I had not seen there before.

'Surely not another scone, William?' she asked. 'You'll not be wanting any supper at this rate.' Although her voice seemed to have lost its usual grudging sigh, William's hand hesitated in response, hovering above the plate of scones, now almost emptied so that the pattern of violets and forget-me-nots on the white china background peeked through at us. But Annie, although she had no children of her own, seemed to know more about the appetites of growing boys than Mrs McCullen did.

'Now William,' she interrupted politely but firmly, standing in the middle of her bright kitchen with her arms folded and her legs slightly apart as though on the deck of a rolling boat, 'I don't often tell children to disregard the words of their parents, but this time I must.' She grinned merrily, firstly at Mrs McCullen and then at William, and from behind her the row of copper pans, burnished to perfection, winked encouragingly down on us all from the top of a full-skirted dresser.

'You'll be out and about on the farm and in the woods and the fields before long, if I know these two at all,' Annie continued, nodding her head so briskly at Amelia and me that her curls jounced about her ears, 'leaving us ladies to catch up on each other's news and gossip in the kitchen.' She paused. 'Well?' she asked us, 'won't you?'

I had just taken a last mouthful of scone and cream and could only nod my head enthusiastically in reply, but Amelia needed no prompting to answer for both of us.

'Oh yes, I can't wait to show William everything.

56

There's all the animals of course, the pigs, the cows, the chickens and things. And then there's the place where we saw the adder last year and the big sycamore tree that's so easy to climb and you can see the lighthouse from the top. Then, of course, there's the duckpond, including the place where Caroline fell in and had to be rescued by Diggory when she was five or six and thought that she could walk on the water and the . . .'

'Exactly, Amelia dear.' Annie cut neatly across Amelia's tumbling flow of words. Amelia hated to be interrupted, but this time she just blinked a little and opened her mouth once or twice as though she might continue. It was almost impossible to interrupt Annie, however.

'Although I shall have to tell you right away,' Annie continued, 'that that old sycamore came down in that terrible storm that we had in February last. Awful it was. Took half the roof off the middle barn as well, it did. It was sad about that poor old tree though. Must have been planted by Diggory's great-great-grandfather. One of the farm hands, Johnny I think it was, the one with the harelip, tried to count the rings, but he gave up at one hundred and fifty. Can you imagine? Still, the logs from that poor ancient tree kept the fires going all through March, so it wasn't really wasted.'

Annie paused, just for a second and not long enough for Amelia to burst forth again with her litany of sightseeing for William. Perhaps Amelia, who usually never missed a chance, had, like me, been struck with a sudden empty sadness by the news about the loss of the old sycamore. I had spent hours in that tree. It had, in its time, been my many-turreted castle and my galleon in full sail, lifting and rolling beneath me. It had taken in my anguished bitter tears when I had discovered the truth of Diggory's elfin ancestry, and it had heard my laughter too. But now it could never, ever hear me read. It had gone in the strange, secret

57

way that so many things tended to disappear. As I grew older, more and more things seemed to slip noiselessly into the irrecoverable shadows of the past, leaving only an ever-diminishing gap behind them.

I brought my thoughts back to the bustle of the farm kitchen and Annie's cheery chatter set against the whistle of the kettle coming up to boil on top of the Rayburn.

'So you see,' Annie was saying, 'when William comes in from romping outside with Caroline and Amelia, I'm quite sure that he'll have plenty of appetite. Just to tempt you now, I'll show you what I've prepared.'

She ducked briefly out of the kitchen into the small chilly pantry and returned bearing a tray of pasties, uncooked as yet, laid out in a row like the corpses of fat silent aldermen or choirboys. Annie was a wonderful pastry cook, and these were monster pasties, a full ten inches long. The crimping, as straight and neat as the frilled seams on Amelia's party dress, seemed to strain against the plumpness of the contents.

As Annie returned the tray to the pantry, the clumping of heavy boots could be heard. After a while Diggory appeared in the doorway in stockinged feet, his boots abandoned outside, for Annie was as strict as Mother about muddy feet in the kitchen.

'Afternoon all,' smiled Diggory and, after Mother's introduction, shook hands with Mrs McCullen and gave William a mock salute. 'Trust you've been keeping these lasses in order,' he said to him and reached out to take the last three scones from the plate. He popped them into his mouth one after the other. For such a petite and delicate-looking character, Diggory had an impressive appetite.

'Won't you get indigestion if you eat that quickly?' I asked with awe, despite a sharp kick on my ankle beneath the table from Amelia. But Diggory only laughed.

'Better indigestion than starvation, young Caroline,'

he said, and wiped the flour off his fingers on the front of his old farm jacket. 'No time for a cup of tea just now,' he added. 'I just popped in to say hello. Johnny is waiting outside in the yard for me, so I'd best be off,' and he slipped quietly out of the kitchen. After a few seconds the clumping of boots was heard again, and through the kitchen window that overlooked the yard I could see Diggory talking to Johnny the farm hand, while the two dogs waited impatiently beside them.

'Let's go outside,' I said quickly, 'and then William can meet Johnny and the dogs before they go off to work with Diggory.'

So began our couple of days at the Pollards' farm, and as the hours passed I was never able to forget completely the wonder of my literacy. I couldn't help worrying about when I would get the chance to show off my newly discovered skill to Mother, and whether I would have forgotten how to do it.

At the farm, as at home in Truro, Amelia and I shared a bedroom. This room was set right up beneath the eaves and in the mornings pigeons cooed and clattered just outside, so close that I felt that I could reach out my hand from beneath the sheets and touch them. Amelia, who hated to be woken up, grumbled at the pigeons and banged crossly on the windowpane to make them scatter briefly away. But I loved to hear their rumbling coos and the scratching of their claws on the leads and slates; it was the first sound of another day at the farm.

The picnic – for, whatever the weather, we always had a picnic during our short visits here – was on our second full day; we were to leave and return to Truro the following day, for Mrs McCullen was due back at work. As the pigeons awoke me with their plaintive, rhythmic calls, Amelia leaned over and tugged at my hand. Our beds were squeezed so tightly together in that small, slant-ceilinged room that there was barely six inches between them.

'Caroline,' she whispered. 'Today's the day. I do hope that you haven't forgotten how to do it.' And my heart pounded in my chest with anxious anticipation.

We always went to the same place for our picnic. Not to the long yellow sands of Godrevy beach as William suggested, his mouth twisting into a petulant bud of disappointment when we rejected his idea, but to a section of heathery cliff top not far from the over-hanging bite into the cliffs that they called Hell's Mouth. I, ever literal, had peered cautiously over the edge once and had fully expected to see, despite whatever Mother and Amelia had told me, a deep black hole going down, down, down into some raging fires with the smell of sulphur and scorched flesh wafting up from it. But there was only the twinkling blue sea far down below me and the dark sulky faces of the rocks, with the seagulls gliding lazily between us.

'Oh Caroline, how can you be so silly?' Amelia had scoffed when I expressed my surprise. 'You know that hell is just a made-up concept by priests and things trying to frighten people into being Christians.'

Annie had laughed as she listened to Amelia's patronizing reproof. 'When the sea's rough, the spray flying up the cliff looks almost as though it could be smoke,' she explained more kindly. 'And the noise of the waves crashing on the cliffs can be quite incredible. You would have to hear it to understand.' She paused for a second and her habitual smile slipped briefly from her face. 'Quite a few people have chosen to end their lives here,' she added. 'Once you're over that edge there's no going back.'

It seemed a shocking and terrible idea to me, but Amelia had little sympathy. 'How silly of them to go over the edge in the first place,' she said.

At the place where we always had our picnic the cliff was perhaps a little less steep. There was a crumbling path which zigzagged down to a narrow stretch of beach and a scattering of rocks dimpled with clear

shallow pools. We hunted for rock gobies, we marvelled at the delicate arms of the tiny brittle stars and
we hit limpets off the rocks with stones and fed their
mashed-up bodies into the dull red, waving tentacles
of the beadlet sea anemones. They called it Smuggler's
Cove, but although I always looked carefully, I never
saw any signs of smuggling activity. The one cave
which tunnelled its way into the cliff with green-
slimed, dripping walls and the cold salty smell of
seaweed stopped abruptly, with no secret passages
that I'd ever found. Once, however, I found a water-
logged leather boot there, flung up by the high tide to
the very back of the cave with its laces snarled and
knotted and its tongue lolling out like a dead black
fish. And once I came across the skeleton of a cor-
morant, its long white bones glittering wetly against
the shingle. But I never discovered any mysterious
wooden chests sealed with rusty iron bands.

This time, as usual, we had our picnic on the cliff
top. Mother and Annie could never be bothered with
clambering down the steep pathway to the beach
carrying the picnic, only to have to scramble all the
way back up again only a few hours later. Mrs
McCullen was nervous of heights anyway, and she had
refused to peer over the cliff edge at Hell's Mouth. At
Smuggler's Cove she peeked over cautiously, although
standing well back from the edge, and shook her head
at the narrow pathway snaking down the cliff. 'There's
no question of me going down there,' she said, and her
mouth snapped shut with an absolute finality.

Mrs McCullen was wearing her long black coat for
the picnic. Although the wind sweeping in from the
sea seemed to hold the garment even closer to her thin
body, pressing it tightly against her, she nevertheless
appeared to have filled out during the short time she'd
spent at the farm. I found her now more human, more
of a real person, and it was increasingly difficult to
imagine her and William up in the distant reaches of
Stonehaven, quailing beneath the menaces from the

huge-knuckled fists of the unknown Mr McCullen. Perhaps it was just the fresh farm food, the creamy milk and fat sizzling rashers of bacon in the morning; the big newly laid eggs and the golden dollops of Annie's clotted cream. Perhaps it was the fresh air, a combination of salty sea and earthy farm, or perhaps it was just the change from her tedious job in the stuffy mustiness of Hurlinghams. Whatever the reason, it seemed to me that Mrs McCullen's face had begun to lose its tired yellowness. Her cheeks had plumped out and become almost pink. Her eyes had become brighter, merrier, and, in tune with her eyes, her lips had begun to smile more frequently and with more enthusiasm. But the greatest change seemed to be in Mrs McCullen's hair. It had been short, dark and straight, but now it appeared to have grown several inches, coppery lights sparkled in it in the sunshine and little curls were beginning to spiral about the nape of her neck. As she walked, they jostled and bounced about her eagerly.

William had carried the big red tartan rug from the farm and Amelia and I took it from him and spread it out on the heather. It flapped like a flag between us as we held it, for despite the brightness of the day there was a brisk wind blowing in off the sea and the blue-grey hillocks of swell were topped with flying white foam.

Annie, helped by Mother and Mrs McCullen, unpacked the picnic bags that we had carried. It seemed a shame to me that Diggory, who had such an appetite for food, could not spare the time from the farm to join us for the picnic, for it was always a feast. Here a cold pigeon pie topped with flaking crispy gold pastry and there two loaves of bread speckled with flour and freckled with poppy seeds, and a round pat of butter wrapped in a sheet of greaseproof paper. Here a bag of saffron buns, tea-treat buns they called them, riddled with sultanas and there two bottles of ginger beer and two bowls of fruit, one of blackcurrants, slightly tart, and one of raspberries, fat and juicy. I always gave the bowls of fruit a particular look which Amelia described as covetous, although I am not sure that it was meant to be. I had a personal pride in those berries because I had picked them myself and therefore regarded them as my own contribution to the picnic.

Annie delegated the task of picking the soft fruit in the kitchen garden to me, something I relished. It was not only because I had the privilege of helping myself as I worked, but also because I loved the warm pink-brick sunlight of the kitchen garden. It seemed to trap birdsong and summer sunshine until late into the evening, and the rich scent of the fruit bushes, bending beneath the weight of their berries, pervaded it. Diggory invariably sauntered past as I picked, his boots clumping on the flagstoned path past the kitchen window where the rosemary, tarragon and parsley grew in chipped and ancient terracotta pots.

'A fine crop there, Caroline,' Diggory would call to me. 'I'm glad they pesky blackbirds have agreed to share them with you.'

The task of unpacking the picnic was always done by Annie, and Mother and Mrs McCullen followed her instructions. I wanted to stay and watch each bag and packet being unwrapped, but Amelia and William tugged at my sleeves and pulled me away.

'Don't go too near the cliff edge,' cautioned Mrs McCullen, and Amelia laughed in a slightly derisory manner.

'I never go too close, Mrs McCullen,' she replied primly. 'I'll keep an eye on William and Caroline though.'

William wanted to go down to the beach, but Amelia told him that there wouldn't be time to explore it properly before lunch. I was glad that she said this, for, to me at least, the whole occasion of the picnic day at the Pollards' farm had become ritualized into a set of unchangeable traditions. It would have spoiled them to have scrambled down to the beach before we had eaten, for that was not the appointed hour. Instead we roamed about the heathery cliff tops hunting for Burnett moths with their unlikely wings of vivid red spots, and Amelia and I gathered, as was another ritual, a bunch of sea thrift and scabious flowers, a tuft of sky of papery pink and purple-blue, to give to Annie.

'You haven't forgotten how to do it, have you?' Amelia and William hissed at me, and I shook my head mutely, my heart racing under the confines of my ribcage. I felt that I was completely incapable of speech, leave alone of reading.

I became too frightened and nervous to eat much of the delicious picnic lunch, despite chivvying by Annie and Mother. I picked half-heartedly at a slice of pigeon pie and nibbled on the corner of my saffron bun.

'Are you feeling unwell?' asked Mrs McCullen, and I nodded, then shook my head in reply, unsure of which was the correct answer. I felt physically sick with apprehension, but I was also ready to burst with joyous excitement at my achievement. I swung between the fear of being unable to remember how to master those printed words, and to the exhilaration of knowing that I could never forget. I felt as though I was flying, spinning with the seagulls from the surface of the waves to high, high in the sky, the merest white speck of freedom against the summer blueness.

The picnic seemed to me to be consumed at a rate that was likewise swooping and soaring. Sometimes it appeared to drag at a tortuous rate of slowness. Sometimes it ricocheted ahead, the knives clattering against the plates like castanets. But when it really was finished, Annie sighed contentedly.

'Why don't you three children dash down to the cove while we three shake the crumbs off the rug for the gulls,' she suggested.

'Be careful on that steep path,' murmured Mrs McCullen.

But William lounged backward with his head leaning against his cupped hands.

'Let's go down to the beach in a minute,' he said, his voice slow, almost careful. 'But I'm too full of picnic just now. Amelia, why don't you read something to us first?' Amelia pulled a worn, red-covered book from a bag, and my heart leaped again with hard, protesting thumps of anticipation.

'Why do I always have to be the reader?' asked Amelia. 'William, you read, or, if you're too lazy, ask somebody else.'

She passed William the book and William, without looking around, stretched his arm backward over his head and dropped it neatly into my lap. I noticed that my knees were trembling and I was grateful that I was sitting down. It was the book of Shakespeare's sonnets and it fell open at number sixty, my first conquest.

'Go on, Caroline,' said William, 'you be reader for once.' His voice was gentle, encouraging and I looked up and saw Amelia staring at me. Her eyes were also encouraging, but they were taunting me, daring me to be unable even to begin to try.

'But William . . .' Mother interrupted quickly; she got no further, for I started to read.

As before I started off slowly and shakily, my voice hesitant. But, as before, the words leaped eagerly off the page at me, shouting out their meanings so clearly that it was no more effort to read each one than it was to pick raspberries, dropping them one by satisfying one into the white china bowl in the kitchen garden.

As I read the last line, the words falling from my lips in strong, steady drops, I looked up again, this time towards Mother, and met her eyes. They were brimming with tears, but her mouth was smiling. She came over quickly and hugged and kissed me, while William, Amelia, Annie and even Mrs McCullen clapped and cheered.

Chapter Eight

Leaving the Pollards' farm had always seemed to mark the ending of the holidays, the fading away of summer freedom. It was no surprise to me that the day that we left dawned through a thick veil of grey sea mist, muting the calls of the roof-top pigeons and clinging coldly to our hair and clothes as we did the obligatory round of farewells about the farm. It seemed strange to be saying goodbye to such dearly familiar, prosaic and yet, for us, unusual objects. Goodbye duckpond; goodbye raspberry canes, blackcurrant bushes and thrushes in the kitchen garden; goodbye laughing farm dogs; goodbye harelipped farm hand Johnny; goodbye five-barred gate which William had taught both Amelia and me to vault. I was very particular not to miss anything, for how was I to know what object that I took for granted now might be missing, vanished for ever into distant yearning, on our next visit to the farm? Last year I had rubbed my cheek against the smooth grey trunk of the old sycamore tree and looked up into its dancing branches. Now there was only an uneven stump, black and rather slimy, with bands of a rubbery grey fungus growing in ridges down its sides.

By the time we had reached Hayle station (goodbye sand dunes; goodbye lighthouse; goodbye narrow winding road; goodbye thatched cottages and winking windows of Gwithian village) the sea mist had condensed into a chilly drizzle that speckled Amelia's spectacles and made Mrs McCullen look chidingly up into the heavy sky as though the weather gods had done this on purpose and needed firmly reproving.

'It always rains when we leave the Pollards' farm,'

explained Amelia to Mrs McCullen and William and anyone else who might be interested. 'Doesn't it, Caroline?'

I nodded, and a puddle of water which had been forming in my collar trickled a trail of coldness down my neck and back. The weather seemed to be quite natural and expected to me. I would have found it so much more difficult to leave the farm if it had still been the blue sky, sunshine weather of our arrival. I would have had to be dragged, I thought, from the tempting and combined loveliness of beach and cliff, sea and farm.

The train arrived, twelve minutes late and panting with effort, and Annie loaded us on and handed our luggage in after us.

'Bye-bye, Annie,' I gasped through the jumble of flailing limbs and bags. 'I can't wait to see you again next year.'

'Thank you for having us, Annie,' said Amelia who never seemed to forget the correct and adult-approved formulae for these occasions. William smiled and nodded agreeably and tried to shake Annie's hand, but Annie grabbed him by the shoulders and kissed him as squarely on the lips as she had kissed Amelia and me.

'Just you look after these two pretty girls for me, young man,' Annie said, and William, too surprised from his kiss to speak, nodded his head so vigorously that I was almost afraid that it might break off from his thin neck and go bounding and rolling down the platform with Annie and Mother and Mrs McCullen chasing frantically after it.

By the time we arrived back in Truro the drizzle had increased in intensity, falling now as a remorseless rain that drummed on the roof of the station and washed the summer dust from the pavements. The gutters swirled and burbled with a grey and scummy liquid that smelt of illness and old age. But even this seemed very proper and fitting to me. It demonstrated that the summer was truly over and that the great brown abyss of the autumn term at school yawned inevitably ahead of us.

For once, however, both Amelia and I were looking forward to the start of the school term. I, of course, was eager to show off my reading skills to the teachers who had long ago given up any hope of my mastering even the basics of literacy. I mused back over comments on the more recent report cards that I had taken home to Mother; she had read them with a sigh.

'Caroline is a friendly and helpful child but I am afraid that she will never master elementary skills such as reading; Mrs Bolivar. Caroline is an obstinate child and has neither academic gifts nor willingness to learn a vocation. I suggest that she leaves education at the earliest possible opportunity; Miss Cutting.'

Yes, humourless Miss Cutting, the headmistress, was going to get a surprise, and I wasn't at all sure how much she was going to like it. Mrs Bolivar too, with her shapeless cardigans of an indeterminate hue that I always mentally described as 'colour of the Pollards' farmyard mud', would be surprised. But she would most certainly be pleased. She would clap her fat little hands together and cry, 'Oh well done, Caroline! Oh, jolly well done!' in that enthusiastic, outdoorsy voice that, I wasn't sure why, reminded me of farms.

Amelia was looking forward to the start of school for a different reason: she was embarking on her first term at the girls' high school. Mother took Amelia to Hurlinghams to buy the uniform and the ugly brown felt hat sat unflatteringly on top of Amelia's head like a decaying leaf. For the summer term she would have an enviable straw boater, but this was the autumn term of brown felt ugliness.

Every sentence that Amelia spoke during those last fleeting days of the summer holiday seemed to begin with the words 'when I start at the High School . . .' until William started parodying Amelia's high-pitched, rather breathy voice and calling her the High School Prodigy. I would have liked to join in and call

Amelia the High School Prodigy too, but I didn't know what prodigy meant and I thought that it might be something rather terrible which could earn me an early night with no supper. I was much too ashamed of my ignorance to ask.

And William himself? 'Are you looking forward to school starting?' I asked him, and he grunted and shrugged in reply as though it made no difference to him.

'All they ever do in schools,' he grumbled, 'is teach you facts. Facts, facts and more facts. And, what is worse, it's the same boring repetition of facts that they taught the last class the year before, and the class before that the year before that.'

'Oh! And what would Mr William McCullen prefer to be taught?' asked Amelia, her voice adopting that challenging tone that I recognized – resigned, but quailing – as heralding an argument. Although I was not feeling as defensive as Amelia about the merits of school, I too wondered what it was that William expected or hoped for from the regimented castles of education. But William did not appear to be goaded into counter-attack by Amelia's battle cries. He shrugged again and scratched his ear without enthusiasm.

'I don't know,' he grunted. 'Ideas, maybe. Theories. Perhaps being taught how to think for yourself.'

'You can't possibly be taught how to think,' replied Amelia very primly. 'You either know how to think or you don't. It's a bit like being able to see or something. You either can, or you can't.' There was a rather superior smile just tickling the corners of her lips and I was suddenly drawn back to that day, weeks or perhaps months ago now, when we had visited Father's grave and Alfred and Dorothy Ambrose. That terrible day when William and Amelia had actually decided that some people would be better off if they were dead.

'You can think, Amelia,' I interrupted, feeling the

hot pinkness spreading up my throat to my cheeks, 'and William can think. But what about me? Can I think? What if I can't? Don't you think that somebody might be able to teach me how to, just like you and William taught me how to read when everybody else said it was impossible?'

It was William who answered, his words leaping on to the tail of my anxious and muddled questioning before Amelia could open her mouth to reply.

'I didn't mean normal, everyday thinking, Caroline. Of course we can all do that – all of us. You, me and Amelia. I meant real, inventive thinking. I meant dreaming up new things, really new ideas, things which nobody has ever thought about before. I don't believe that many people can think like that, but I'm sure we could learn something from being shown examples, given suggestions about how the really great brains, the brilliant minds, the da Vincis of the world, thought and think. I'm not sure that any one of us three would be able to think like that, but how do I know? Perhaps just you can, Caroline. Perhaps Amelia. Perhaps even me. Perhaps all of us, or, more probably, none of us.'

I didn't really understand what William was trying to say about this special, clever, incomprehensible thinking and I was almost certain that da Vinci was the name of a famous painter. Of course a painter would have to be clever to be famous, but a brilliant mind? Despite my doubts about da Vinci, I gazed in fascination at William's glistening eyes and his arms waving energetically as they tried to assist his explanations. His voice had quite lost its previous grumbling tone and throbbed with enthusiasm, making me feel gawky and dull in comparison.

I glanced sideways at Amelia to observe how she was responding to William's strange, excited words. The traces of a smile still glimmered tolerantly around the corners of her mouth and her fingers fiddled with the ribbon which corrugated around her school hat, as yet unworn apart from for demonstration purposes. Although some innate sense of modesty was preventing Amelia from speaking out, every signal from her silent being was that she was quite convinced of her own capabilities. Da Vinci or not, she was certain that she at least was the master of every variety of thinking imaginable.

The three schools, or indeed four schools including Mother's, commenced their autumn terms on different days, as was their almost bolshily distinctive wont. William's school began first, and Amelia and I waved cheekily at him from our garden wall as he set off down the street in his grey school shorts and silly peaked cap, relishing our extra moments of holiday freedom. But for Amelia it was only two extra days and for myself just one, and Mother began back at her teaching post last of all, the day after Amelia.

On my very first day at school I demonstrated for anyone who was interested, teacher and fellow pupil alike, my recently discovered skills of literacy, perhaps still requiring some polishing, but an impressive improvement nevertheless. As I had predicted, Mrs Bolivar, my class teacher for the year, was delighted. The sagging corners of her cardigan flapped in the air like chicken's wings as she clapped her hands to her face and then to each other with undisguised pleasure and amazement.

'But Caroline, that's marvellous!' she exclaimed. 'And how wonderful to be taught this by your dear sister and the little neighbouring boy! Your mother must be so pleased. We must certainly tell Miss Cutting straight away.'

Mrs Bolivar and I, she still beaming and occasionally clapping, went to Miss Cutting's cold little cell with the etched glass door and the brass plate which read (for I could read it now, rather than just trace the engraved letters with my finger), 'Headmistress. Please knock and then wait'. So we knocked and waited until Miss

Cutting's clipped tones summoned us to enter.

Miss Cutting's little cell – and with its windows very small and high up in the pictureless wall, the row of sullen-faced grey metal filing cabinets, the atmosphere of frostiness and restriction, it did seem terribly prison-like to me – was not a place that I associated with celebration. Here excuses were handed in and punishments were handed out. Here I had once been rapped very sharply across the palm of my hand by Miss Cutting, wielding the short ebony cane that usually hung from a brass loop on her belt, swinging softly and menacingly amongst the folds of her skirts as she walked. My sin, as I recall it, had been relatively minor, either speaking when I should have remained silent or remaining silent when I should have spoken, and the punishment, although it had been quickly delivered, had seemed disproportionately severe. The red weal with its white central line, no wider than a hair, had remained on my hand for several days, smarting and uncomfortable, and somehow reminiscent of the grim slit of Miss Cutting's mouth. But this time in the chilly cell, with Mrs Bolivar's plump and be-ringed hands pressing reassuringly into my shoulders as she shepherded me in front of her, things would surely be very much better.

Miss Cutting was sitting at her desk when we entered. There were five piles of papers, very correct and orderly, on her left and to her right her pens and pencils, the latter sharpened to hard little points, in a neat row and a jug of water with a glass, upside down, on a prim white coaster. I observed all these details of object and position as Mrs Bolivar's eager voice lapped over and around me, telling Miss Cutting of the astounding progress made in the summer holidays by their previously illiterate pupil.

'So Miss Caroline West can read now?' Miss Cutting asked me at last, firing a stare at me down the long ridge of her nose.

'Why yes Miss Cutting.'

'And you can write as well, I imagine?'

'Not yet Miss Cutting, but I mean to learn as soon as possible.'

'I find it hard to believe, Caroline West, that a child that is capable of reading is incapable of writing.'

I remained silent and looked away from Miss Cutting's accusatory, disbelieving eyes to the rows of fat morocco-bound books which stood to attention on the shelves behind her.

'Many children,' said Mrs Bolivar gently, her voice slow and rather cautious, 'seem to need a while to adjust to the joy of reading before they can overcome the hurdle of writing.'

'I thank you for your opinion, Mrs Bolivar,' said Miss Cutting coldly, 'but I hesitate to exchange my greater experience for your lesser knowledge. The question that I feel obliged to put to you now is this: has Caroline West indeed managed to grasp, as she claims, the privilege of reading? Or has she, by recitation of simple verses and sentences that she has learned by rote, merely duped you?' Miss Cutting's lips twitched a little as she finished her sentence, and her eyes were cold pebbles in her face.

'Oh Miss Cutting!' I gasped, but I believe my words were inaudible, for Mrs Bolivar came promptly to my defence.

'With due respect, Miss Cutting, I really do not think this is the case.' Although Mrs Bolivar's voice was polite it was also firm and I felt her hands, warm on my shoulders, pressing down on me a little harder, a little more reassuringly.

'Caroline West has been before me in my office on a previous occasion, Mrs Bolivar,' Miss Cutting replied, her voice matching her eyes, 'and, I might add, under circumstances that were entirely reprehensible. However, there is no necessity for us to disagree, for we can very easily test whether Caroline West is trying to deceive us, right here and now in my room. Let us give her some prose to read aloud to us.'

'I shall get something from the classroom directly,' said Mrs Bolivar.

Miss Cutting shook her head slowly and deliberately. I had an image of snakes and helpless rabbits and I felt my legs trembling beneath me. I was certain that whatever easy sentences were placed before me now, I would be quite incapable of reading a single word, or pronouncing a single syllable or letter.

'No, we won't bring some simple primer from the classroom, Mrs Bolivar.' Miss Cutting's voice was steel piercing ice, ice piercing steel. 'I have plenty of reading material available here.'

She stood up from the chair at her desk, and I realized anew how tall and straight she was. With another quiver of fear I glimpsed the short ebony cane glinting as it swung beside her from her belt. Miss Cutting selected a book from the shelves behind her and my mouth felt as though it was suffocatingly crammed with a dry and crumbly cheese that clogged my palate and made my breath come in short sour gasps.

'Miss Cutting,' broke in Mrs Bolivar, 'these books of yours are learned works. Surely you must agree that they are quite unsuited to a child who has only mastered the art of reading some few weeks ago, and that with considerable difficulty of which we both are fully aware.'

'Words are but words, Mrs Bolivar,' replied Miss Cutting, placing the chosen book before me on the desk. 'It is not the inner meaning of great literature that I am expecting or asking this Caroline West to attempt to interpret for us. I am merely requesting a demonstration of this reading skill on which I have already wasted too much time, and of which I must admit to being highly sceptical.'

By this point I felt so terrified and so certain of my fate looming close, of another encounter with Miss Cutting's cane, that any printed words, not just verbose and erudite text but even the easiest nursery rhyme,

74

would have been impossible for me to read. But, to say that any words were beyond my grasp is to exaggerate. Miss Cutting opened the book before me and the faint, dry aroma of disuse came dustily up.

'I expect, Caroline West, that you are acquainted with the name of the author of these words, although I should not imagine that you have much close knowledge of his works.' My gaze, which, if it had been focused on anything at all, had been trained upon the grain of the wood in Miss Cutting's desk, jumped to the book. It appeared that my heart must have previously stopped beating, for it leaped alive now with such a sudden, kicking jerk that I was surprised it did not make a hole in my ribcage and go dancing wildly about the room, enlivening the blank walls with bursts of scarlet blood.

Shakespeare! I nodded my head mechanically, for I still could not trust my voice.

Out of the corner of my eye I saw Miss Cutting's hand, thin and pointed, and with irregular blotches of melanin marking the skin like coffee stains, slide to her waist and unclip the cane from the hoop on her belt. She placed it very deliberately upon her desk beside the water jug. There was a click, as she positioned it, of wood tapping wood; it sounded impatient, as though longing to progress to flesh.

Behind me, poor Mrs Bolivar, who had surely never envisaged the passage of events presently unfolding before her, gave a little gasp and the pressure of her plump hands on my shoulders became slightly more urgent. Her palms seemed to be clutching at me and burning through my thin school blouse. I imagined that she would leave two hand-shaped scorch marks there, for which Mother would surely scold me.

'Well?' prompted Miss Cutting.

With automatic fingers which appeared to operate without needing command or effort, I turned some of the pages of the unloved book. They were of thick, good-quality paper and the typeface was superior and clear, quite unlike the book of Shakespeare in its stained red jacket that I was used to handling. And then, suddenly, it was there before me: my party piece. For a few brief, elastic seconds the letters stayed in their jumble of angry barbs against the slightly yellowed paper, and only the number which headed the page sang out to me.

In my mind's eye I saw the glowing, triumphant eyes of Amelia and William; as that image faded, it was replaced by the tear-brimmed eyes of Mother, the warm, salty smell of cliff tops and the mingled harmony of waves and seagulls and clapping.

'Well, Caroline West?' repeated Miss Cutting. With my voice slow, but steady and gathering confidence and volume, I began to read.

After a week or so of the new term had elapsed and faded into the past, the three of us, Amelia, William and I, had become accustomed to our new roles in school and life seemed to have settled down into that series of comfortable, comforting patterns that they call routines.

My ability to read was no longer a source of wonder to people other than myself. Although Mrs Bolivar now treated me with a special, undisguised warmth and enthusiasm and although Miss Cutting swept past me without ever looking down at me and acknowledging my presence, it all seemed terribly normal now and not worthy of either comment or criticism. For my own part, I was still struggling to form letters, and hopefully later, words, myself.

I was naturally a left-handed individual, but according to the rules laid down by Miss Cutting left-handedness was not to be tolerated. Left-handed people were sinister, Miss Cutting said, and she called on the Romans to support her claim. It was the work of the devil to be left-handed. Amelia would probably have relished the chance to prove some sign of Christian ignorance in this matter and would even have dared to flaunt left-handedness, but I was much too willing to conform and thus be camouflaged. I forced my recalcitrant right hand to tumble out rows of clumsy, ugly letters, distressed to find that they always seemed crippled and sad.

Meanwhile William had apparently resigned himself to the constraints of factual teaching and the endless schoolboy teasing about his Scottish accent, and Amelia, who had initially been besotted by her new school to the point of wide-eyed entrancement, now treated it with the mundane, Monday to Friday matter-of-factness which it deserved. The ugly brown hat was no longer hung up reverentially on the peg in the hallway as soon as she got home to avoid being damaged by William or me or Hilary the cat, but flung carelessly down on the cushions in the sitting-room along with her brown gaberdine raincoat and satchel. Here it was at risk of being sat on, or patted to the floor by Hilary, pounced upon and dented.

We were both glad, William and I, and perhaps even Mother, that Amelia had mastered her infatuation with her new school and was capable of speaking about it in a normal, no longer reverential, tone of voice. Better still, she seemed quite content to not speak of school at all. She even suggested that we might meet in town to walk home together at the end of the day.

We began to meet outside a small newsagent, not far from the cathedral, called Worthingtons. It was pre-sided over by Mrs Worthington herself, a grey-haired, rather dumpy lady who snorted frequently and loudly into a white handkerchief. After use, she would throw the handkerchief carelessly down on top of the counter, regardless of the health or sensibilities of her customers.

As well as stocking the regional newspapers, the *Western Morning News*, the *Falmouth Packet*, the *West Briton* and the *Cornishman*, and the national papers too, Worthingtons sold cigarettes, writing paper, bottles of royal blue and permanent black ink, erasers that could sit proudly on the end of your pencil, candles, Brasso, marbles, light bulbs and tins of golden syrup. These things were in the window display that Mrs Worthington dusted and rearranged slightly every week.

I was invariably at the meeting point before Amelia, for she, unlike myself, who hurried from the school gates as soon as I possibly could, trying to diminish the possibility of Miss Cutting's cold eyes alighting unfavourably upon me, tended to linger a little after her lessons were over. Perhaps she was chattering to a friend, for Amelia had always been convivial. Perhaps she was stacking her books neatly in her desk, for she was strictly and maddeningly methodical in such things. Perhaps she was even ingratiating herself with her teachers, as was her custom. Whatever the reason, I surmised that she must be lingering because a group of four girls from her school always arrived at Worthingtons before Amelia and had left by the time she got there.

I could recognize this giggling gaggle of four as being high school girls by their own cowpat headgear like Amelia's. I guessed, not only from their size and the hint of curvature of their pre-pubescent breasts, but also from their brashly confident voices, that these were not new pupils like Amelia, but perhaps one, or even two, years further up the educational ladder.

Every day, one or other of the party of schoolgirls would go into Worthingtons and emerge with some offering to be shared amongst the four friends. Perhaps a small paper bag of sticky sherbet lemons or jelly babies; sometimes a bottle of ginger beer or lemonade. These items were not part of the window display, but kept by Mrs Worthington behind the counter. She was never very punctilious about demanding sweet coupons from her customers. First come, first served appeared to be her guiding principle. The sweets were stored in tall glass jars with fat glass stoppers, and stood on a shelf just above the height of Mrs

Worthington's head. She had to stand on a low wooden stool to reach down the customer's desired jar, before weighing out the sweets on the big scales which stood beside the till. The bottles of drink resided in a crate at her feet. Sometimes she would stub her toes on the bottle crate and mutter 'bother' or 'blast', but she never moved fast enough to hurt herself too severely. She lumbered from one end of the counter to the other like an ancient, snorting toad.

I rarely had any spare pocket money to spend in Worthingtons, but when I did, I would buy a quarter of jelly babies – if they were available – and Amelia and I would share them on the way home. It was a rule that neither of us should look into the bag when picking out a jelly baby, for both of us for some reason favoured the black ones, although I must admit that they all tasted very similar. We both had our different ways of eating those little effigies too. Amelia would start at the feet, then the arms would be nibbled off, the body would follow in one bite and finally the head would be eaten. It seemed cruel to me, almost a form of torture, and I would always decapitate my jelly baby, black or orange or red or green, in one swift clean bite to prevent the possibility of any unnecessary suffering. But purchases of these sweets, and the subsequent rituals, were relatively rare and I was mostly restricted, as I waited, to contemplating Mrs Worthington's window display.

I like to think I had a critically appreciative eye. I would notice with approval the small changes in the juxtaposition of light bulbs and candles, the elegantly balanced pyramid of pencil-end erasers and the light glinting off the blue, white and gold tins of Brasso. I would listen to the chatter of the trio of girls waiting for their friend as she made the daily purchase inside the shop. They took no notice of the stoop-shouldered, brown-haired girl that was myself, waiting silently, peering intently into Worthingtons window.

Meeting Amelia here soon became absorbed into the

routine of the school day, and sometimes William too might join us. However, his school placed much emphasis on participation in extra-curricular activities, and the first hour of almost every evening would be taken up with his football, chess club, or choir practice. It was therefore quite exceptional for William to turn up at Worthingtons, his fingers splotched with ink and his red hair poking out, this way and that, from beneath his school cap. On those occasions when William was not committed to some school endeavour, and appeared to join us walking back to Treddanick Close, he always arrived after me but before Amelia, and before the four other high school girls had sauntered off together in the direction of the cathedral, passing their paper bag of sweets or bottle of drink to and fro and chattering all the while.

Whenever William did turn up at the shop he always seemed to have a few pennies to spare, and he would invite me to accompany him inside to spend his money. With the door jangling shut behind us, William would make his careful selection from Mrs Worthington and as she tipped the sweets into the weighing pan of the scales he would enquire of her very politely as to the state of her health and wasn't the weather mild?

William tended to favour bull's-eyes and another type of confectionery, spherical in shape and of a rather unappetizing translucent green. Its taste reminded me unpleasantly of mouthwash, although Amelia told me that it was aniseed. Perhaps because of his politeness, or perhaps because he reminded Mrs Worthington of her own son who had died in the war almost ten years before, she always put a few extra sweets into William's paper bag.

On the third time that William joined me at Worthingtons to await the arrival of Amelia I noticed that he was making some sort of impact on the four girls. Previously they had ignored me totally. I was as invisible to them as the shreds of grey cloud in the late afternoon sky; I was of less importance than the leaves, just curling brown now, on the trees.

With William beside me, however, they took some notice of me. They shot covert, winking glances towards where we leaned together on the brick wall beside the window display, each of us sucking on a bull's-eye. Their giggles were more strident and seemed, if not actually directed at us, to wish to involve us. But William, whistling through an awkward combination of teeth and bull's-eye, appeared quite oblivious. As the four of them moved off down the street towards the cathedral, they bobbed furtive glances over their shoulders towards us and tossed their hair about as though it should command attention.

'Do you know them?' I asked William curiously, for I could not envisage how their paths might previously have crossed.

'Who?' asked William.

'Them,' I replied and pointed at the four receding figures, their high voices still fluting back to us up the street.

'No, of course I don't,' answered William. 'Just a handful of silly schoolgirls. Why on earth should I?'

Amelia, of course, would have responded with vigour to William's implication that schoolgirls were necessarily silly, but I was more struck by the lack of interest in William's voice. It suggested to me that I must have imagined any change in the behaviour of the four girls. So I shrugged an equally disinterested 'I don't know,' and changed the subject.

Yet it hadn't been my imagination after all. The following day, a cool and foggy Thursday with the sun sliding cautiously through layers of mist that rose trembling from the grey surface of the Fal and swathed the whole valley, one of the girls actually approached me and spoke to me. Another had gone in through the jangling door to Worthingtons and the other two remained at a distance, giggling encouragement. The spokesman for the quartet had thick brown hair and big brown eyes, almost exactly the same dull mud shade as her school uniform. Her face was puppy-plump and there was an ugly acne spot on her chin that had been prodded and squeezed into an angry eruption.

'Was that your boyfriend who was here yesterday?' the girl asked. Her teeth were bared in a grimace that could have been a smile, but could equally well have been a sneer or a snarl.

I don't know now whether it was the unexpected words which startled me most, or the fact that one of these girls had approached and spoken to me at all. I felt quite incapable of verbal response, and I shook my head mutely.

'I bet he is your boyfriend really,' the girl said defiantly, stretching out the last word to a screech and baring her teeth again, although this time it seemed to me to be less probable that she was smiling.

Again I shook my head.

The girl turned to her friends; by now the third had emerged from Worthingtons bearing a bottle of ginger beer, the door jangling closed behind her.

'She's shaking her head,' my interrogator told them as though they were not watching our every movement eagerly, 'but she's not speaking.'

'Maybe she's mute,' suggested the girl who had bought the ginger beer, and the others giggled raucously as though a tremendous joke had just been cracked.

'Perhaps you're right,' gasped one of them, her long dark hair swinging in a braid down her back. 'She goes to the retard school, doesn't she? Try and get her to speak, Alice. Oh, do try.'

And Alice, with her chin-side pimple glinting savagely, said, 'What's your name, dumby? What's your name?'

It wasn't the first time I had been teased about my slowness and clumsiness, but it was certainly one of the most vicious, unprovoked attacks, and the tears of shame were already prickling demandingly behind my eyelids. I had to gulp twice before I was able to answer, and even then my voice was reedy thin and trembling.

'My name is Caroline West and the boy who was here with me yesterday lives next door. We sometimes walk back home from school together.'

Alice turned from me to face her trio of giggling friends.

'My name is Caroline West . . .' she mimicked cruelly and the four of them clapped their hands with delight and hooted gleefully.

Alice faced me again. How I hated that sueted face and despised that pustulating spot. I bit my lip to try and stop its spontaneous trembling and to hold in my tears.

'Has he stood you up today then?' asked Alice and, like a line of ill-trained chorus girls, the cluster of her friends started a taunting chant behind her.

'Stood you up . . . Caroline West has been stood up . . . poor little Caroline . . . retardy Caroline West . . . Caroline goes to simpleton school . . .'

'I'm waiting for my sister,' I muttered miserably, and then I realized that Amelia would soon arrive. I desperately wanted to see her, a familiar, loved and loving face amongst all this hateful mockery, but also I was ashamed. I could not bear the thought of her witnessing my humiliation by the sharp tongues of her fellow pupils.

But one of the girls was getting anxious about the time, and before Amelia appeared my tormentors had already left, laughing down the street towards the cathedral. The girl who had bought the ginger beer turned to look at me.

'See you tomorrow, Caroline West?' she called down the street in her taunting voice of silvery superiority, and her friends, pausing for her, laughed the more.

'Oh Tamsin!' I heard one of them say, 'you and Alice don't half make a pair.'

Alice and Tamsin and the other two girls, their friends, who I later found out were Katherine and Julia, the one with a pretty pink and white face and an ever so slight lisp and the other with big, rather bulging eyes of a bog-alder greenish-grey, now became the four nightmare menaces of my existence.

I was too ashamed to tell Amelia and William, and it didn't cross my mind to run whimpering to Mother or Mrs Bolivar. Although either of the latter two might have acted as most able and discreet benefactresses, they were, or so it seemed to me, far away from my plight, up there in the distant and incomprehensible world of adulthood and authoritative responsibility. Besides, every schoolchild has it impressed upon them by their peers that blabbing, telling tales, sneaking or otherwise reporting to the world of dictatorial adult-dom the crimes of other children is an unpardonable sin. Instead I began to linger around the gates of my school, hoping to avoid a meeting with the quartet. I scuffed my shoes amongst the wind-banks of mushy brown leaves beside the low brick walls and wished that a thunderbolt, even a gargoyle from the cathedral, might kill them all.

The school days crept tortuously past now, dragging through October, and the evenings became damper, darker, drizzlier. I was afraid of the hard, taunting faces and the jeering voices, and I lingered outside my school all the more. Often, by the time I had arrived at the Worthingtons rendezvous, my four tormentors had long since left and Amelia would be there waiting for me impatiently. She tended to suffer from chilblains and she would be puffing on her hands and stamping her feet.

'Where on earth have you been, Caroline?' Amelia would ask me, her voice high with peevishness. 'Is Miss Cutting keeping you back after school?'

I, too lumberingly slow in imagination to think up credible excuses, would shake my head dumbly and resolve not to be so late next time. And, arriving earlier on the following day, I would again have to face Alice, Tamsin, Katherine and Julia, not yet felled despite my most vindictive and terrible thoughts.

If William was with me I would be spared all but the most cursory of mocking glances that seemed barely to brush against me, but if I was alone I became the object of all their ridicule and derision. I could see this torture lasting for ever, following me out of childhood into the mysterious far-off ways of being an adult and finally into even more mysterious and distant old age, an inevitable and infinite spiral of contempt. But, of course, things seldom follow such simple patterns.

October faded, misty grey and damp with puddles on the pavements, into a crisper and bleaker November. The light from Worthingtons window threw a golden rectangle into the street where I waited for Amelia. It made a spotlit stage for Alice, Tamsin, Katherine and Julia to play out their games of cruel mockery.

The leaves by the wall around my school were all swept away now, and I wasted time picking at the moss in the cracks, uncovering woodlice which had presumed themselves to be snuggled safely away. I arrived late at Worthingtons. Amelia was waiting for me, stamping her feet and blowing on her fingers, her plaits sticking out from beneath her school hat at their usual hectic angle. Although on this occasion William was waiting with her too, chess club cancelled due to the master succumbing to a bout of influenza, rather than being less impatient she seemed to be even more so, and both her posture and expression were more than typically alert. William, as usual, had his bag of Worthingtons sweets, this time the green mouthwash spheres, and as I took one and popped it in my mouth for the walk home he said, 'I'm glad you're here at last, Caroline. Amelia said that she couldn't possibly tell me what the matter is until you had arrived.'

I looked sideways at Amelia and although, as I have said, the impatience and excitement in her face and bearing were both magnified, she also seemed strangely reluctant to speak.

'Well?' prompted William, but she just looked crossly at him and said that her feet were cold. I remained silent and sucked harder on the nasty sweet, until I could feel the insides of my cheeks all dry and rasping.

'Oh Amelia!' said William, his voice exasperated. 'You told me that you would say what was wrong when Caroline got to Worthingtons, and now look at us, practically halfway home and all you want to do is whine about your toes.'

'But . . .' said Amelia, and paused. It was unlike her to be so hesitant.

'Yes?' said William encouragingly.

'It's got absolutely nothing to do with you, William McCullen,' Amelia burst out, 'but since you insist on pressing me . . .' William interrupted sharply.

'Oh, a secret!' His voice was hard and cold. 'I must apologize. I didn't realize that you and Caroline had secrets from me.'

All three of us had stopped walking now and were standing in an ill-humoured little triangle in the middle of the street, blocking the pavement. Two men dressed in suits, one youngish and with an earnest face and the other older, florid and fat with a watch-chain stretched across his paunch, had to step on to the road to get past us. The older man tutted crossly at us.

I probably noticed the two suited gentlemen because I was not really listening to Amelia and William. I had no idea what they were squabbling about. They argued so often and with such vehemence over the most trivial matters that it didn't seem terribly import-ant to me; it was just another of their hateful quarrels.

Amelia and William, however, were so involved in their argument that I'm sure neither of them noticed the two men, nor do I think that they noticed the lady who followed behind a few minutes later in a coat and matching hat of mottled orangey fur. She tutted also, if anything more crossly than the watch-chained man, as she skirted around us. But Amelia and William were intent on glaring at each other and the lenses of Amelia's spectacles glittered furiously, the way that they always did when she was annoyed.

'Oh, do come on you two and stop being silly,' I said in an attempt to be peacemaker. 'Of course we don't have secrets from you, William. Please don't quarrel now. We're in the way here, and Amelia, you must be getting cold.'

'Do shut up, Caroline,' William rounded on me fiercely. 'You don't have a clue what we're talking about.'

Amelia, almost simultaneously with William, snapped, 'Well, if that's the way you feel, Caroline West, then I'll stop worrying about your precious feelings and show you both.'

As she spoke, Amelia put her hand into the pocket of her gaberdine, and after some fumbling extracted a piece of folded paper with some strands of silky pocket lining still attached to the corners. Amelia unfolded the paper and smoothed its creases before holding it out for William and me to see. It was a note, neatly written in squat black capital letters and Amelia read it to us in her cold little voice, although all of us could read, of course. In the dark autumn air her words sounded sharp and brittle.

'Amelia West has a dumbo sister. Amelia West's sister is a retard.'

The green mouthwash sweet in my mouth, now sucked to a smooth small bullet, was swallowed in surprise, and apparently catching in my throat, made me gag and splutter.

'Oh!' I cried. 'Oh!' It was an automatic, hopeless reaction. I wanted to clap my hands over my ears and run away as I had in the summer when William and Amelia had discussed the deaths of handicapped children. This time, however, I was a little braver and stood my ground, still repeating my foolish, helpless cries of despair.

'But who on earth wrote that?' William was asking and Amelia shrugged and shook her head. Her mouth was buttoned into a thin and angry line.

'I thought that Caroline might know,' she said.

They both turned their bright eyes on me and I knew immediately who the perpetrators of that note must be.

'Oh!' I repeated.

'Well?' asked Amelia and William in unison.

'I want to sit down,' I said.

Our route home led us close to St Michael's church where William and Mrs McCullen attended the morning service every Sunday. Beside the railings there was a bench with wooden slats painted in a pale green and deeply scored with initials. We sat on it in the darkness, in a cold and therefore huddled row. Amelia sat to my right and William to my left.

'Oh!' I said yet again and William and Amelia chorused, 'Well?'

So it all came out: Alice with her glowering spot and suet-pudding face, Tamsin with her swinging black plait, Katherine with her strawberries-and-cream complexion and Julia with her bog-alder eyes; all four of them taunting and mocking me outside Worthingtons while I waited for Amelia.

'But why didn't you tell us?' demanded Amelia, and I shrugged helplessly.

'Don't tell Mother, though,' I pleaded.

'Of course not,' said Amelia and William.

Revenge is reputed to be sweet, but the taste that filled my mouth was the metallic flavour of nauseous trepidation as William and I lurked cautiously across the street from Worthingtons on the following day and watched Amelia confront my four persecutors. Her voice carried to us clearly. It was shriller than I had ever heard it, as she accused and admonished with fury.

'My sister,' I could hear her shrieking at them, 'has

more intelligence than the four of you combined. I'm surprised that your mothers didn't suffocate you at birth.' The girls, not expecting this wild attack, huddled together briefly, reminding me of the cattle at the Pollards' farm before a thunderstorm. It was Alice who regained her poise first.

'It's only Amelia West from the first year,' she jeered. 'Have you come to protect your imbecile sister? Where's poor little Caroline West now? Is she still up at the retard school, learning to tell the time and tie her shoelaces?'

Alice thrust her plump, sneering face out towards Amelia, and Amelia, who never missed a chance, took a single, calculated step backwards and thumped Alice hard and squarely on the nose.

The scrap, for it was too brief and much too messily flailing to be called a fight, was soon over. Alice's nose began to bleed. Tamsin hit Amelia, but it was an awkward, ill-prepared hit that grazed against my sister's cheek and knocked her spectacles sideways on to the ground. Amelia kicked Tamsin in the shins and tugged hard on her long black plait and punched Julia in one of her bulging, bog-alder eyes. William, who had dashed across the street to join in the fray at the first sound of flesh colliding with flesh, thumped out wildly, and Alice, snorting back her blood, pulled off Amelia's hat. Then, just as William lined himself up for another thump, Mrs Worthington, alerted by all the commotion, pulled open the shop door.

Alice, Tamsin, Katherine and Julia looked fearfully up at Mrs Worthington's bulky form, handkerchief in hand, silhouetted in the doorway. They ran off quickly down the street towards the cathedral, Alice still in possession of Amelia's hat.

Running away implies guilt, and, rightly or wrongly, Mrs Worthington assumed us to be the innocent party and gathered us quickly into the security of her shop. William, of course, had often been treated favourably by her, and Amelia, without her glasses (for they had

been trampled underfoot, and, although easily
mended, were presently bent into an unwearable
shape), had an endearing look of defenceless innocence. Her hair was awry and her precious school hat
was missing in the hands of the enemy, but her eyes,
unprotected, glowed. Mrs Worthington gave us each a
quarter of jelly babies to take home with us.

Chapter Nine

After Amelia's triumph, life seemed to settle down for a while and jog along at a more comfortable and ordered pace. Mother, of course, was curious as to why Amelia's spectacles were misshapen and where on earth was her school hat which had cost no mean amount of money. Amelia, however, was quicker by far than me at producing convincing stories and Mother, although she gave a sniff to let us know that she wasn't entirely deceived, was appeased.

As Amelia had predicted her hat was returned to her, anonymously, the following day. She related with glee that Julia had apparently inadvertently walked into the corner of a door at home the previous evening, for her eye was swollen and puffy and a glorious array of colours, from purple through to yellow like a sunset. But I never saw Julia's sunset eye, nor indeed did I see Alice, Tamsin or Katherine, for they stopped visiting Worthingtons after school. I was able to wait for Amelia, and sometimes William, outside the shop window with an easy heart.

Mrs Worthington used to look out for us now and, when it was rainy or there was a particularly biting wind, she would come to the jangling door and suggest that I waited inside. It was pleasant being the favoured patrons of a shop stocking sweets, for she often gave us a free sherbet lemon and at Christmas she presented us each with a large bar of milk chocolate in shiny purple paper. But the season of goodwill was a little way off yet, and before Christmas that year there was one more episode to be played out.

It was traditional for each of our schools to perform a

simple Nativity play for friends and relatives to attend. A small entrance fee was charged, and donated by the school to some worthy cause. As far as I recall, and my memory is hazy, Amelia's school chose some war-widow fund, mine selected a trust for the blind, and William's school, I believe, decided that the lifeboat men should receive their offering.

Unlike Amelia, whose forthright opinions about the ignorance of Christians could not be suppressed and who evaded any participation in her Nativity play, I was too frightened of Miss Cutting and too willing to conform with my peer group, to refuse a minor role as an angel in part of the heavenly host. Also, I had never been on stage before and I had an irrational desire to perform.

Amelia, of course, was scornful of my spinelessness and Mother sighed wearily when she realized that she would have to help in the construction of my costume. But it seemed easier to face Amelia's scorn, to which I was accustomed, and Mother's sighs, than to back out of my acceptance. In the camouflage of a flimsy white sheet and a cardboard halo, I was glad, not only to have my stage début, but also to escape being a dissenter and thus easy game for Miss Cutting's eye.

William, however, was quite careless of Amelia's scorn. In many ways he seemed to welcome it. He landed a star part in his school Nativity play: he was to be one of the three kings, either Balthazar or Melchior if I remember rightly. For his role, he had a snazzy little costume of which I, and I believe Amelia, was secretly jealous. Baggy red satinette trousers William was dressed in, and a velveteen jacket of black and purple with gold braid around the cuffs and six gold buttons down the front. The best bit, however, was his fez, which was also black and purple velveteen and sported a long central tassel of some gold and glittery woven fibre. On close inspection the costume was rather elderly: the gold was peeling off the buttons at the edges and the seams were sorry affairs, held together with looping tacking stitches and safety pins. From a distance, however, and especially when draped about William, it looked quite sumptuous and most wonderfully impressive and theatrical.

Both William and I had to bring home our costumes for fitting and we spent an evening prancing about our living-room in them, while Mother and Mrs McCullen, with their mouths full of pins and tape measures looped across their shoulders, made adjustments to lengths and widths. Amelia lounged by the window with Hilary the cat on her lap.

How dowdy I felt in my flimsy angel costume compared to William in his king's attire, but Amelia kept nagging at him and complained that his pantaloons clashed with his hair.

'Do let me try on your costume,' she said to him when Mother and Mrs McCullen had finished their tightenings and turnings. But William was regally lofty in his reply.

'No, Amelia,' he said. 'You told me that it was ignorant to be participating in a Nativity play,' and, despite the persistence of her requests, he refused to change his mind.

Rehearsals, both in plain clothes and in costume, took place during lunchtimes and after school, but those with minor parts were seldom required for evening rehearsals. As an insignificant angel (second to back row, fourth from the left) amongst the heavenly throng appearing on just two occasions, first to the shepherds in their tea-towel headdresses and secondly in the final tableau gathered around the crib, I was very much a minor part.

I sang choruses with the other angels; I was supposed to be an alto, but I was never quite sure what that meant. I tried instead to follow the tune of the rather loud angel who stood to my right. I also had to clasp my hands before me and smile in the prescribed manner of an angel, nothing too coarse and toothy. I tried my best to perfect this smile at home in the bathroom mirror, but Amelia mocked me and told me that I looked as though I had stomach ache.

Chorus angels, like myself, were such a minor part that they were even denied the privilege of wings. Only the angel Gabriel in our production, a girl with frizzy blonde hair called Shirley, was allowed wings. Hers were of gold-painted cardboard strapped to her waist by a silver belt. But Shirley's wings seemed to be more of an encumbrance than a privilege, and she was not adept at managing them. They were invariably rather wonky by the final scene and gave the angel Gabriel a rakish appearance, as though too much celestial activity had intoxicated her.

William's major role meant that he never had to appear in the middle of a cluster of semi-clones. He had three full scenes in which he was centre stage, with words to speak and even a solo to sing. It was his singing voice which had, apparently, earned him his part. Although his east-coast Scottish accent would always sound harsh and rasping to us southerners when he spoke, when he sang the rusty nails and wave-clattered pebbles would mysteriously have disappeared, leaving only a sweet harmonious richness.

As the term rumbled through the end of November and slid into December, the nights swept across the hours ever earlier. The evening air developed a sharpness that made the stars and moon, hanging in the sky above us, seem very cold and close and white. The windows of the houses that we passed beamed warm, reassuring glows across their gravel paths and dark humps of flowerbeds.

Often, in the morning, each blade of grass crackled with the whiteness of frost that crunched delightfully underfoot, although Amelia complained that it aggravated her chilblains.

School always seemed to switch down a gear at this time of year, or at least it switched to a different channel. The priorities were no longer concerned with the addition of columns of awkward figures and the careful formation of letters, but the more exuberant application of crêpe paper in red and green, cotton wool in abundance and the deliciously pervasive smell of Copydex glue.

While school itself was winding down, rehearsals for the Nativity plays wound themselves up. William had a sore throat that Mrs McCullen was afraid might develop into laryngitis which he had suffered from the previous year; but then, Stonehaven was so cold, I imagined that everyone who lived there would be likely to develop such a complaint.

For my part, I perfected in my sleep an awful nightmare about the play. In this nightmare, the final tableau was taking place with a critical audience watching, and there I stood amongst my fellow angels of the heavenly host, second row from the back, fourth from the left, and absolutely desperate for a pee. In my nightmare the awful, onstage urination never actually happened, although it was anticipated in full and terrible detail. I would awake just at the point when I knew that my powers of bladder control were waning, with my heart beating wildly in my chest, and I would be amazed at the quiet calm of the bedroom. My bladder would be pressing, uncomfortably full and stretched to capacity, against my abdominal wall. Of course, my nightmare was never realized just as William never developed the suspected laryngitis.

There were to be two performances of our play on subsequent nights and I rather hoped that William and Mrs McCullen might be able to attend the first, while Mother and Amelia came to the second. However, William had a rehearsal for his own play on the first night, and so all four of them came together.

Amelia complained bitterly, of course, about having to comply with this pageant of ignorant Christianity, and kept reminding us that she had managed to avoid the slightest participation in such an event. She glossed over as best she could, however, the compulsory carol service that the high school enforced as though it were a visit to the dentist or some other necessary evil. The high school carol service was in the cathedral, the building that both Amelia and I loathed and that I blamed for the death of my father.

Mother, who, I was certain, was just as scornful as Amelia of Christians and all their accompanying baggage of ritual and ceremony, although, like most adults, she could convey her displeasure without the necessity of clumsy, restrictive words, was strangely biased over the matter of the Nativity plays.

'If you don't want to come, Amelia,' she said with her eyes glittering in that peculiarly reproving and threatening manner that she often used to silence us or to make us behave, 'then you can stay at home and keep the living-room fire stoked up for our return. Or, perhaps, while you're waiting for us, you might care to do the ironing.'

So Amelia, somewhat subdued by Mother's betrayal, came with her and William and Mrs McCullen to watch my school Nativity play. I am sure it was not the threatening pile of sheets and blouses waiting to be ironed that persuaded her, but the idea of being left out. Amelia always wanted to be included in any activity, preferably to be right at the very heart of it, and this seemed to apply however hateful or Christianly ignorant that activity might be.

'Oh, I want to come,' Amelia sniffed crossly at Mother. 'I'm just glad that I'm not acting in the silly Nativity play at the high school.'

Mother smiled in response and said nothing. She often told me that it was frequently wiser to say nothing, but it was a principle that neither she nor Amelia generally adopted.

The performances of my play went well, as far as my limited assessment could tell. The first night was exciting for being just that: it was the first time before a real audience. One of the shepherds, who were, like the angels, barefoot, stubbed a toe and said 'Ow!'

rather loudly and the innkeeper was nervous and had to be prompted more than once by Mrs Bolivar, but other than that everything seemed fine to me. But it was nothing compared to the second performance, for this had all the excitement of being the last night, the end, the climax, and also there were four people in the audience who had come expressly to see me.

'You were lovely, Caroline dear,' Mother said to me afterwards. 'You made a beautiful angel.'

I could feel my face, all flushed pink from the excitement of the occasion, burn a little hotter with pleasure at her compliments.

'We could only see your halo and the top of your head,' said Amelia, 'and your left arm and your left ear. That angel in front of you kept fidgeting and getting in the way. I never knew that angels fidgeted. Besides, she was much too fat. Whoever heard of a fat angel?'

I thought of the plump little cherubs that I'd seen grinning out at me from the pulpit stairs in St Michael's church, but I didn't mention these. Instead I snapped roundly back at Amelia.

'I know why you could never be an angel anyway. You couldn't be an angel because you've got to wear spectacles. Whoever heard of an angel that couldn't even see properly?'

'I thought that you didn't believe in angels anyway,' William interrupted crossly. 'Neither of you – fat angels, fidgeting angels or even blind angels. According to you, angels are a sign of ignorance.'

Surely William should have known better? Maybe he was purposely goading Amelia into an argument.

'Caroline might believe in angels,' she replied irritably, 'but I don't.' Off they went again, their voices raised in another of their endless spirals of quarrelling.

'Children, do stop bickering so,' said Mother. Mrs McCullen, who had been a silent presence until then, took my elbow gently.

'Here, Caroline,' she said. 'I'm sure you would like your own copy of the programme.'

I went straight to the list beneath the title ANGELS OF THE HEAVENLY HOST and found my own name, typed a little unevenly, just one from the bottom, beneath Eleanor Wade, but above Victoria Williams: Caroline West. It was wonderful being able to read one's own name in print.

William's Nativity play was being held the following week and again had a two-day run. If anything, Amelia seemed more disgruntled by his involvement in this pageant of ignorance than she had been by my wingless angeldom.

'Kings never had red hair,' she muttered crossly to William. 'Especially kings from the East.'

'Just you wait and see,' he replied, apparently quite unperturbed by her criticism. 'You haven't yet seen me in my full costume.'

'Two silly Nativity plays in less than a week,' Amelia continued peevishly, still keeping her voice down in case Mother should overhear and again suggest that she stayed at home stoking the fire and tackling the ironing. 'I hate Christmas,' she added.

'I bet you still get Christmas presents,' replied William. 'And I bet you like getting them.'

Amelia gave him her most disparaging and exasperated sniff and did not deign to reply. Although we were 'that peculiar atheist West family, you know' Mother still bought Amelia and me presents at Christmas, and we still had a celebratory meal on Christmas Day. We had crackers by the plates and streamers of red and green crepe paper in the sitting-room, pinned on to the picture rail and looping out to the central light like a carnival carousel. We even had a Christmas tree in the bay window of the living-room.

Amelia, although she would never have admitted it to William, enjoyed decorating the tree with Mother and me. We had silver tinsel, small red candles in tiny brass holders and about two dozen glass baubles, but their number reduced every year, for they always seemed to leap carelessly from my fingers and crash to the floor, shattering into a million shining smithereens.

'We celebrate the capitalist Christmas, not the Christian Christmas,' I had once heard Mother explain laughingly to a friend. The friend had first frowned, and then joined Mother in a merry smile. Amelia had not been there at the time and I was pleased, for although I did not properly understand Mother's words, I knew that this was the sort of sentence that Amelia would love. I planned to use it myself one day when the occasion was appropriate, and watch a new glow of respect dawning in Amelia's eyes. But William, who, I was sure, had not overheard Mother either, got there first.

'You do celebrate Christmas,' he said accusingly to Amelia and me, 'but you don't celebrate a Christian Christmas; you celebrate a capitalist Christmas.'

Although William had managed to steal my words almost exactly, he had also succeeded in changing the emphasis completely from the one that I, and surely Mother too, had intended. Mother had made us sound endearingly and intelligently eccentric. William had merely made us sound greedy and cheap.

My Nativity play was rapidly becoming no more than a memory and the programme that Mrs McCullen had given me, which sat on top of the bookshelves in the sitting-room. It was gently yellowing, too precious to discard, but a pointless object to keep. Our attendance at William's play was fixed for all of us, Mrs McCullen, Mother, Amelia and I, as the second day, just as it had been for mine.

'You mustn't laugh when you see me,' William instructed Amelia and me gravely.

'Why should we?' I asked. 'Do you have to do something funny?'

'I expect it will be nearly identical to Caroline's boring old Nativity play, and I'll have fallen asleep by the time you appear on stage,' said Amelia stuffily, and followed her words with a prolonged sniff.

I thought that was a terribly rude thing to say, for William had not yet got through his production and might be suffering who knew what terrible nightmares in anticipation. Curiously, my own nightmares had ceased as soon as the rehearsals had given way to the actual performances and had not recurred. I felt that Amelia was being cruelly devoid of artistic empathy. But William did not seem in the slightest offended or worried.

'I bet you won't be asleep, Amelia West,' he replied happily. 'I bet you stay awake right to the very end.'

When she was out of the room he told me that he wore a wig of black hair for the play and had a curly moustache drawn on to his face with a burnt cork by Mr Churchton, the art teacher.

'Don't tell Amelia,' said William, 'it can be a little surprise for her.'

For once I felt drawn into a conspiracy against my sister. To my dismay, it was not an unpleasant sensation.

We didn't see William after his first performance to enquire as to how it had gone, as to whether his solo had been successful and whether anybody had stubbed their toes or forgotten their lines. I, at least, was eagerly looking forward to watching him the following night, and I'm sure that Amelia must have been too, albeit from behind a sniff and a peevish frown.

We had an early supper before going to the play, and Mother made us brush our hair and button our coats correctly before going out. I had managed to mislay one of my gloves.

'I'll go and fetch Mrs McCullen,' Mother said, 'and Amelia, do help Caroline to find her glove. Caroline, you are the most careless girl I know.' She went briskly out of the front door. I knew how much it annoyed her that I could be so clumsy and forgetful, not a bit like herself or Amelia. I clung to the hope that Father would have been just as careless as me, and surely Mother must have loved him dearly.

Mother was away several minutes at the McCullens' house; long enough for Amelia to find my glove, while I managed to lose its partner, and then for Amelia to find the now-missing partner while I, on her instruction, sat tight on the settee in the living-room with Hilary the cat on my knee. Mrs McCullen, however, was not accompanying Mother when she returned, with a vaguely worried look creeping into the corners of her eyes and mouth.

Like Amelia, Mother had a face which expressed her emotions clearly, particularly negative emotions such as anger or fear or anxiety, and these were especially obvious in the set of her lips and the brightness of her eyes. Both Amelia and I said almost immediately, 'Where's Mrs McCullen, Mother? What's wrong with Mrs McCullen?'

'I'm sure that there's absolutely nothing wrong with Mrs McCullen,' replied Mother crossly; cross that we should be able to detect her edge of worry and also cross that she was worried. 'She just isn't home from work yet. No doubt she's been delayed by all the poor fools caught up in the Christmas rush at Hurlinghams.'

'But she must be at home,' replied Amelia, who by this time was kneeling on the settee and peering through the curtains at the McCullens' house. 'Their sitting-room light is on and the curtains are drawn.'

'I know,' said Mother. 'But they maybe forgot to open the curtains this morning and they could easily have left the light switched on by mistake.'

'You're probably right,' agreed Amelia, sitting back on the settee, her interest dimmed by explanation. 'It's William's job to open the curtains in the mornings and he's probably so worked up over his stupid play that he forgot.'

Mother didn't even comment on Amelia's derogatory tone, but smiled gently. 'See,' she said. 'A simple explanation like that. You two run along now and get us seats, while I wait here for Mrs McCullen. We'll catch you up as soon as we can. If the play starts before we've managed to get there, then Caroline please remember not to fidget and Amelia, keep your voice down if you're chattering before the play begins.'

I looked hard at the sagging curtains of the Mc-Cullens' house, quiet and forbidding across the street, as I waited for Mother to entrust Amelia with the necessary small change for our entrance to William's play. Their sitting-room curtains were not fully closed and a narrow sabre splash of light appeared between them, white and rather cold.

'I'm sure that William *did* open the curtains this morning,' I said slowly. 'I remember standing here and thinking that their windows needed to be washed.'

'That was probably yesterday, Caroline you silly,' said Amelia, and Mother nodded and smiled, and then kissed the top of my head, as though in apology for my clumsy memory.

'Perhaps,' I assented. Amelia and Mother would know best. After all, they always did.

Amelia and I ran through the darkness to William's school, not because we were late, but because we felt excited and as if there were springs in our feet that pushed us along and made us leap and bound. It seemed to me to be quite grown-up to be running through the night-time streets without any adult presence walking sedately and reprovingly along beside us.

Perhaps because of our enthusiastic bounding through the quiet streets, we were among the first of the audience to arrive. We secured four of the seats that we considered to have the best view of the stage: right in the front and in the centre of the row.

It was warm to the point of stuffiness in the school hall and there was a smell of polish and plimsolls. We took off our coats and draped them conspicuously over the chairs beside us, reserving them for Mother and Mrs McCullen. The chairs had fold-up seats of a pale wood slatting, polished to a high sheen by years of bored bottoms.

'Much more comfortable than the chairs in your school hall,' said Amelia.

'Don't talk so loudly,' I said primly. 'Remember what Mother said.'

'Don't fidget then,' answered Amelia and went to buy a programme from a man sitting at a table at the back of the hall where the doors were situated.

It was a much grander programme than the one that had been produced for my school Nativity play. The paper was of a thicker, superior quality, the typeface very black and all of it quite straight. On the cover was a pen and ink drawing, a robin perched cheekily in the centre of a star, and at the bottom of the drawing was written, very neatly, David W.T. Churchton, December 1950. We both knew, Amelia and I, that this was the name of William's art teacher, but I also knew, and, better still, I knew that Amelia didn't know, that this same David W.T. Churchton was, maybe at that very moment, to draw a curling, burnt-cork moustache on to William's upper lip.

'I wonder what the W.T. stands for,' said Amelia.

'Walter Thomas,' I suggested.

'Oh no,' said Amelia scornfully, 'that's much too boring for an artist. Warring Tornado, maybe; Wolfgang Torenskio.'

'Sssshhh!' I replied and opened the programme to look for William's name.

The three kings appeared in a very prestigious position: after Mary, Joseph and the angel Gabriel of course, but before the innkeeper, the shepherds and certainly before the chorus of angels, as the angels of the heavenly host were described here.

'They've spelt McCullen wrongly,' said Amelia, tweaking the programme off my lap and on to hers. This time I didn't say sssshhh, but leaned over towards her to see that the programme-makers had inserted an 'a' between the 'M' and the first 'c' in McCullen, where no 'a' rightly belonged.

'Stop fidgeting, Caroline,' said Amelia triumphantly.

The aroma of sweaty plimsolls and floor polish was being slowly swamped by a sweeter, yet only marginally pleasanter, smell of perfume and powder and stale cigar smoke. The hall was gradually filling up with parents and siblings and friends of the cast, all shuffling and creaking in their fold-down seats. Occasionally people tried to move our coats and sit down next to us in our prime viewing position, but Amelia could always be relied upon to speak up in plenty of time.

'Oh, please excuse me, but those seats are actually reserved,' and the offender would apologize and move away sheepishly to find an unreserved place, with a much less satisfactory view. I had always been impressed by the easy authority that Amelia used to manage people with, even adults.

One person who attempted to move our coats was a stout man with large hairy ears and a restrictive white collar at his throat.

'Ignorant Christian,' muttered Amelia at his stooped retreating back after she had successfully scared him away.

'That's the Reverend Peploe from St Michael's church where the McCullens go every week,' I said unthinkingly.

'How do you know?' asked Amelia, but before I had time to formulate a suitable reply she continued, 'he smells horrible: wet dogs with terminal diseases.'

The play began and, whatever Amelia might have anticipated and wherever my loyalties should have lain, it was immediately obvious to both of us that this was not going to be 'nearly identical' to my Nativity play; it was destined, from the very first scene, to be a much grander, richer, more professional show. The costumes, the lighting, the singing, everything, were so much better than my impoverished play, and now I felt sad and embarrassed and wished that things might have been different. Even Mary, who of course had to be played by a boy, was a better, more convincing,

Mary than ours. He was prettier than our Mary and they had even given him a bulge, presumably a cushion pushed up his long blue dress. Our Mary had had a receding chin and an ugly nose and had shown no alteration in physique. She was narrow-waisted and flat-chested before giving birth to the baby Jesus, and she was exactly the same shape afterwards.

Of course, Amelia and I were waiting, in the most part, for William's appearance. On he came to the clash of cymbals and the important rattle of drums, the second king in a line of three, in his red satinette trousers and black and purple velveteen jacket. None of his red hair was visible and from beneath his tasselled fez peeked a fringe of jet black curls. Also, as promised, a black moustache wriggled convincingly across his upper lip.

He strode very stiffly and proudly on to the stage, looking neither left nor right, and – apart from being slightly undersized – quite magnificent, and certainly every inch an oriental king.

I stole a quick sidelong glance at Amelia to see if she was laughing, but her face was serious and she looked straight ahead to where William strutted proudly across the stage. I could tell by her bright gaze and her mouth, hanging a little open, the pink tip of her tongue just visible between her teeth, that she was terribly jealous and immensely impressed.

Then came William's first lines. He stepped forward from his two companion kings and pointed to the top right-hand corner of the stage where a big gold star had magically appeared.

'I have seen a bright star in the east,' he declaimed. His voice was nervously high but it was clear and resonant too, and I wondered at the rumble of subdued laughter that emanated gradually from the audience. I realized with a flash of inspiration, unusual for me, that they were laughing at his accent. I had become so used to it that I no longer registered its hard east-coast Scottishness, but to the rest of the audience it was perhaps surprising to hear these scratching tones issuing from the small thin king from the orient, attired in his fez and his satinette trousers.

I felt glad that Mrs McCullen wasn't there to witness her son's voice being laughed at, and then instantly I was worried, my worry briefly spoiling all that I was relishing and envying of William's play. Where on earth were Mrs McCullen and Mother? It would be terrible, despite the laughter, for Mrs McCullen to miss this sumptuous performance, with William such an important character in it too; our second-hand programme would be a very poor compensation. And what about William? I knew that I would have been terribly upset if Mother had missed attending my Nativity play.

It was the scene with the shepherds now, and offstage were the faint sounds of sheep baaing plaintively. I half-turned in my seat, looking for Mrs McCullen and Mother. Maybe they had come in late and got themselves places at the back of the hall. But there was no sign of them, and I could see that there were no free seats either if they turned up now. Amelia nudged me hard in the ribs with her elbow. She had ferocious pointed elbows which she could use to good effect.

'Don't fidget,' she hissed at me.

In the next scene involving William he was carrying a cylinder, much the same size as a pickle jar, but this cylinder was sleekly wrapped in shining red paper with a gold ribbon about the centre. It was either frankincense or myrrh. I can't remember which of these two it was, but I am sure that it was not gold. Gold was the only gift from the kings that I felt I might recognize. I had no idea what frankincense or myrrh might be. They were strange, exotic goodies to be carrying, and therefore much more exciting.

This was the scene in which William was to perform his solo. Two verses of 'We Three Kings', the first and the last, all three kings sang in unison, but they each had a verse to themselves too. William was, without a doubt, the best singer of the three. His voice was clear and supple, and there was not so much as a thread of laughter from the audience as he sang. I held my breath, worried that my breathing, booming hoarsely in my ears, might put him off. It seemed terrible, almost wicked, that Mother and even more so Mrs McCullen, should miss William's solo.

All too soon, for Nativity plays are short and have an uncomplicated plot, it was the final tableau. Mary, just as pretty as in the first scene, but no longer bulging at the waist, sat on a low stool beside a straw-filled crib from which peeped the pink and white face of the newborn baby Jesus, with a mop of yellow wool hair. Joseph stood behind and to the left of Mary, one hand pressed reassuringly on to her shoulder. On the other side of the crib the shepherds knelt in adoration in their tea-towel headdresses accompanied by two sheep, slightly balding along their backs and with wheels where hooves might be expected. Ranged behind the crib, centre stage and directly opposite where Amelia and I sat, were the three kings, with William, the shortest but indubitably most classily dressed, in the middle.

The choir of angels, also barefoot, came trooping on to the stage last of all. All these angels had wings, silly little silvery affairs, more in the shape of butterfly wings than anything else, especially compared to the angel Gabriel whose massive gold wings swept the floor and came to a triumphant arch more than a foot above his head. Unlike our angel Gabriel, Shirley, this Gabriel could manage his wings. They never slipped sideways, and he could even manage to give them a little waggle occasionally as though warming up for flight.

I had already noted, in previous scenes, which angel occupied my position, second row from the back, fourth from the left. This angel, his face largely obscured by the halo and wings of the angel in front of him, who was not fat and did not seem unduly restless, had a boring, nondescript type of face and blondish-brown hair with a parting so severe and straight that it appeared to have been cut with a scalpel. Despite the parting and the bland face, I liked to think of him as 'my' angel. I even thought that I might recognize him as the son of Mr Mayberry the fishmonger, who brought in the fish heads for Hilary while we had been away at the Pollards' farm.

As the angels shuffled quietly into their respective positions at the back of the stage, the light glittering prettily off their tinselled butterfly wings, I heard the door at the back of the hall opening and closing. A man's voice whispered loudly to the late entrants, presumably and hopefully Mother and Mrs McCullen, that there were a couple of free seats at the front, next to two little girls.

Despite another elbow-sharp nudge from Amelia, I had a quick look over my shoulder to see if I could see our awaited companions making their way down the aisle to witness the last tableau of William's Nativity play. But it wasn't them at all; it was a scrawny man with scrunched shoulders and gingery hair streaked with silver. He had a weaselly face and he was dressed in an ugly suit of navy blue. He glanced furtively from side to side in his quest for a free seat – this gave him a sharper, greedier look, as though he were an animal hunting. He saw the chair beside me, and I gently lifted my coat from it and spread it across my lap; Amelia would surely not try to chase him away now, in all this anticipatory silence with the end of the show so close.

The latecomer stood still beside me for a few seconds, staring intently at the children assembled on stage. Perhaps it was longer than a few seconds, for a couple of impatient voices behind us hissed 'Sit down,' in irritated whispers. The man's hands fumbling behind him for the seat, were nervous and pale, with badly bitten fingernails and ugly yellow stains of cigarettes between the fore and middle fingers.

Perhaps it was the nervousness of the fingers which betrayed him, for the seat, which he had surely meant to handle gently, escaped him and, lowering itself rapidly, made a loud wooden clatter as it reached the horizontal position. The noise, placed as it was between a silent, waiting audience, and an even more silent assembly of actors, seemed magnified. Some of the audience looked towards us and tutted not quite beneath their breath at this unseemly sound, but the effect on the cast was greater. They all looked, from the pretty, seated Mary, to the last angel, still just getting into his position at the very back, towards the source of this unexpected noise.

The middle king, the smallest one with the sweetest singing voice and the harshest, most improbable spoken accent, the king with the red satinette trousers and the tasselled fez, suddenly raised his hands to his face, his gesture so clearly involuntary that I was glad that his gift, whether frankincense or myrrh, had already been safely delivered. He took a lurching step forward, and another backward. He gasped something, but the words were unintelligible, even to those in the front row who stared at him in helpless amazement. Then, with a singular lack of grace, the middle king fainted.

The fez, with an attached ring of black curls, slipped sideways from his head, revealing an untidy mess of red hair. He slumped to land sideways on Joseph, who, with un-Josephlike thoughtlessness, slid the burden of the king's little body forward on to Mary. Mary was clearly made of sterner stuff than her husband, for she clasped the little king firmly around the waist and held on. But she couldn't save her baby, for the king's leg, in its satinette pantaloons, had managed to get caught beneath the sturdy wooden legs of the crib, and he now seemed to kick it away from her. The crib toppled over and, in a mess of straw and wood shavings, the baby Jesus rolled out.

The distance between the edge of the stage and the

crib's original position was little more than a foot, and although the baby Jesus rolled slowly, his motion slowed by his yellow wool hair catching on the straw and wood shavings, he still rolled as far as the edge of the stage and toppled slowly over it. He landed right in front of the first row of the audience.

Before our startled and amazed eyes, the head of the newly born baby Jesus shattered into hundreds of shards of pink and white china, while his eyes, a brilliant blue in colour, which appeared to be on springs, shot dizzyingly out from his eyesockets and vanished somewhere beneath our chairs and feet.

Chapter Ten

I had been looking forward to Christmas. Looking forward to helping Mother and Amelia prepare the Christmas lunch while Mrs McCullen and William were at church, and then looking forward to showing them both our own traditions for Christmas afternoon: the walk beneath grey December skies across bare December fields to Father's grave; the Christmas tea with Alfred and Dorothea Ambrose, mince pies and fruit cake in front of the fire. But now it was different, all different, and William didn't even come and say goodbye to us, nor did he wish us a happy Christmas.

They left very early in the morning, before even the first pale wash of cold winter light was filtering across the eastern sky. The stars were still absurdly bright and the moon swung across the darkness like a shining silver penny. Why Amelia, who normally slept so soundly through the night, never troubled by anxious dreams, was awake I don't know. Perhaps the creak and clatter of the McCullens' sagging gate woke her, perhaps the cough of the taxi engine, protesting in the coldness. Perhaps the taxi driver had slammed the door or perhaps Amelia hadn't slept at all that night anyway, too charged up after the excitement of the previous evening. Certainly her face seemed particularly pale in the moonlight and there was none of her usual disgruntlement from her sleep being interrupted. If there had been any noises in Tredannick Close, then they did not disturb my sleep; it was Amelia who awoke me. She bent over me, her cold hand shaking me by the shoulder as her hair, loose for the night, fell across her face, and she hissed loudly in my ear.

'Wake up, Caroline. Wake up, Caroline, they're leaving.'

Amelia's bed was closer to the window, and we knelt on it, side by side in our long flannelette nightdresses, our cold bare feet just touching and our faces close together as we looked out on the street. Our warm breath misted the window, and Amelia wiped at the condensation with an impatient hand.

'Stop breathing so much, Caroline,' she muttered and I tried to twist my lips into a strange tunnel and direct my obscuring breath away from the cold pane of glass.

The taxi driver, capped and rather corpulent and whistling a sad, repetitive tune between his teeth, was outside the McCullens' gate, walking slowly up and down and rubbing his hands against his waist. He had already turned the taxi around, and whenever he walked into the beam of his headlights the shadow that he threw on to the pavement was huge and solidly black.

Mr McCullen came out of the house first and walked slowly down to the waiting car. He was wearing a long overcoat and there was a scarf wrapped around his throat. Two cardboard boxes, bound up roughly in string, swung from each hand and one of them hit against his shin as he walked. He handed the boxes to the driver and rubbed at his leg with his hand; those pale and anxious hands, not the huge hairy fists that I had imagined.

I wondered what the boxes that were now being stowed in the vehicle might contain, but I didn't want to ask Amelia. She was staring hard at Mr McCullen, her mouth hanging slightly open and a frown puckering her forehead; that was her characteristic expression of concentration and I knew that she wouldn't want to be interrupted. Also, I was afraid that if I spoke my breath might mist the window again. Mr McCullen went back up the path to the front door, leaving the gate swinging open behind him. From this angle he looked stooped, and his legs had a worn bandiness about them. He seemed like a shrivelled old man, too exhausted by age to inflict damage upon anything or anybody.

He came out of the house again, and this time his wife and son followed reluctantly behind him. He closed the front door quietly, but with a firmness that I imagined as finality. Unable to stop myself I whispered to Amelia, 'They'll never open the front door again.'

'Ssshhh,' replied Amelia and rubbed her hand over the windowpane.

Mrs McCullen was holding William by the hand. They both looked so thin beside the round bulk of the taxi driver, it was as though they were figures drawn by a child. Mrs McCullen was so long and drooping that she could have been fashioned from a single length of string. In their free hands they each carried a Gladstone bag. I recognized them as those same battered Gladstones that had accompanied us on our summertime trip to the Pollards' farm, all those many months before. Both William and Mrs McCullen were dressed as though it were a Sunday, Mrs McCullen in her black hat with the purple-dyed feather curling backwards – although, of course, at that distance and in that light it was impossible to detect the purpleness of the feather – and William in his kilt, his knees looking trembly and pale in the little light that there was. Neither of them looked up to where Amelia and I watched from the bedroom window. Indeed, just as when they went to church, neither of them glanced towards our house at all.

We only had a brief glimpse of Mrs McCullen and William, for they were soon engulfed into the fat carapace of the taxi. Mr McCullen, after shutting the gate, climbed in after them, another two boxes in his hands. The taxi rumbled off down the street and the sound of its engine and the rumble and clatter of its wheels on the cobblestones soon faded into the distance. The house across the street stood cold and deafeningly silent, a dark hump of emptiness.

'They didn't even say goodbye,' I said plaintively. 'They didn't even wish us a happy Christmas.' I assumed that it was all right to speak now, for surely it wouldn't matter if my breath obscured the window. There was nothing to see outside but an empty street.

For a while Amelia continued to stare out at the darkness, her chin cupped in her hands. Then she sighed and shrugged and sat back from the window.

'Let's go back to bed now, Caroline,' she suggested, her voice perfectly, and somehow unnaturally, normal. 'I'm sure my feet will have developed hundreds of terrible chilblains by the morning.'

I lay silently in the cool sheets, unable to drowse and drift off into the embracing gentleness of sleep. I wondered if we would ever see William or Mrs McCullen again. Although Amelia did not speak, I could tell by her breathing that she was not asleep either. Eventually the silence was broken by the pained mewling of a cat somewhere down the street, and a little afterwards by the plaintive, drawn-out hoot of a train whistle.

'Caroline,' hissed Amelia from her bed. 'Are you awake?'

'Yes.'

'Did you hear that?'

'Yes. It's only a train.'

'That's William saying goodbye,' replied Amelia softly. 'That's William saying happy Christmas.'

I was silent then. Amelia, usually so sensible and factual, was not given to fanciful ideas like that. To my surprise, I felt tears welling up irrepressibly. They spilt noiselessly down my cheeks, and, because I was lying on my back, ran down my cheekbones and trickled, cold and unpleasant, into my ears. I wriggled from side to side to shake them out.

'Caroline,' murmured Amelia from her bed.

'Yes,' and I sniffed a little. I felt cold now and sorry for myself.

'Go to sleep now, Caroline,' Amelia advised gently. 'Don't you worry about William and Mrs McCullen. I'm sure they'll be back after Christmas.'

'What about Mr McCullen?' I asked.

'No,' replied Amelia slowly. 'No, I don't think Mr McCullen will come back. I think that he'll stay in Stonehaven now.'

The weekend seemed confused and sad without the reassuring presence of Mrs McCullen and William. Hilary the cat was missing too, and I suggested that Mr McCullen might have stolen Hilary away, perhaps in one of those cardboard boxes he'd been carrying. I wondered how on earth Hilary would manage in Stonehaven, but Mother told me that I was being silly.

'Cats often go out prowling at full moon,' she said. 'I'm sure that Hilary will be back later on this morning, all paws and mischief.'

But Hilary was not back later that morning and neither were William and Mrs McCullen, although, of course, they were not expected. Like Amelia, Mother was sure that those two would be back after Christmas, but she differed from Amelia in her opinion of whether Mr McCullen would accompany them.

'Maybe he will come back with them,' she said thoughtfully. 'Maybe. And maybe he won't. We'll just have to wait and see.' Then Mother blinked at me as though something had got into her eyes or she had just been woken up. 'Do run along now, Caroline,' she added, her voice suddenly sharper. 'You're getting as bad as Amelia with all your endless questions.'

Yet Amelia didn't seem to be asking endless questions. Not then anyway, and certainly not about the McCullens. She sat amongst the cushions on the living-room sofa, reading occasionally, but more often just gazing into space, gnawing absent-mindedly at her bottom lip. She didn't once glance out of the window at the house across the street which had, already, picked up the mantle of neglect that deserted houses so easily assume. She didn't even have Hilary to stroke

115

and to distract her with occasional taps of his paws, his claws unsheathed.

'What are you doing, Amelia?' I asked, bored and almost scared by this strange lethargy that seemed to have sunk over Amelia like a damp cloud.

'I'm thinking, Caroline, thinking,' Amelia snapped back at me. 'Something that you obviously don't know how to do.'

'I'm sorry,' I replied humbly. I was too ashamed to ask her if this was the special, clever thinking that William had once been so excited about or just the usual mundane, everyday sort of thinking.

In the afternoon, Mother went down to Hurlinghams to tell them about Mrs McCullen.

'What are you going to say to them?' I asked her as she stood in the hallway pulling on her winter coat.

'I'm not quite sure yet,' said Mother. 'I'll see when I get there.'

'Can I come too then?' I asked. But she was adamant.

'No, Caroline, you can't. This is something for adults to discuss.'

I pouted my lips, because this was the sort of answer that I hated. There was simply no room for persuasion in that type of response. Mother kissed me on the nose and smiled at me.

'Cheer up, sweetie,' she said. 'Don't you worry yourself about all this McCullen nonsense. Why don't you and Amelia go out and see if you can find Hilary?'

Once Amelia had been persuaded to leave her thinking and her brief bursts of reading, grumbling about her chilblains as she pulled on her mittens and changed into her lace-up boots, it didn't take long to find Hilary. I was surprised that nobody had found him earlier and come to tell us, for the unlucky cat really hadn't strayed far from home at all.

His body lay in the gutter at the corner of Tredannick Close and the main road, on the opposite side of the street to the postbox. Although his fur was clogged and heavy with cold and lingering dew, there was not a mark or scratch that we could see. No torn ears or signs of a fight, just the slumped body and the heavy reality that Hilary was quite dead.

'I bet a passing vehicle must have hit him,' said Amelia, looking up at me from where she crouched on the edge of the pavement, rubbing gently at a splodge of dirt on Hilary's side.

'But no vehicles ever come up Tredannick Close,' I said doubtfully.

'One did last night,' said Amelia and I could only nod silently in response. Mr McCullen and his taxi. He had taken away Mrs McCullen and William. He had killed Hilary.

We carried Hilary home on a stretch of old pale blue towelling that Amelia found in Mother's collection of cleaning rags. His body slumped between us, heavy and rather awkward, his claws snagging on the loops of thread and his tail flopping inelegantly this way and that. At least our little cortège didn't have far to walk.

We buried him in the front garden. Amelia thought that this would be more appropriate than the back yard.

'That way Mother can see the grave straightaway,' she said, 'and she'll know what's happened.'

'She might just think that we've been gardening,' I ventured, but Amelia didn't agree.

'She's not that stupid, Caroline,' she sniffed. I had never intended to suggest that Mother might be stupid.

We dug the grave between us, but Amelia's role was confined to sitting on the low garden wall and giving instructions. She thought that the actual digging would aggravate her chilblains, although I tried to reassure her that it actually made me hot. The ground was hard and recalcitrant. The soil was riddled with long tough dandelion roots, old crumbling half-bricks and small pieces of broken blue and white pottery. I pulled out the roots as best I could and threw them away and I piled up the bits of brick and the shards of broken chinaware beside me. I thought that perhaps they could be used for decorating Hilary's grave.

117

'You can make a sort of drink like coffee out of those roots that you're throwing away,' said Amelia from the wall. I didn't answer. It didn't seem a particularly funny joke to me, and it was annoying only having a short-handled trowel to dig with. I knew that proper grave-diggers like Alfred Ambrose stood up to dig, instead of grovelling on their knees in the dirt as I was having to do. I was sure that Alfred Ambrose didn't have a supervisor either, sitting on the wall dangling her legs and complaining about her chilblains.

'Remember it's got to be at least six foot deep, Caroline,' said Amelia. I straightened up quickly then, for all this crouching was making my back ache.

'Six foot deep? That's enormous. That's taller than me. That's taller than Mother. I'd never be able to dig down that deep.'

'Oh well, we'll just have to see how far you get,' replied Amelia.

I took off my coat and put it over the wall beside where Amelia was sitting. She wriggled over quickly and sat on top of it.

'Mmm, that's better. The wall's awfully cold.'

'You'd better make sure that you don't get chilblains on your bottom.'

Much cheered by my own joke, at which Amelia scowled and remained silent, I returned to my grave-digging with renewed zest.

The combination of cold and boredom defeated Amelia just before the digging defeated me.

'That's enough now, Caroline, surely,' she said. 'There aren't any wolves or lions around here to dig up poor old Hilary's remains anyway.'

We lowered the cat's body on its blue towelling stretcher very quietly and soberly into the grave. Any words would have been a sign of Christian ignorance, I was sure. We looked down at him. His front paws were tucked neatly beneath his chest in a position reminiscent of one of his dozy loungings in front of the living-room fire.

'Rest in peace,' I said tentatively, looking at Amelia for signs of disapproval, but Amelia only sniffed.

'Start shovelling the earth back in again, Caroline,' she said.

I scraped the soil from the crumbling half-bricks as best I could with the end of the trowel, and arranged them in a neat row at the foot of Hilary's grave.

'Do you think we should make a cross?' I asked. 'A gravestone, I mean,' I corrected myself before Amelia could reply. She shook her head.

'Even ignorant Christians don't believe that cats go to heaven,' she said.

'How about flowers?' I asked. 'We always put flowers on Father's grave.'

'All right,' conceded Amelia. 'Flowers.' But it was, of course, winter time, nearly mid-December, and there were none. Instead, Amelia arranged the chips of blue and white pottery in the shape of a five-petalled flower, in the centre of the small bare mound of earth.

'Poor old Hilary,' she muttered. 'I bet you would prefer a mouse to a flower, but it's only broken china anyway.' She stood up and stretched and, for a brief few seconds, she gazed across the road at the secretive face of the McCullens' empty house. 'Come on, Caroline,' she said. 'Let's go in and make a pot of tea. Mother will be back from Hurlinghams soon and I'm freezing.'

The schools had all closed for Christmas, and Christmas Day itself was less than a week away, but now Mother had managed to acquire another job. She had taken Mrs McCullen's place behind the haberdashery counter in Hurlinghams.

'It was too near Christmas for them to get a temporary assistant in,' she explained to us. 'And if I don't do this then when Mrs McCullen returns from Stonehaven, she won't have a job at all, and then what will she do?'

'But what if they don't come back?' I couldn't help

119

asking, although Mother and Amelia were still quite convinced that they would. Their conviction, albeit without explanation, quietened my questions, but I could still feel the uncomfortable nigglings of doubt and apprehension. How could they be so sure? Mother had told me that Hilary would come back, and look what had happened to Hilary. But, as Mother and Amelia both pointed out to me with exasperation echoing through their words, I would just have to wait and see.

Mother was, therefore, at work in Hurlinghams, measuring out lengths of ribbon and counting out buttons, on the Tuesday afternoon when there was a hesitant knock at the front door. Amelia usually loved to answer the door, but she still seemed more subdued than usual and, besides, she was engrossed in a book.

'You'll go Caroline, won't you?' she asked without even looking up.

I recognized the smell first, the decay and the wet dogs, before I recognized the large hairy ears and the dumpling nose, for the Reverend Peploe was out of uniform; there was no dog's collar biting at his throat beneath the nervous tremble of his Adam's apple. Instead he had on a shabby fawn jumper and a derelict tweedy jacket with the collar fraying and the leather elbow-patches hard and shiny with wear. I wondered if he had discarded his dog's collar because he thought it would be unwelcome at the front door of us atheist Wests.

I had never expected to see the Reverend Peploe at our house, and perhaps he had not expected the door to be answered by me, for his face looked startled and his mouth opened once or twice without any sound, leave alone any words, emerging.

'Have you had a death in the family?' he asked at last awkwardly, and he gestured vaguely over his shoulder to where Hilary's grave stood, naked and somehow rather obscene, beside the wall.

'Hilary,' I said. 'Hilary the cat got run over.'

'Poor creature,' murmured the Reverend Peploe and I wondered whether to ask him if he thought that cats went to heaven. Amelia, however, was beside me before I had managed to decide. Her curiosity had overcome, as I knew it would, her interest in her book.

'Can I help you?' she asked, and from the distant formality in her voice I knew that she too had recognized the Reverend Peploe, despite the lack of dog collar. Amelia's appearance seemed to jolt the Reverend Peploe out of some misty reverie, for he blinked rapidly and, tugging at the cuffs of his too-short jacket sleeves, he cleared his throat loudly several times before speaking.

'I have come to speak to your mother, if I may,' he said, and there was a sound of shy apology in his voice, as though he knew that he was intruding and wasn't really welcome.

'I'm afraid that she's out at present,' replied Amelia, still frostily remote. 'She should be home in an hour, if you would care to come back.'

But the Reverend Peploe hesitated, and even Amelia was not brutal enough to shut the door in his face.

'Our mother is at work,' Amelia added by way of explanation.

'At work?' asked the Reverend Peploe.

'At work,' repeated Amelia firmly.

'I thought that she was a teacher at the grammar school,' said the Reverend Peploe, and still he stood on the doorstep waiting.

'She is,' answered Amelia and I thought that this time she might really close the door between us and the shabby figure of this ignorant Christian, albeit without his dog collar.

'But surely . . . I mean . . . well . . . hasn't the . . . I mean to say . . .' The Reverend Peploe seemed to have some difficulty in organizing his sentences and I wondered whether his sermons, which William and Mrs McCullen must have listened to on all those Sunday mornings, were as painfully constructed.

'Hasn't the school term finished?' he managed at last.

'Yes,' replied Amelia. And then, apparently taking pity on him, she added, 'She's working in Hurlinghams at the minute.'

Eventually, of course, Amelia suggested that the Reverend Peploe should come inside and wait for Mother there. We might have stood on the doorstep for an hour otherwise.

The Reverend Peploe sat down awkwardly in the living-room, perching at the very edge of the settee as though afraid it might swallow him if he leaned back amongst the soft tide of cushions. He looked up at the crêpe-paper streamers that the three of us had put up the previous evening.

'Very pretty,' he murmured and he smiled at us.

'Can I take your jacket?' asked Amelia. 'Can I make you a cup of tea?'

But the Reverend Peploe didn't want to take off his jacket, nor did he want a cup of tea. He sat there lumpishly, humming tunelessly under his breath and drumming, out of time with himself, on his thigh with his plump fingers.

'He's horrible and pathetic,' hissed Amelia in my ear in the kitchen, making a pot of tea anyway, for Mother would want a cup when she returned from Hurlinghams. She clutched my wrist in her strong little hand. 'How can he believe in God,' she asked, 'when he doesn't even believe in himself?'

I shrugged my lack of answer carelessly and remembered the spring flowers and friendly warmth that I had once sensed in his church. He had frightened me then, but he had been kind. He had given me a sweet and offered to show me something. What was it? The altar? A brass? I couldn't help but feel sorry for him now; he seemed lonely and out of his depth beneath our bright, unChristian carousel of Christmas streamers. He also seemed weak and frightened of Amelia. I pulled away from her grip and went back into the living-room.

'I was in the Nativity play at my school this year,' I said softly to the Reverend Peploe. 'I was an angel in the heavenly host, but we didn't have wings. Only the angel Gabriel had wings. Would you like me to show you the programme?'

I remembered that I had run away that time when the Reverend Peploe had offered to show me around his church, and I was almost afraid that he might run away now. But he didn't. He held out his hand, his plump pale fingers looking soft and dead.

'I'd love to see it, Caroline,' he said.

The Reverend Peploe had come to see Mother about the McCullens, of course. Mother sent Amelia and me into the kitchen, for this was adult talk again, and we stood pressed up close against the door, our noses squashed against the tea towels which hung there, in the hope of overhearing what was said.

Amelia said that she clearly heard the words William, father, train and Stonehaven, but even if she did, they didn't tell us anything. I heard only the gentle murmur of voices undulating incomprehensibly together and once or twice the clink of a cup on a saucer as Mother drank her tea. Her voice was usually like Amelia's, ringing out clear and high. She must have guessed that we would be listening and was intentionally speaking quietly.

'I bet he didn't realize that that was Mr McCullen who came in at the end of the play,' said Amelia, her words whistling hot and moist in my ear.

'He must have guessed when William fainted,' I answered.

'He might have thought it was because of the heat,' suggested Amelia. 'Or the excitement. I wonder if William will be allowed to go back into church now, after murdering the poor little baby Jesus.' Her mirthless laugh was too close to my ear for comfort and I jerked away from her and went and sat down at the kitchen table. I couldn't hear what Mother and the

Reverend Peploe were saying to each other anyway.

Their conversation showed no sign of coming to an end, and after a while Amelia got tired of having her ear pressed against the kitchen door and came and sat beside me, perched on the edge of the table, swinging her thin legs impatiently.

'I wish he'd go back to his stupid church,' she said. 'Ignorant Christian, wasting all Mother's time.'

Eventually we heard Mother's voice raised into the recognized formula of farewell, and the shuffle of them moving out of the living-room and towards the front door.

'Amelia and Caroline,' Mother called. 'Come and say goodbye to the Reverend Peploe.' The three of us stood in the doorway as the Reverend Peploe moved his clumsy, wet-dog bulk down the short gravel path, past Hilary's grave and out of the gate into Tredannick Close.

'Goodbye,' he called back to us. 'Thank you so much, Mrs West. A happy Christmas to you all.'

'Ignorant Christian,' muttered Amelia.

'Poor man,' said Mother, giving a final wave and shutting the front door. 'I do hope you were polite to him, Amelia. He does worry so and then there's that sister of his.'

'What sister?' asked Amelia suspiciously.

'Penelope Peploe,' answered Mother, a trace of weariness in her voice now. 'She has some kind of dementia and is locked up in an institution somewhere.'

'Perhaps she drove him to turning into a Christian,' suggested Amelia with interest.

'Maybe dear, maybe,' said Mother, and smiled at Amelia fondly.

Christmas Day passed. As usual we had a tree in the living-room window dressed up in its silver tinsel and baubles, and the dusty spider plants were temporarily relegated to the kitchen. It was a smaller tree than previous years, I thought, but perhaps I just received that impression because I was bigger. Twice we lit the candles in the little brass holders, and the reflections of the tree in the night-time windowpanes danced brightly back at us. On Christmas morning there were presents beneath the tree for Amelia and me: three each from Mother and also interesting parcels wrapped up in brown paper and string with masses of postage stamps pasted untidily over one corner, which Amelia took for her stamp collection.

One parcel was from Uncle Tommy who had moved from Edinburgh to Harrogate, and had sent us a flat blue and silver tin of hard toffee. One parcel, very exciting before it was opened, was from the Marsdon family in Africa. Friends of Father's father, they owned a huge tea plantation in the Kenyan Highlands, and had sent us a pleasantly fragrant but otherwise unimaginative parcel of tea. Annie and Diggory Pollard had sent us a parcel too, and inside were individually wrapped presents for all of us; mine was the biggest and heaviest, a beautiful book of poems and stories about the sea.

'The weight of that book,' said Mother wonderingly. 'No wonder the postage was so dear.'

And of course, Amelia and I had combined our limited resources to buy Mother a present too, and she smiled warmly at us as she opened it; it was just what she had always wanted and had been hoping for, or so she said anyway.

Then we had a roast chicken for lunch with crackers to pull beforehand and little glasses of a sweet nutty wine that I knew Amelia didn't like by the way she twitched her lips and screwed up her mouth as she swallowed. She drank it all without comment and had a second glassful. We had Christmas pudding with a sprig of red-berried holly in the top. A silver sixpence had been stirred into it with our wishes; not just our wishes, either. I knew that William and Mrs McCullen, too, had given that pudding a stir when Mother had made it. We were not hungry enough to eat more than half and the silver sixpence must have been in the other half, for none of us found it in the portions on our plates.

After lunch we put on our coats and boots and gloves and Amelia and I wrapped our new scarves, Christmas presents from Mother, three times around our necks, and we set off on our walk out of Truro to Father's grave, tramping stolidly up the hill and calling out 'Happy Christmas' to everyone we passed. We didn't enquire as to whether they were celebrating a Christian Christmas, or just a capitalist one like ourselves.

We looked into the lit and friendly windows of the houses, admiring and comparing Christmas trees and laughing at the numbers of stout old men stretched out in fireside armchairs, their cheeks flushed, their hands folded across their paunches and their eyes closed.

'They need a walk after their lunch,' said Mother.

'Christmas has killed them,' said Amelia. I said nothing. I was wondering what William would have said if he had been with us. He and Amelia would have probably been deeply buried in an argument by then.

Father's grave seemed cold and damp in wintertime; we only really came in the summer apart from Christmas Day, and so I always imagined sunlight and warmth there. Nevertheless, the graveyard was peaceful still, full of a soft and lingering sleepy greyness and an all-embracing quietness in which the repeated calls of a blackbird rang out like a bell above the eternal flickering of the brook.

The bare limbs of the beech tree above Father's grave were like leadwork tracery against the heaviness of the sky, and I leaned against Mother and held her hand.

'My heart has left its dwelling place and can return no more,' I read softly to myself and Mother smiled down at me.

'It's a shame that there are no flowers at this time of year,' she said.

'Do you think that Father is cold in there?' asked Amelia, rubbing her hands together.

'No,' replied Mother, a touch of sharpness in her voice. 'Of course not, Amelia,' she added more gently. But I could feel a shiver going through her body and I wondered what she might be thinking.

'We're the ones who are cold,' I said. 'Let's go and say happy Christmas to Alfred and Dorothea Ambrose.'

Alfred Ambrose's motorbike stood, as ever, bright and gleaming by the front door of their cottage, and the tiny mullioned windows winked merrily at us. A thread of smoke came trickling from the chimneypot into the still afternoon air. There was a wreath of ivy tied to the knocker on the red front door with a length of white ribbon. Alfred Ambrose opened the door for us. His trousers bagged, as they always did, about his thighs and his kindly eyes sparkled.

'Look who it isn't!' he exclaimed and Amelia and I chorused our 'Happy Christmas' while Mother smiled from behind us and held out a gift-wrapped box of Furnesses fairings; we had brought these spiced biscuits as a Christmas present for the Ambroses for as long as I could remember.

'Do come in, won't you?' asked Alfred and he took our coats and scarves from us in the hall, little more than a narrow stone-flagged passageway, and ushered us into the sitting-room. Their fat cat Claudia, Hilary's mother, lay stretched out asleep before a fire of logs that glowed and spat contentedly in the grate. Despite the crackle of the fire, I noticed an unusual air of stillness in the room almost as soon as I was through the door, and I looked around in confusion, trying to see what it was that I missed. But Amelia and Mother had always been so very much faster than me.

'But Alfred,' said Mother and Amelia simultaneously, 'where is Dorothea?'

Alfred led us from the fireside without a word or a glance.

'Where are we going?' I muttered fearfully to Amelia, for, in all the times I had visited the Ambroses, I had only ever been in their tiny hall, the sitting-room, and on one occasion, when I had been very much younger, the lavatory out at the back.

'She must be sick in bed,' Amelia muttered back at me and made a grimace of disgust. Amelia always felt revolted by other people's afflictions, especially as she was so seldom ill herself. Mother gave us a quelling look over her shoulder and followed first in line as Alfred led the way up the steep and narrow staircase, and through a whitewashed door into a bedroom. He took a little step to one side, and the three of us crowded forward, with Mother in front, to give Dorothea our Christmas wishes.

'Oh!' gasped Mother rather faintly and held out an arm as though to restrain Amelia and me. But it was much too late. We could already see the small single bed with its patchwork coverlet and dark wood headboard; we could already see the small chest of drawers with its free-standing oval mirror and the white lace-trimmed square laid in front of it like an altar cloth. We could already smell the faint grey smell of fear and loneliness, made all the more terrifying by the twofold overlying layers of odours, a heavier one of ammonia and a lighter, sweeter one of rose petals.

Dorothea Ambrose lay in the bed. Her face was grey and sagging and there was an unpleasant waxy look about it. Her jaw drooped flaccidly on to her chest and her eyes were wide open. They gazed blankly upward, towards the whitewashed ceiling. It was horribly obvious that she was quite dead.

'Oh!' repeated Mother, and Alfred replied softly, 'Yes?'

I felt that we were trapped in this small clean room, and I longed to run from it and escape, but I could not. I stared at the face which had been that of Dorothea

Ambrose, and I could not move; my legs were no longer operated by my mind.

'It was last night,' said Alfred, and there were tears rolling down his face now. They fell so openly and so unashamedly that I wondered if he even realized that he was crying. 'I was out at Midnight Mass,' he continued. 'If I hadn't gone she would still be . . .' he paused and gulped loudly, like a child. 'She choked,' he said. 'I don't know what she choked on. Something she ate, I suppose. I don't know how she choked. Nobody was here to help her. She choked and she died.' Alfred took a step towards the bed. 'I let her die,' he cried out despairingly. 'Oh my God, I let her die.'

He was down on his knees beside the bed now, and he fumbled awkwardly beneath the sheets while we three stood and watched him, unable to move, unable to respond at all. He pulled out Dorothea's dead and flopping arm from beneath the covers and clutched the fat freckled hand between his own. His tears streamed down on them and he looked up imploringly at Mother.

'I can't close her eyes,' he said. 'I keep trying to close them, but they just open up again. Please close her eyes, Mrs West, and let her sleep.'

Chapter Eleven

We went to Dorothea Ambrose's funeral of course, Mother, Amelia and I. It was the first funeral that I had ever attended, and the first one that Amelia could remember, for she had been only a snivelling and querulous three-year-old at Father's funeral. Mother bought a black wool skirt for Amelia from Hurlinghams especially, but my navy blue school skirt was considered to be both new enough and sober enough for the occasion.

The funeral was on the last day of December, the last day of 1950, and it had snowed during the night. Snow is a relatively unusual event in Cornwall, and this snow, which squeaked underfoot like cotton wool, was no more than a couple of inches thick. Nevertheless, it covered the fields in a pristine whiteness and rimmed the walls of the churchyard prettily, reminding me of the iced Christmas cake that we usually had with Alfred and Dorothea Ambrose on Christmas afternoon. We hadn't had any this year, of course.

After the brief service in the church, which was cold and draughty, the coffin rested for a while on the granite table in the lych gate as we filed through. That was where my father's coffin had once lain, I thought. But the image which was foremost in my mind was of William lying there, complaining of the hard coldness of the granite, his thin arms folded across his chest. William, of course, did not even know that Dorothea Ambrose was dead. It seemed a terrible thing to me that he was ignorant of her absence.

The dark hole for Dorothea's coffin lay close beside where the small marble tombstone marked the grave of

130

her nameless baby. There were two dozen or so people gathered around the grave, their faces serious and rather strained. They shuffled uneasily on the snowy ground, turning what had once been crisp and white and beautiful into a formless grey slush. Everything seemed harshly black and white and grey; black silhouettes of gravestones and of trees, black hole, black clothes; white snow, white marble gravestone for baby Ambrose, white faces; grey slush, grey churchyard wall, grey sky. The unrelieved monochrome made my eyes ache and I longed for colour, some colour, any colour.

We waited silently as the coffin was lowered into the hole – which, I presumed, with a gulp of horror, Alfred Ambrose himself had probably dug – and the vicar, in the black and white uniform of his profession, said some words. Brief words, Christian words, monochrome words. He finished speaking and a grey 'amen' came rumbling coldly and uneasily back from the huddled shiver of mourners.

Perhaps because it was so cold, the burial ceremony was very soon over, and we filed out through the lych gate again. The mourners stood awkwardly on the road and spoke to each other in gently regulated murmurs, muted voices suited to funerals.

'In peace at last,' I heard them say, and 'at least it was quick,' 'at least she didn't suffer.' They seemed silly, unkind phrases to me; they sounded as though they were the trite mottoes that they had found in their crackers at their Christmas lunches.

Alfred Ambrose – I had only seen his long sloping back during the church service, and I had been unable to look at him at the graveside, afraid of his guilty tears – stood by the entrance to the lych gate and shook hands with everybody. He seemed to be quite calm and composed now, so upright and correct in his dark old-fashioned suit that I could hardly believe that this was the same man whom I had seen in a crumpled heap, sobbing on his sister's body.

'Good of you to come,' he murmured to Mother. 'Good of you to come.' But he gave Amelia and me a slow wink, as though this formal sobriety was only a pretence.

'Look who it isn't,' he said softly, and for a brief second I thought that I saw tears glinting in his eyes.

There were cups of pale, insipid tea then, and thin slices of bread and butter with the crusts removed, in the sitting-room of Alfred's tiny cottage. It was all prepared and served by a plump rosy-cheeked lady, with her skirt of black and white dog's-tooth pulling tightly, perhaps even a little indecently, against her ample rear; Mrs Forsyth the vicar's wife, Mother told us, although I don't know how she knew. Perhaps the same Mrs Forsyth had arranged a similar such occasion of weak tea and bread and butter for Mother after Father's funeral all those years ago.

Fortunately the majority of mourners chose to decline the tea, for there would not have been room enough for everyone. Instead they crept discreetly away, perhaps relieved to escape the colourless sobriety. As it was, with the vicar, presumably Mr Forsyth, and his round wife, us three Wests and four or maybe five other people, either singly or in pairs, the little room was crowded, with everyone trying to nudge their way as close as possible to the fire while pretending not to, and also trying not to slop their tea or drop crumbs from their bread and butter triangles on the floor. I had had no appetite at breakfast and only swallowed a few mouthfuls of porridge to please Mother, but now I was suddenly ravenous and took three of these dainty slices from the proffered plate. One, of course, fell to the floor.

'Caroline!' hissed Mother, but at least it had landed butter-side up.

After the empty teacups had been piled up on a tray and taken away by Mrs Forsyth, bustling importantly as only vicars' wives and home helps know how, there was nothing left for us to do apart from say goodbye to

Alfred Ambrose and go home. As soon as the first person had made a move to leave, everybody quickly followed, as though afraid that they might be left behind for ever. Apart from Mrs Forsyth and her husband, the one presumably washing up the tea things in the kitchen, for there was the sound of running water and the organized clink of china, and the other straddling the hearth now, warming his hands at the fire, we were the last to leave.

I took a long look at Alfred as we said our goodbyes at the red front door, the ivy wreath now taken down, and I saw that his face was gaunt and grey and that his eyes looked tired beyond exhaustion.

'You two young ladies will still come and visit me, won't you?' he asked anxiously, and even Amelia had no reply other than to nod her head.

'And bring that young Scottish laddie with you again,' he added. Again both Amelia and I nodded, but I couldn't help bursting out, 'William has been taken back up to Stonehaven by his daddy.'

Mother and Amelia shot me fierce, silencing looks, but Alfred did not appear even to have heard me, for he nodded automatically and asked Mother about the welfare of Hilary. Mother, usually so confident, so rarely at a loss for words, paused, and this time I did not burst in with a clumsy sentence. Even I could see that it might be painful to bring up the subject of death and loss with Alfred Ambrose.

'We lost Hilary shortly before Christmas,' Mother ventured cautiously, and although Alfred nodded again as though in automatic reflex, he must have heard her words for he paused briefly and then said, 'You must take Claudia then, Mrs West. Please, as a replacement for Hilary.'

'We couldn't possibly, Alfred, could we, girls?' Mother replied. 'She would be lost without you.' And dutifully Amelia and I chorused, 'Of course not, Mr Ambrose.'

But Alfred was adamant. 'Claudia is already quite

lost without Dorothea,' he said gravely. 'I cannot bear to see her moping about the house. Please take her, Mrs West. She's no mouser as Hilary was, but I am sure that Dorothea would have liked her to go to a good home.'

I was equally sure that Dorothea would have preferred, if she had had any preference at all, that Claudia continue her fat, lazy existence about the churchyard and neighbouring fields, dozing in front of the fire whenever the weather was damp or cool, rather than adjust herself to a paved and grimy urban existence. But how can a recently bereaved brother be contradicted about the wishes of his dearly-loved sister?

We found Claudia hunched up against Alfred's motorbike, banished from the fireside and the warmth of the cottage by Mrs Forsyth and her tea party. Amelia scooped her up, mewling her protests half-heartedly at this unaccustomed rough treatment, and plonked her unceremoniously in a lidded wicker basket for the journey to her new home in Tredannick Close.

Claudia had still not become fully accustomed to her new life in her new home when William and Mrs McCullen returned, just as Mother and Amelia had predicted that they would, from Stonehaven. Just as Amelia had said, Mr McCullen was not with them.

It was not the sort of return that I had envisaged when I had sometimes allowed myself to picture this event, forgetting that it might never happen. Homecomings should be great triumphant occasions, or so I had thought: events which generated both laughter and tears and which lasted in the memory like beacons of shining hope. I never really considered the practicalities of such a celebration. If I had thought about it at all, I would probably have imagined that Mother would organize something, for I was still at an age when the fallibility of adults, especially mothers and, in particular, my mother, was not something that had occurred to me.

As seen in my mind's eye, when . . . if . . . William and Mrs McCullen came back to Truro, leaving behind them that stooped yet terrifying man with nervous hands, for I could not imagine that of which I knew nothing, we would have a huge meal together with crackers and glasses of that sweet nutty wine that Amelia disliked but drank anyway. It would be like Christmas all over again, but this time better, and we would stay up late, talking and laughing. There would be tears too, but tears of happiness, and they would brim in our eyes and only one or two would be shed, for we would be content in a feeling of renewed security. But, of course, it wasn't like that at all.

Mother, and Amelia too, could doubtless have warned me that I would be disappointed if I had revealed this imagined jubilant homecoming to them, but I had not. I was afraid that if I mentioned the event, then spiteful fate would ensure that it never occurred. By not speaking of the resplendent return of mother and son to Tredannick Close, I was safeguarding against it never happening at all. But the actual return of William and Mrs McCullen to Truro, to Tredannick Close, to our lives – if they had actually left the latter at all, for distance can be a poor divider when it chooses – was so unlike what I had envisaged, so undramatic and with so little triumph or festivity, that I never even noticed it happening.

To be fair, however, the reason that I missed their arrival, the reason that I was not out in the road waving flags of welcome, and it was not just I who missed it, but Amelia and Mother as well, was because we were all out.

The new school term was little over a week away and Mother was still working in Mrs McCullen's place behind the haberdashery counter in Hurlinghams. If Amelia had been like me, clumsy and foolish and slow, instead of the brightly sensible girl that she was, I am quite certain that Mother would never have trusted us to be left alone for so long. But she had confidence, quite rightly placed, in Amelia and none of the disasters which Mother's tut-tutting acquaintances suggested might befall us, from chimney fires to accidentally drinking paint stripper, ever occurred. Amelia was much too sensible for that.

It so happened that the afternoon of the return, Amelia and I were out visiting; visiting Alfred Ambrose. It had been Mother's idea and Amelia had been a reluctant participant.

'But he'll be all mopey,' Amelia had protested, grief apparently as unacceptable to her as illness.

Mother said nothing.

'I keep thinking about the way he cried over Dotty Ambrose's hand when she was lying there all dead and cold,' Amelia continued. 'It was the most horrible, horrible thing that I've ever seen.'

'Perhaps you're right,' said Mother quickly. 'Perhaps it would be better if you didn't go to see Alfred just yet.'

I wondered then whether Alfred Ambrose's tears, falling over that cold fat freckled hand, had been the most horrible, horrible thing that Mother had ever encountered too. But Amelia was contrary as well as sensible and clever.

'Oh no,' she said, tossing her head so that her hair, still twisted into hard little plaits, bounced as though the plaits were made of wire. 'We'll go and visit Mr Ambrose today, won't we Caroline? After all, we did say that we would.'

'He might be lonely on his own,' I suggested. 'He doesn't even have Claudia with him now.' And, as though on cue, Claudia came slinking around the edge of the table, for even the fattest cats are endowed with their measure of feline grace, and rubbed herself against Mother's legs, arching her back and purring sycophantically.

Claudia knew, as pets always do, who was the provider of her meals, and Mother, worried that Claudia might pine away and die in her new home and with no familiar friends, spoiled her terribly. She brought Claudia fish heads from Mr Mayberry the fishmonger every other night, and on Saturdays she went to Mr Mayberry's shop and bought Claudia a whole mackerel. She gave Claudia the mackerel in the back yard and the cat would play with it exuberantly on the back step before devouring it, leaving the step covered in a dull sheen of fish scales and producing later pungent and oily defecations. Claudia was not a typically fastidious cat in respect of her lavatorial arrangements, and her attempts at burying these foul-smelling turds were, at best, cursory. It also seemed, to me at least, in exceptionally poor taste that her favourite patch of soil for such purposes was the slightly raised mound in the front garden: the grave of Hilary, Claudia's own offspring who had never once been indulged with a whole mackerel.

Over breakfast, however, Mother had little time for Claudia. She could not afford to arrive late at Hurlinghams and she pushed her away quite crossly.

'Well, I leave the decision with you two,' she smiled at us. 'I really must hurry off now. If you do go out then, Amelia, be sure to lock up properly and do make certain that Claudia is not left in the house. Take care crossing the road both of you, and, Amelia, please do keep an eye on Caroline.' As Mother spoke she bustled about getting ready to leave, adjusting her hair with a distracted hand and, as she squinted, frowning slightly, into the mirror which stood propped on the shelf beside the sink, putting a faint covering of lipstick of the palest pink, ice rose they called it, on her lips. She came and kissed each of us on the forehead before she left the house. 'Oh Amelia,' she added, looking back from the doorway to where we sat at the kitchen table, 'do give Alfred Ambrose my very kindest regards if you decide to go and see him.'

Alfred was in the graveyard when we got there, planting out a rose bush on to the painfully new grave not far from the lych gate. There would be two

137

beautifully manicured graves in the churchyard now, I thought: the tiny grave with the small marble headstone of Dorothea Ambrose's child, and the grave of Dorothea herself.

Alfred looked up from his work as he heard the sound of our feet.

'Look who it isn't,' he said and smiled up at us, but the smile only spread as far as his lips, leaving his eyes utterly weary and devoid of pleasure. His fingers, stained with the soil, continued to tamp down the earth around the grey wrinkled base of the rose bush. 'There'll be crocuses and snowdrops blooming on her babe's grave,' Alfred continued in a conversational tone, 'a spring showing before the summer pansies and violets, and I just couldn't bear to think of her grave lying here all completely bare beside it.' He stood up and brushed the loose soil from his fingers. 'It's an early bloomer,' he said. 'A May one, Pink Cloud it's called, pale pink petals. Very pretty. She would have liked it.' It sounded like another shade of lipstick for Mother to wear.

'Suffer the little children to come unto me,' I read again on Baby Ambrose's headstone, and wondered vaguely what inscription Dorothea's stone would bear. 'At least it was quick'?

Alfred led the way back through the lych gate towards his home. It was the first time that I had been in the churchyard without visiting Father's grave, for even at Dorothea's funeral there had been a few minutes spare in which I, Amelia and Mother had stood quietly at his graveside. I apologized wordlessly to Father for this betrayal as we followed Alfred out of the peaceful arena of the dead. I wondered if Amelia, who had fallen uncharacteristically silent, was also apologizing to Father.

Outside his front gate Alfred paused for a second and ran a caressing hand over the seat of his motorbike.

'Oh,' said Amelia, breaking free from her thoughts.

'Do you remember William, Mr Ambrose, our friend from Stonehaven?' Alfred nodded. 'He liked your motorbike very much,' Amelia continued. 'Didn't he, Caroline? Wasn't William impressed with Mr Ambrose's lovely motorcycle?'

I agreed and Alfred, perhaps encouraged by Amelia's words, took a strip of worn chamois leather from his pocket and gave the badge on the tank a brief rub.

'My Triumph Tiger?' he smiled. 'I was giving it a clean this morning, you know.' He nodded slowly a couple of times, ponderous, heavy nods, and his eyes shone for a moment as he gazed at the gleaming workmanship of black and chrome. 'You might not believe this, girls,' he continued, his voice dreamy now, sinking to a whisper, 'but I reached a ton on that bike once. A ton on my Triumph Tiger, clean as a whistle.'

Neither Amelia nor I knew quite how to respond to that, and I for one, was not entirely sure what Alfred was talking about. But the moment passed; the glow faded from his eyes, and they resumed their hollowness, their aching tiredness. He thrust the leather back into his pocket with a sigh. 'I suppose we'd better go inside,' he muttered.

There was, to my surprise, no fire burning in Alfred's sitting-room. Instead there were the cold and black remains of a fire from a previous evening, dead in the grate, and an unpleasant feeling of chilly dampness in the air. This room, which had once appeared to me to be the very hub of the Ambroses' existence, cheerful and unfussily friendly and warm, now seemed inhospitable and neglected. It reminded me of the unloved and empty house that stood across the street from our own home.

There were two mugs with cold, half-drunk tea in them on the mantelpiece above the dead fire, and already there was a dull coating of dust around them. On the gate-legged occasional table with the circular brass top there were three unwashed glasses and two empty bottles of whisky. 'Distilled and bottled in the Highlands of Scotland', I read on their labels, and, inevitably, I thought again of William.

'Shall I make up the fire, Mr Ambrose?' asked Amelia, after glancing quickly around and giving her verdict of disapproval with a couple of sniffs.

Alfred looked about him too, almost as though he had never been in the room before, and he seemed to notice the air of neglect that hung about the dusty furniture and abandoned crockery.

'You've caught me out, I'm afraid,' he murmured. 'I would have tidied up if I'd known that you were coming. I never expected visitors today.'

He'd never expected visitors on all the other occasions that we'd called after visiting Father's grave, and yet the sitting-room would still always be bright and cheerful: flowers in a cut-glass vase on the mantelpiece in summer, a fire crackling in the grate in winter. But then he had always had Dorothea previously. And Claudia.

After a few half-hearted protests, Alfred agreed to let Amelia set the fire with kindling and logs from the wicker baskets, and coal from a great iron bucket. He took the cups, glasses and bottles away and later returned with the usual mugs of milk and slices of bread and honey, carried through from the kitchen on the usual wooden tray, although the traycloth looked grubby and wrinkled.

On all the previous occasions Alfred had watched us partaking of our refreshment, but this time he joined us. Not with bread and honey and a mug of milk, to be sure, but with a glass half full of a clear amber liquid. From my usual place on his comforting knee, I could smell a rich, hot flavour coming from the glass as he raised it to his lips. I touched the glass tentatively with the back of my hand, and was surprised to find that it was quite cold.

'What are you drinking, Mr Ambrose?' I ventured, but Alfred just smiled up at me and drooped an eyelid over one of his sad old eyes, so that it was Amelia who answered first.

'He's drinking whisky, Caroline. Aren't you, Mr Ambrose?' and she sniffed twice rather loudly and pursed her lips. Behind her spectacles her eyes shone cold and hard. I could sense Amelia's displeasure like the scent of thundery rain approaching and I wondered what I had done wrong. But I knew that I would find out soon enough, and I was presently more interested in trying Alfred's whisky. I imagined that it would conjure up William and Mrs McCullen and bring me closer to them.

'Please, Mr Ambrose,' I said carefully, knowing that adults had a hypocritical attitude to children trying out the indulgences reserved for older people. 'I would very much like to try a little tiny weeny sip of your whisky, if I may?' For a while I thought that Alfred Ambrose would remember the unfair baggage of adult responsibilities that he, as a grown-up man, should be bearing. He did not answer for several long seconds. Then he gave a rather mirthless laugh and handed me the glass. 'It's only a cheap brand, I'm afraid,' he said.

The whisky seemed to burn an entirely new route down my throat and into my stomach. It made me gasp and it brought tears to my eyes, and it left every unfortunate cell that had been in its path, tingling and horribly fearful of future contact.

'Oh!' I said. The slightly sour aftertaste that the whisky left in my mouth and at the back of my throat reminded me of vomit. 'I don't like that,' I added decidedly, and then, fearing that I was being rude, quickly tacked on, 'not much anyway.' Amelia gave a single prolonged and unnecessarily loud sniff.

'Would you like to try some, Amelia?' asked Alfred, but Amelia, who would normally try anything and had once eaten a woodlouse when William had dared her to do so, crunching into its shining grey back with her teeth, shook her head very firmly.

141

'No thank you, Mr Ambrose,' she said and sniffed again.

All the way home I waited fearfully for Amelia to tell me what it was I had done to cause her unmistakable displeasure at Alfred's house, but she remained stubbornly silent for most of the walk, only speaking to urge me not to dawdle and not to walk in the centre of the road.

'But cars don't come along these back roads,' I protested.

'That's what you said about Tredannick Close,' returned Amelia sharply, 'and look what happened to poor old Hilary.' There was no answer, of course, to that.

Eventually, as we descended the hill into the brooding valley of Truro, I forced myself to ask Amelia what it was that I had said or done at Alfred's cottage that had displeased her so. She looked at me with bright, curious eyes, as though I had said something very strange.

'Come on, Amelia,' I said quickly. 'I can tell when you're cross. You're just like Mother – you sniff so, and even behind your spectacles I can see your eyes glinting at me.'

Amelia gave an impatient snort and sighed loudly, raising her hands skywards and rolling her eyes in a pantomime of exaggerated exasperation.

'But Caroline,' she said, 'it wasn't you.'

'Wasn't me?'

'It was Alfred Ambrose.'

'Mr Ambrose?'

'Oh, do wake up, Caroline,' said Amelia, sighing again, 'surely you saw?'

'Saw what?'

'The embers in the grate? The dust on the furniture? The unwashed mugs? The glasses? And the bottles? The bottles, think of the bottles, Caroline. That man is just collapsing. He doesn't care, he's letting himself go. He'll be a drunk before we know it.'

Again, of course, there was no answer to that and we walked the rest of the way home in an uncomfortable silence.

I was pleased to be the first to notice the changes that had occurred in the McCullens' house while we had been out. It wasn't because I was more observant than Amelia, merely that she studiously avoided looking towards their house, whereas my gaze was drawn to it almost irresistibly, horrified and yet fascinated by its air of empty loneliness.

The actual physical changes are hard to recall: perhaps the curtains in the sitting-room window had been closed more completely, perhaps there was a light on in one of the upstairs rooms or maybe one of the upstairs windows was open. The overall change, however, is much easier to remember. Simply, the house no longer seemed cold and neglected; it was a house that was lived in once again. It was a house that somebody, somewhere, referred to as 'home'.

'Look!' I said eagerly to Amelia, all thoughts of Alfred Ambrose immediately dispelled. 'Look!' And Amelia paused mid-stride and viewed the house contemplatively for a minute with her head on one side. 'Well?' I asked, ready to bound around the street in my excitement. Amelia nodded her head slowly.

'Yes, I believe you're right, Caroline,' she said. 'They're back.'

I, of course, wanted to rush up to their front door at once, but Amelia restrained me and we went first to our own house to take off our boots, damp and slightly muddy from the graveyard, and to set the fire. When we went outside again William was sitting on our front wall, stroking Claudia. He looked the same as ever, thin and angular and pale, his red hair sticking out from his head in untidy tuffets and the tilt of his face and the set of his mouth both cheeky and defiant.

'Hello Amelia, hello Caroline,' he said as naturally as though he had never been away. 'I suppose that's

Hilary's grave, is it? Whatever happened to the poor cat? I rearranged the bits of china in the shape of a fish. I hope you don't mind, but it somehow seemed more appropriate than a flower for Hilary. And whose fat cat is this one, anyway?' He prodded Claudia's swinging belly as he spoke, making her snarl and swipe ineffectually at William's hand. 'She reminds me of that cat that belonged to those friends of yours with the Triumph Tiger. You know, that nice sexton chappie and his mad sister.'

Chapter Twelve

It was strange how quickly, with the start of the new term and the new year, we slipped again into the old familiar routines.

William was reticent about his trip to Stonehaven; when Amelia asked him what they had done on Christmas Day he shrugged noncommittally. When pressed, for Amelia could exert a persuasive pressure when she wished to do so, he said that they had gone to church. Amelia gave one of her sniffs.

'And your da?' she probed. 'Did he go to church with you too?'

'Of course,' William retorted. 'He's got a lot more sins to pray for forgiveness for than me and Ma.'

William's voice was hard and bitter as he replied and the look that he gave Amelia was so fierce that the sniff that was about to emerge from her nose became tangled up inside her and came out as a strangled cough. It was not easy to scare Amelia out of her sniffs, and she hadn't been defeated yet.

'So why did you come back to Cornwall?' she asked. 'And why didn't your da come too?'

William's gaze was fiercer now and brighter too with the unshed tears glistening in his eyes, and he clenched his small pale hands into fists of misery and anger. When he spoke, his voice was low and even, but there was a dark warning running through it.

'Why do you think, Amelia West?' he answered, and I shivered at that voice of suppressed fury. 'Why do you think?'

But even Amelia was not prepared to hazard an answer to that one and so, for a while at least, the subjects of William and Mrs McCullen's travels over the length of Britain, and their Christmas celebrations in Stonehaven with Mr McCullen, were dropped. I, for one, had no intention of encouraging these subjects, with their attendant cold and anger, to be mentioned again.

Mrs McCullen, however, frequently referred to the whole episode, but she contrived to do so in a manner which was both cautious and oblique. For her, the whole event, from Mr McCullen's unexpected appearance in Truro to the return of William and herself in the New Year, could be conveniently amalgamated under the one umbrella-like euphemistic phrase of 'at Christmastime, if you get my meaning'. This would be accompanied by a sideways look from beneath puckered eyebrows and a wry twist of the lips which the generous might describe as a smile.

'I can never repay your mother,' Mrs McCullen told Amelia and me, 'for taking on my job at Hurlinghams, you know, at Christmastime, if you get my meaning.'

And there would be the eyebrows slanting towards each other and the thin, humourless smile.

'What would you have done if Mother hadn't been able to keep on your job for you, Mrs McCullen?' I asked, looking up at her sad thin face.

'Caroline!' said Mother warningly.

'I don't know, dearie. I really don't know.' Mrs McCullen's voice quivered a little and now I didn't need Mother's sharp, silencing glare to stop me asking any further questions. I felt ashamed of my own inept clumsiness, and I hung my head.

The school terms had begun again and the sky was grey and gusty. There were flurries of hard bouncing hail amongst which bright patches of sunniness shone briefly before disappearing, reappearing some time later with all the chilly inconsistency of early spring.

Twice the coincidence of a high spring tide and a heavy rain swelled the river Fal until it flooded. It

146

oozed moodily over the grassy banks and then slid slowly down the streets, lapping at the doorsteps and lamp posts. When it retreated, sinking sullenly back on itself as though exhausted by its effort, it left a layer of green-grey slimeyness on the cobblestones and glinting puddles in all the hollows.

On the occasion of the second flooding, more wet and more dramatic than the first, with families carrying provisions and treasures upstairs and talks of possible evacuation, Mr Churchton, he of the Nativity play programme and William's curly burnt-cork moustache, found a fish when the river receded, stranded in a shallow puddle on Lemon Quay. The newspapermen put his picture on the second page of the *Western Morning News* holding the fish, a small pathetic thing with an ugly blunt nose, by the tail between forefinger and thumb. Mr Churchton's hands looked pale and long, as artists' hands should be, and the expression on his face was one of utter boredom and disdain.

Amelia and I still met at Worthingtons to walk home together, and William joined us more frequently now. He said that he wanted to get home early to light the fire and set the table. I thought he might be worried in case his father turned up again while he was out, but when I tentatively suggested this, William only scowled.

'Da won't be coming back down here again,' he said, thrusting his hands deep into his pockets and hunching his shoulders. 'It ain't Da I'm worried about,' he added. 'It's me ma. She's not well at the minute. She needs to rest.'

It was Amelia, of course, sniffing just a little, but also twisting her face into her expression of mild disgust, who asked what was wrong with Mrs McCullen. But William didn't reply. His frown deepened and his pace quickened as he walked away from us up the road, leaving us sucking on our balls of mouthwash sweet.

'Don't you know what's wrong with her?' Amelia

shouted after him, hating to be ignored. Despite the strident insistence in her voice, so loud that he could not have failed to have heard her, William's hunched back never even faltered. I thought that perhaps he had another reason for wanting to be home early, some ulterior motive that he was too ashamed to confess to us. I put my suggestion to Amelia's peeved and pale face, and she tossed her plaits and fiddled with the elastic of her school hat beneath her chin.

'Maybe, Caroline,' she conceded, but she sounded unconvinced. I knew that she was still raging because William had walked away from her without even acknowledging her question.

After that I kept a careful watch on Mrs McCullen, trying to detect signs of disability or sickliness. Ever since we had known her she had seemed worn and scrawny, with her deep-set eyes and her yellowish skin. Her height and slenderness had always made her appear stringy and undernourished. But now I looked closer and I thought that perhaps her aura of weary gauntness had increased, that the skin of her face was drawn tighter across her cheekbones, that her eyes had sunk yet deeper into their shadowed sockets, that maybe the pucker in her forehead had become a permanent score of three parallel grooves. The mole on her cheek also seemed enormous now, but perhaps that was because I kept staring at it. It began to haunt me, a huge dark island floating treacherously across the stark landscape of troubled, half-remembered dreams.

'Do you think Mrs McCullen looks sick?' I asked Amelia as we brushed our teeth together in the bathroom. The next day I watched as Amelia gave Mrs McCullen a long and appraising stare, her gaze darting from the shadow stroke of a moustache line on her upper lip, up to the mole and back again. But she seemed unaware of Amelia's scrutiny.

'Not any sicker than she usually does,' said Amelia that evening, standing barefoot in her flannelette nightgown and brushing out her plaits with the ebony-backed hairbrush. 'I think that she looks scared.'

'Scared?' I repeated wonderingly, ignoring Amelia's derisive sniff.

'Nervous, frightened, worried, anxious, fearful,' suggested Amelia, each word being pronounced in time to a brisk stroke of her hairbrush. She had finished her brushing now, and she took off her spectacles and climbed into bed. 'Scared,' she repeated, gazing vaguely towards me. 'Good night, Caroline,' and she was almost immediately asleep. She nearly always fell asleep first.

I was at the McCullens' house rather early one Saturday morning, for Mother had taken Amelia into town to see Mr Geoffrey Quigley, the optician. This was an annual event that both Mother and Amelia took very seriously. Mr Quigley was a widower with bright eyes, a large nose and a loud booming laugh. Mother knew him well and they were of similar age; he had been a friend of Father's, or she had been a friend of Mr Quigley's wife who had died years before of something unpleasant and painful that adults spoke about in subdued, respectful voices. Mother called him Geoffrey or Geoff, and sometimes Amelia hinted to me that she thought Mother and Mr Quigley might get married again one day, to each other. But Mother insisted that Amelia address him as Mr Quigley rather than Geoffrey, and Amelia had seen the photograph of Mr Quigley's children, two daughters and a younger son, on the windowsill in his office. The girls, at least, were much prettier than Amelia or I could ever be, and therefore Amelia disliked them.

'I expect they're stupid,' she said crossly.

'But Amelia, I'm stupid,' I replied hesitantly, and Amelia was too annoyed to contradict me or even to soften the blow by saying that I was kind or generous.

'Exactly!' she sniffed. 'Two stupid stepsisters and a stupid stepbrother as well as you would be too much to ask. No, I hope that Mother doesn't marry her Geoffrey.'

And Mother, coming into the room on the tail of this sentence, said sharply, 'Amelia, you're too young for such familiarity and informality. His name is Mr Quigley until either he or I tell you otherwise.' And Amelia blushed, afraid that Mother might have overheard more than Amelia would have liked her to.

So while Amelia and Mother were at Mr Quigley's premises, halfway up Lemon Street, behind a crisply painted door with a brass knocker in the shape of a lion's head, Amelia reading out letters of diminishing size from a board, while Mr Quigley obscured one of her eyes with his clean pink hand smelling of violet soap and talcum powder, I went to visit William.

It was, as I have said, rather early, and William was in the kitchen making tea and toast, and raking the ashes out from the fireplace.

'Where's your ma?' I asked him, and William shrugged one shoulder towards the ceiling.

'Upstairs,' he said. 'She's getting up. She always gets up a little later at the weekend.'

'Mother has taken Amelia to see Mr Quigley, the optician,' I explained. 'Amelia thinks that Mother and Mr Quigley might get married to each other one day, but she's worried about his children.'

'Why?' asked William, looking up at me from where he crouched by the fireplace, his hands grimy with coal dust. But he didn't sound very interested, and he got up quickly and turned on the tap full blast and started rattling the cups and saucers together noisily.

'Either because they're pretty or because they're stupid,' I answered, having to raise my voice to be heard above the racing splash and dash of the water into the sink, and the clatter of the crockery. But William didn't appear to be listening to me. From the angle of his head and his expression of concentration I could tell that he was listening to something else.

Above the noise of the water and the china a

different, painful noise came rasping down to us, and I could see now that William was trying to hide it beneath the medley of other sounds. Despite his efforts, however, it was too insistent and too loud to be disguised. He looked sideways at me and saw that I had heard. He made a wry face then, a thin tight-lipped smile with a frown above it, and he tilted his face defiantly. He turned off the tap and the cups sat silent on their saucers as that strange and painful sound repeated itself, this time more clearly, this time more anguished. It was a peculiarly familiar noise, or at least one that I thought I had heard before some-where. It was a snorting, choking, gurgle that reminded me of fat puffing aquatic animals, walruses perhaps or hippopotami. It was a desperate and unhappy sound.

'Is that your mother?' I asked, for it was indubitably drifting down to us through the kitchen ceiling. William nodded and sighed, a deep lugubrious sigh.

'Don't tell Amelia,' he pleaded, touching my arm. 'It happens every morning.'

And, yet again, that awful throat-grappling sound. Mrs McCullen was upstairs in the bathroom, retching and vomiting and retching again, and all the time choking on huge and gulping sobs of despair.

So I said nothing to Amelia, but I touched Mother's arm at the elbow as she put out the mackerel for Claudia on the back step.

'Mother, what's wrong with Mrs McCullen?' I asked, and she wiped her hands on her flowery apron with the broderie anglaise trim and gave me a hard, appraising look.

'Now, what do you mean by that exactly, Caroline?' she asked, and when I had told her, in uncertain snatches, she turned away from me and looked out, beyond where Claudia flipped at the mackerel, to our unappealing square of back lawn, more dandelions than grass, with the clothes line flapping across it, to the door of the coal shed with its paint peeling off in ragged strips.

'Poor Mrs McCullen,' she murmured. 'Poor William.' And that was the only answer that she gave me, for, at that moment, Amelia appeared, diffident in a new and uglier pair of spectacles with stronger lenses, and hungry for lunch.

March was fierce with gales which felled an elm tree near St Michael's church and chased shreds of grey cloud across the sky. Slates were blown off houses and whisked sideways through the air like playing cards, clattering and breaking on the street as they landed.

'A child could be hit by one of those slates and killed,' said Mrs McCullen.

'So could an adult,' said William.

Up near Amelia's high school somebody was killed, a retired dentist from Essex called Mr Wiggens, crushed by a falling chimney, and, off the south-west coast of Cornwall, a fishing boat, the *Morwenna Rose II*, sank in heavy seas with all the crew lost. It seemed a furious, violent month to me and I made my way to school cautiously, keeping a vigilant eye out for killer slates and murderous chimneys. The branches of the trees creaked and moaned as the wind pushed them against each other. It was a bruised and dismal sound and I thought of the beech tree behind Father's grave.

'Should we go out to the churchyard?' I asked Mother and Amelia. 'A tree might have fallen over Father's grave.'

'What difference would it make if one had?' snorted Amelia.

'It's sheltered in that valley,' said Mother. 'I expect the trees will be all right.'

'I think that we ought to go anyway,' chimed in William, and Amelia looked at him crossly.

'You just want to go and look at Alfred Ambrose's motorbike,' she said, sniffing again. 'Why don't you and Caroline go by yourselves?'

'All right,' replied William, who could tilt his chin every bit as defiantly as Amelia. 'We will.'

We went on a showery Sunday afternoon when the gales had abated and Amelia had homework to do. Homework was called 'prep' at the high school, a short, stiff word which seemed to me to epitomize both the superiority and the snobbery of the place. We walked quickly up the hill out of Truro, William striding on ahead while I huffed and puffed behind him.

'Come on, Caroline,' William goaded. 'You're like an old lady.' I had to run a few uneasy steps then to catch up. Once out of Truro and walking downhill towards the green valley where the graveyard lay, William walked more easily. He wanted to talk to me now and we went side by side along the road with him testing me on the correct spelling of words. He was curiously fascinated about my progress in all things literary now, and I was ashamed that I could not be a more able and rewarding pupil.

'Spell coffin,' William suggested. 'Come on, Caroline, spell tomb; spell burial; spell cemetery; spell sepulchre.' I was a hesitant speller with neither confidence nor skill, and I got no further than the second or third letter of each word before giving up with a helpless shake of the head.

'I can't do it,' I told William sadly. 'I know I won't be able to get it right. I can't see the words in my head like you and Amelia can.'

So instead we kicked a smooth oval pebble up the road between us, in a companionable silence broken only by our footsteps and the sound of the stone being kicked and rolling on ahead of us.

The churchyard was shining wet, pearly in the grey dampness. There were snails on the wall and twigs strewn on the paths and scattered amongst the graves, torn from the trees by the racing winds. These twigs had a ripped, abused look about them, but there were

153

no trees fallen, nor even any branches, for, as Mother had said, it was sheltered there. The beech tree behind my father's grave seemed to be veiled in a meniscus of green: a sign of spring, of resilience and hope.

I showed William where Dorothea Ambrose had been buried, the rose bush planted by her brother still ragged and lonely in the mound of soil.

'Do you think that the worms will be chewing her up down there?' I asked him, recalling a conversation I had once had with Amelia, but he didn't answer. He was bending over Baby Ambrose's grave admiring the tufts of rain-wet snowdrops, the hard, pale green points of crocuses already two or more inches above the ground.

Alfred Ambrose answered the front door after we had knocked and stood for a few uncertain minutes on the step. He looked tired and rumpled, as though he might have slept in his clothes. His braces were twisted and there was a smear of something glutinous, which could have been scrambled egg, on his shirt. His hair was dishevelled and there was a greyish fuzz of stubble over his chin. He stared blearily out at us, as though the watery Sunday-afternoon light hurt his eyes. As William started up hesitantly, 'Good afternoon, Mr Ambrose,' he gave a fleeting smile.

'Look who it isn't,' he murmured, and then, more loudly, but also more gently, 'I'm afraid that I overslept.' He peered out behind us and added anxiously to me, 'You haven't brought your mother with you, have you?'

'I'm afraid not, Mr Ambrose,' I replied apologetically. 'Nor Amelia. It's just me and William. You do remember William, don't you? He came with us to see you in the summer. He would like you to show him your motorbike.' My voice gabbled on, quite unstoppable, like the brook behind the graveyard, as I tried to mask my shame that Mother had not been to visit Mr Ambrose since Dorothea's funeral. But Alfred didn't seem to mind and his eyes softened at the mention of his motorbike.

'My old Triumph Tiger,' he said. 'Well, if you've come to see that, I'll put my boots on and join you.'

I looked quickly down and saw his big toes on both feet, with their corrugated yellowish nails that looked as hard as horn, and their tufts of coarse grey hair at the joints, poking out through holes in his knitted socks. And then, abruptly and to my surprise, he closed the hectic red door and left us standing on the step in the drizzle.

Despite the drizzle, a fine misty rain which speckled the chrome and gleaming black paintwork of the motorbike, and stuck to our hair as though it were gossamer, the enthusiasm of both William and Alfred for the Triumph Tiger seemed not to be dampened at all. Alfred had brought a kitchen chair from his home and I sat on this sipping a mug of milk, which tasted slightly sour, as he showed off the machine to William. I listened vaguely to his voice, soft with pleasure, quick with enthusiasm, running through a litany of incomprehensible words.

'Magneto, dynamo, exhaust manifold, cylinder barrels . . .' His voice drifted over me like the chimes of bells, strangely foreign, and I wondered again about Dorothea Ambrose in her wooden box beneath the ground. Would the worms have gnawed their way into it yet? Would they go for her vacant pale blue eyes first? Or her dimpling chin? Or her fat freckled hands? And then of course I thought of baby Ambrose, and of Hilary the cat, and of Father, and I shuddered.

A barking roar startled me from my morbid thoughts, and there was the briefest puff of white smoke. Alfred had started his motorbike.

'Just going for a quick spin, my dear,' he called to me. 'Up you jump, William. Careful now. Put your feet on the pillion pegs.'

And off they went up the road, the engine thumping regularly like a heartbeat, increasing slightly and then gradually fading into the distance, leaving me sitting by the side of an empty country road in the drizzle. I poured the remains of my glass of milk on to Alfred's garden, and the church on the opposite side of the road gave a cold and disapproving stare.

When William and Alfred returned from their ride their eyes were shining and their cheeks flushed. Their hair was blown into wild damp tufts like moorland grasses and they spoke to each other excitedly, William asking questions, Alfred replying. Then Alfred's voice became languorous with reminiscence. 'You might not believe this, William,' I heard him say, 'but I reached a ton just once . . .'

Before we left there was small talk, with all the drawn-out politeness of goodbyes between acquaintances.

'May I come again, Mr Ambrose?' William asked and Alfred laughed and nodded.

'You'll be coming to see the old Triumph Tiger, not me,' he said. Then he asked me how Mother and Amelia were keeping, and without waiting for my reply, for he probably knew that they were hardly ever unwell, he asked William how his mother was too. William shuffled his feet awkwardly before replying.

'Ma?' he said. 'Actually, Mr Ambrose, Ma isn't very well at all. You see, she's going to have a baby.'

Chapter Thirteen

Mother, of course, knew already. William was quite certain of that. But he asked me if I would tell Amelia.

'I just don't want to have to see her face,' he said, and I thought that I knew what it was that he wanted to avoid. I, too, could picture the mixture of incredulity and contempt, the bright curiosity that would burn in Amelia's eyes and the derision that would twist her lips into countless questions. So I agreed, and it fell to me to tell her that evening as we climbed into bed. But my predictions of her response, although not entirely wrong, were also not entirely correct, for her eyes were soft and reflective as well as curious and there were no questions at all, not then anyway.

'I wonder . . .' she murmured as she scrunched herself down beneath the blankets, but even her wondering was soon lost beneath the easy rhythm of untroubled sleep.

We watched Mrs McCullen more carefully now and saw that the severe, straight lines of her dresses were gradually softened into garments that billowed about her like sails. Frequently in the evening she came to our house to borrow Mother's sewing machine, sitting quietly in a corner of the sitting-room adjusting seams and adding panels of material into skirts. Only the steady chugging whir of the treadle betrayed her presence, and the satisfying slicing of Mother's sewing scissors through the material.

The harshness of March blew into the soft showers and watery, silver-green sunshine of April, and in the streets beside the cathedral the pale blossom of the ornamental cherry trees fluttered like clouds of soft confetti. Mrs McCullen seemed to have absorbed some of that light merriness of springtime. Her hair, which had been cut severely short after her return from Stonehaven, grew thick and lush and curled softly around her ears. Her face lost some of its yellow weariness and became less harsh, and although it could never be described as pink, there was a rosy warmth glowing in her cheeks. Her ever-increasing plumpness softened the angles of her figure and I thought that I had never seen her looking healthier. I could not believe that she still sobbed and retched in their bathroom every morning and when I asked William, he conceded that she no longer did.

William seemed to hate to talk about his mother's pregnancy. Amelia said that perhaps it scared him and I thought that she might be right, but I also thought that it was because it reminded him of his father and 'Christmastime, if you get my meaning'.

'Aren't you excited?' Amelia asked him. 'Don't you wonder whether it will be a boy or a girl?' But he only shuddered and shook his head.

'It makes Ma's back ache,' he said. 'It makes her tired.'

'But don't you wonder what it will look like?' pressed on Amelia, who could not easily be persuaded to abandon a topic that interested her. 'Haven't you wondered about what it's going to be named?'

William shook his head again and his hard blue stare was a warning against further questioning, but Amelia could be heedless and she ignored the danger signals.

'Why aren't you interested, William?' she asked. 'We're interested, aren't we Caroline? Why don't you want to know too? It's going to be your little brother or sister after all.'

But William went off without replying and for a full week refused to see or speak to either Amelia or me, walking home from school alone and playing by himself in the McCullens' dreary house. Even Mother noticed and questioned his absence, and, when Amelia explained, she scolded her crossly: a rare event, for she and Amelia usually thought alike.

'I would have thought that you knew better than that, Amelia West,' she chided. 'Can't you see that the poor boy is frightened? Can't you see that he doesn't want to be reminded of his awful father?' Her words confirmed both our theories as to William's reticence.

May was a month of light, warm days. Grass grew over Hilary's grave, hiding the pieces of china, and Claudia basked on the garden wall, fat and lazy as ever. Mrs McCullen complained, in thin murmured sentences, of swollen ankles and tired calf muscles. William went once more, this time by himself, to visit Alfred Ambrose and his motorbike. Mother bought Amelia her school summer uniform from Hurling-hams, a plain gingham dress and a blazer, and a straw boater with a ribbon around the rim.

'You ought to rest more,' Mother told Mrs McCullen. 'You should give up your work in Hurlinghams. You must get William to help you more about the house, and Amelia and Caroline should give you a hand too. I know that they would be glad to do so, wouldn't you, girls?'

Mother had always said that it was her prerogative to land us in situations like that, and although I was unsure what prerogative meant I knew that there was only one answer, and both Amelia and I nodded.

'The three of them could start on your back yard while the weather is fine,' Mother suggested.

The McCullens' back yard was rank with tall stinging nettles and a mess of pampas grass that cut the soft flesh of our fingertips with neat painful slices. The fluffed and tufty pampas flowers made Amelia sneeze. Beside the coal shed William found two dead fledglings with ugly pink bodies, naked apart from bedraggled clumps of downy feathers. I buried them in our garden, close to Hilary's grave. Amelia scythed down the nettles, complaining and singing alternately. William poured paraffin over the pampas grass and set it alight.

It burned with a surprising quantity of choking grey smoke and somebody further down the street, we never found out who, called the fire brigade. Three doors along, Mrs Hanson had hung out bed linen to dry, and the ash settled on the damp sheets and stuck. Mrs McCullen had to mollify the unwanted firemen with apologies and cups of tea and rewash Mrs Hanson's sheets, returning them to her not only washed and dried, but also ironed.

The whole exercise was pointless, however, because even with the nettles trimmed down, the pampas grass reduced to a charred stump and the door of the coal shed repainted, the McCullens' back yard still seemed dank and drab in the shadow of their house. On sunny Saturday afternoons, when Mrs McCullen wanted to sit outside knitting small yellow and white fluffy things for her ever-increasing bulge, she invariably came and sat in our back yard anyway.

June and July were hot, glaring months. The windows in all the houses looked streaked and dirty and the streets smelt of melting tar and excrement. When the tide was low, a miasma of decay came drifting muddily up from the river and settled over the town as though it were punishing it.

There were end-of-term tests being set in all the schools, and William and Amelia attacked them with competitive relish. Mother brought home her marking and wouldn't let us touch the pile of papers. William came top in English, biology and Latin, and Amelia came top in physics, history and mathematics. They argued querulously over whose achievement was the greater.

'I am surprised that you didn't manage better in French, Amelia,' said Mother, who had always given Amelia extra tuition in the subject. I said nothing at all. I had never performed well in school tests.

Mrs McCullen's ankles had swollen yet further and the veins behind her knees and on the backs of her hands stood out lividly, like purple embroidery silk. She waddled rather than walked now, ungainly and uncomfortable with one hand pressed into the small of her back. When she lowered herself into the striped deck chair in our garden to drink Mother's iced lemonade, her feet flew up into the air and she found it hard to stand upright again.

She had planned to work until August, but the management at Hurlinghams said that she was putting off the customers, and by mid-July Mrs McCullen had left the haberdashery counter to fend for itself. She became slovenly in her tiredness, and she never seemed to change out of a floral curtain of a dress and a pair of slopping, broken-down slippers with a band of tatty red velvet across the toes.

I looked grumpily at the five of us: Amelia and William quarrelling noisily, Mrs McCullen fanning at herself with a book, trapped in her own ungainly body, and Mother squeezing endless lemons in the kitchen and scolding William and Amelia when their voices became too loud and petulant. Even Claudia seemed fed-up with the heat and sat in the shade of Mrs McCullen's deck chair, occasionally flicking irritably at flies with her tail.

'I think we need a holiday,' I said to Mother. 'When are we to go to the Pollards' farm?'

Mother looked up from her lemon squeezer, her face flushed with effort and tendrils of hair smeared to her forehead with sweat.

'We won't be going to the Pollards' farm this year, chickadee,' she said. 'We can't expect poor Mrs McCullen to travel down there, can we now? And we can't leave her here on her own.'

My face must surely have expressed the horror that I felt as I heard her words. They rang through the air like warning bells, crackling in the heat of the fissile July afternoon. It was the first year ever in the placid history of my memory that Mother had suggested we should be deprived of our annual summer visit to the farm.

Mother smiled at my stricken expression and kissed me, her face hot and sweatily sticky against mine.

'We'll go in the spring next year, Caroline,' she promised. 'We'll go during the Easter holidays. You'll enjoy seeing the farm then with all the baby animals about.'

But spring seemed an indescribably long distance off. I couldn't imagine all those days and nights passing until the Easter holidays. I felt both trapped and cheated and my heart's desire was a trip to the countryside, now: an escape, however brief, from the town's stifling heat to the fresh sea air. I longed for this freedom with a burning intensity, made all the more fierce by the knowledge that I was to be deprived. By nightfall I was running a fever, my head ached and throbbed and my eyes, reflected in the bathroom mirror, glittered back at me with an unnatural brightness.

I was ill for four days and five nights and Mother was worried. I twisted and turned in my bed in a delirious mixture of sleep and wakefulness. I poured sweat until my nightdress and sheets were drenched and I shivered so vigorously that Mother had to hold me down to prevent me from falling out of bed. I bit my tongue so hard that my mouth slowly filled with the salty warmth of my own blood. Amelia was sent to sleep in the big double bed in Mother's room. Mother took over Amelia's little bed, getting up in the night to change my sodden sheets and night clothes and to make me fresh hot-water bottles. She held my hand during terrifying, muddled nightmares about Father, about Dorothea Ambrose, about Mr McCullen, about Mrs McCullen's morning sickness. All the unexplained mysteries of my small life twisted themselves into garbled costumes of horror and dread as I tossed and turned and sweated and shivered.

On the third day of my illness, Mother took the unusual step of calling in Dr Donnelly. He had spectacles and a smooth, round, reassuring face. He liked cats, children and women, in that order, or so he told me, but years later I heard rumours that he actually liked men best and lived with a younger man, an unsuccessful artist or poet I was told, and a French poodle called Dauphine. But it was much later that I heard that, and besides, it was only a rumour. For now, Dr Donnelly took my temperature and my pulse, looked down my throat and made me cough while he put something cold and hard on my chest. He asked me questions that I was too exhausted to answer and he made notes on a piece of paper in spiky royal blue writing. Mother hovered anxiously at the bedroom door while he spoke and wrote and prodded and poked, but he told her to wait for him downstairs, and that was when he told me that women were in third position in his list of priorities.

Dr Donnelly prescribed for me two sorts of tablet, one which was large and had to be taken twice a day, and one which was small and had to be taken with a drink at night time. There was also a sticky red medicine whose blackcurrant flavouring enhanced rather than disguised the taste of unpleasant bitterness.

Two days later my fever had abated, the nightmares faded and William and Amelia came to see me. They sat on Amelia's bed and told me how thin and white I looked. They had a jigsaw with them, which they did together on an old tin tray, and they told me that Mother had arranged a surprise for me.

Three days later, Mother wrapped me in a blanket and allowed me to sit in the bright afternoon sunshine with Mrs McCullen. We were a strange couple: Mrs McCullen lumbering and enormous with beads of sweat glistening along her moustache line, and me, pale and thin and still trembling slightly from my illness. Mrs McCullen showed me all the baby clothes that she had knitted, four bonnets in pale yellow and white and blue with little satinette ribbons to tie beneath the chin, six pairs of bootees, two fluffy jackets and one blanket. I thought they were all quite

163

delightful. I hoped that she would have a girl and I told her this, but she only smiled and dabbed at her sweaty upper lip with a lace-trimmed handkerchief.

'I don't mind a boy or a girl,' she said with a tiny sigh and she pressed my hand, still sickly translucent pale, against the side of her bulge. Beneath my fingers I felt something moving inside her. It was a small and secret movement, like a sleepy fidget. It occurred to me briefly that this might be Mother's surprise of which William and Amelia had spoken. But it was not, of course.

The real surprise took place some five or six days later and I wondered if Dr Donnelly, who had expressed a preference for children above women, had suggested it. The trip to the Pollards' farm was going to take place after all, but, unlike previous years, Mother was to stay behind in Truro with William and Mrs McCullen, while Amelia and I made the trip alone.

Mother took us to the station, kissed us goodbye, sent her love to Annie and Diggory, urged Amelia not to forget any of her instructions and told me to listen to Amelia. She stood on the platform waving to us as the train drew away from Truro, moving with every inch closer to the Pollards' farm.

Amelia was in charge on the train. I was not to fidget, speak to strangers other than the guard, or take off any clothes. Because of my illness I was bundled up in a wool jacket that restricted movement and had an itchy collar. Amelia, however, swung from the luggage rack, said hello to everyone she could, accepted a toffee from a fat man with a Panama hat and a blue and white spotted handkerchief in his breast pocket, and stuck her head out of the carriage window as far as she dared when we went roaring through the brief black tunnels.

'Why can't I?' I asked Amelia.

'You've been ill,' said Amelia. 'You've got to be careful. Mother said that I had to make sure that you were careful.'

In Amelia's book, illness deserved punishment. My punishment was being careful.

Annie met us at Hayle station and kissed us both warmly.

'Caroline's been ill,' Amelia warned her. 'She needs to be careful.'

'She needs fresh sea air and good farm food,' Annie retorted gaily. 'Your mother wrote and told me all about it. Come on Caroline, take off that thick woolly coat now, it's much too warm inside there surely, and doesn't that collar tickle your neck?'

'She might be ill again,' Amelia said threateningly. 'Surely Mother told you that Caroline had to be careful.'

But Annie's only reply was a laugh, and with that laugh I could feel the hot burden of the city summer days puffing away from me like old dust, and I laughed too and even Amelia smiled.

It was a week blessed with sunshine and happiness. Johnny, the harelipped farm hand, taught Amelia and me how to ride on a fat-barrel pony with a whiskery nose called Nutmeg. Amelia rode well, with confidence and even with style, although Nutmeg was really too round and whiskery for elegance. Amelia and Johnny constructed small jumps out of planks and gorse bushes and Amelia and Nutmeg gambolled easily over them, while I stood beside Annie and Johnny and watched. Johnny and Annie clapped Amelia's performance, although it was Nutmeg who had done the jumping, and Annie said that Amelia looked like royalty. It was the sort of compliment that my sister revelled in, and she tossed her blonde plaits and flushed. Behind her spectacles her eyes shone with pride.

'I'll have a stable of thoroughbreds of my own when I'm a grown-up,' she declared, and, as though in preparation for this, she spent hours brushing Nutmeg's coat, plaiting his mane into ugly bobbles and oiling his saddle. But I could not share her enthusiasm.

Perhaps because of my recent illness I felt uneasy on Nutmeg's broad back, too high up from the ground and insecure as he trotted around the paddock on the end of a long rein held by Johnny.

'Rise in rhythm with his trotting, Caroline,' Amelia urged me from her perch on the paddock gate, but I clung all the tighter to the joggling saddle and tugged on the reins to make him stop so that I could climb down to the inferior safety of the ground. I preferred to feed Nutmeg carrots, feeling his lower lip rubbing against the palm of my hand, or, when Amelia was riding, I would stay with Annie in the kitchen garden watching the thrushes banging snails on the flagstones while I picked raspberries and ate them by the handful. Alternatively I would follow Diggory around the farm as he worked, keeping my distance from him to avoid getting in his way and being a nuisance, leaning lazily on farm gates, vaulting them as William had taught us the previous summer, and gazing absently at the velvet ears of cows twitching away the summer flies.

We went on our picnic too, Annie, Amelia and I, but that was less successful than usual for the tide was so high that almost all of the little cove was covered with water, and Annie had forgotten to pack the ginger beer. It seemed quiet without Mother or William there, and we returned early to the farm, hot and thirsty. I wished it had been the previous year again with my triumphant reading beneath the smiles and the proud eyes. Amelia was particularly quiet on the walk back to the farm, and she crept so close to the cliff edge at the place that they called Hell's Mouth that Annie called her away anxiously.

'You'll be throwing yourself right over the edge if you get any closer,' she chided.

'As long as you're careful,' Amelia said, 'you couldn't possibly go over. Except on purpose, of course.'

Back at the farm Amelia went quickly to nuzzle

Nutmeg, and I wondered if she might be missing William and their endless circular quarrelling. But, later that evening as we sat at the kitchen table with a plate of Annie's thick farm soup before us, and the comforting whistle of the kettle coming up to boil on the Rayburn, Amelia gave me her usual derisive sniff.

'Me? Miss William and his arguments?' she said, raising her eyebrows and grimacing. 'Of course I'd sooner talk to Nutmeg. Nutmeg understands me. And he doesn't answer back.'

Our time at the Pollards' farm slipped sweetly past, in that secretly paradoxical way which time alone has mastered. Lying on my back on the grass in the kitchen garden, watching the clouds floating past in the summer sky, minutes lasted hours and longer. But days flew past, rushing into minutes, gobbled into seconds, into brief blinks of time, until, suddenly, there we were in the farmyard with our bags packed, saying goodbye to Diggory and Johnny. Diggory kissed us each on the cheek, but Johnny, to my relief, didn't take such a liberty. He hurried away after Diggory to attend to his farming tasks, while Amelia called out goodbye to Nutmeg over and over again, although she she had already had a much more intimate session of farewell with him that morning.

And then we were at the station in Hayle, with Annie bundling us along amongst all the busy station bustle. The train, our train, at Platform Two was already eighteen minutes late, and the smell of the estuary mud, warm and dank, was all about us.

Annie held me out at arm's length and surveyed me proudly.

'Brown as a berry,' she said. 'And as strong and as plump as a young jack hare. There's nothing like fresh sea air and good farm food when you're feeling sickly.'

She kissed me roundly and then kissed Amelia too, 'the young horsewoman', as she liked to call her, to

Amelia's blushing pride. And Amelia, who never forgot, despite the flattery, said, 'Thank you for having us, Annie,' and I added, 'Mother said we could come in the spring next year, Annie. I can't wait to see you again in the spring.' Both Amelia and I hung out of the train window, waving at the diminishing figure of Annie until our arms ached and a curve in the track obliterated her from our view.

I had expected Mother to meet us at the station in Truro. I had imagined her there waiting, hugging and kissing us and saying how much she had missed us and how well we looked, especially me, while all the while Amelia chattered on and on about Nutmeg. But there was only William at the station. He was sitting on a bench sucking a humbug and reading a comic and looking cross.

'Your ma sent me to meet your train,' he explained. 'I've been waiting here hours and hours. It was late. Half an hour late at least.'

'Oh, I'm sure we're not that late,' Amelia interrupted defensively. 'Not as much as half an hour late, anyway. You must have got to the station early.'

'Twenty-eight minutes late, if you want to be precise,' said William, and I sighed softly to myself. Amelia and William were arguing again already, the urban air smelt of dust and drains, and from outside the station entrance I could see the cathedral, squatting broodingly over the huddle of the town as though threatening to gobble it all up.

We walked for a while in silence, three abreast along the pavement. I knew that Amelia was desperate to tell William about our visit to the Pollards' farm, in particular about her riding skills upon Nutmeg's trusty back. But, for the moment at least, she was maintaining a chilly silence. She would not speak unless asked. This silence weighed down heavily upon us, inescapable and cross, like a bad smell. It was broken only by the sound of the passing traffic and the beat of our feet on the paving stones. I tried to will Amelia to speak, but she refused. I turned my concentration on William, but he also remained quiet.

'How's your ma?' I asked at last. William snorted.

'She's had it,' he said.

'Had it?'

But Amelia was always faster than me and her brief quarrel with William and his refusal to ask us about our trip, thus depriving her of a chance to mention Nutmeg, was immediately forgotten.

'Oh William!' she exclaimed. 'Why didn't you say so at once? It was early, wasn't it? And is it a boy or a girl? And what's it called?'

'Yeah, it was early,' William said. 'Ma was shelling peas in the kitchen when . . .' he paused, but neither Amelia nor I were interested in pea-shelling. We were much too eager to hear what happened next. William sighed.

'I got your ma,' he said, 'when my ma asked me to. And she, your ma, sent me out to telephone for the midwife.' We walked in silence for a few paces, our feet slap-slapping timelessly on the pavement.

'And then?' asked Amelia, her voice breathy with excitement.

'And then? Oh then they sent me out into the back yard to play. Your ma told me to go outside and play quietly.' There was bitterness and resentment in William's voice, but Amelia and I were too interested to enquire whether this was due to the indignity of being sent out to play, or for some other reason.

'And then?' repeated Amelia.

'Then your ma called me in again and Mrs Gibson, that's the midwife, told me to go and telephone for that Dr Donnelly,' William continued. 'But he was out on a case, and it was born by the time he arrived. She was born, I mean. It's a girl. She's a girl. Ma's called her Phoebe. Don't ask me why. Phoebe Alexandra Louise McCullen. I think the Louise must be after your ma.'

'But what's it like?' asked Amelia. 'What's the baby like? Has she got dark hair like your mother? Or red hair? Or is she still completely bald? Is she sweet? Does she cry all the time? And has your mother gone all thin again now that the baby's been born?'

William stopped on the pavement and we stopped too. He stood in front of us and turned to glare at us with a mixture of anger and hate and puzzlement in his eyes.

The afternoon sun was still August hot, and I lowered the bag that I was carrying to the ground, leaning it carefully against my leg. I wiped the sweat from the palm of my hand on to my skirt.

'There's something wrong with her,' William said fiercely. 'There's something wrong with the baby.'

He paused and, in a nearby garden, a blackbird gave three falling, liquid notes.

'I think,' said William, his voice low and harsh, 'that Phoebe would be better off dead.'

Chapter Fourteen

Phoebe McCullen was pinched and tiny. She had a
wizened little face, more suited to an ancient crone
than a baby, and her eyes were small and blue and
empty. Her wrists reminded me of the necks of the
dead fledglings William had found in his back yard
and that I had buried, and her hands, at the end of
those wrists, flopped as limply as the heads of those
ugly nestlings had done.

I looked at her tiny fingers, the skin waxy, warm and
translucent, and I marvelled at the thought that before
we had left for the Pollards' farm these fingers had
been invisible, hidden inside Mrs McCullen's uncomfortable enormity. Now I could touch them. I
could feel their hard, minute joints. I could stroke the
pearly smoothness of their fingernails.

It seemed an amazing thing to me, quite miraculous.
It was nearly enough to make me convinced of the
existence of God; but it was still not quite sufficient.
Amelia's derision was one thing, but also, despite the
wonderfulness of the baby's appearance, I could
almost see what William meant. There was something
not quite right with little Phoebe McCullen. And yet, in
retrospect, I find it difficult, impossible even, to define
what it was that I thought was wrong with her.

She was particularly small of course, and her head,
especially, seemed to be not only undersized, but also
lopsided, and there was a tracery of pale blue veins
beating tremulously between her eyes and ears. But
her appearance was not the main thing: it was more
her dead-nestling limpness, her lack of enthusiasm for
existence. She lay heavily in my arms when I picked

her up ('Remember to support her head, Caroline,' Mother called anxiously across the room) and I thought I could feel, in her inert, drooping weight, her complete lack of interest in being alive.

Her pink pale-lashed eyelids closed as I gently stroked her scalp, still horribly naked and fragile-looking, and it seemed to me not that, as William said, she would be better off dead, but that it wouldn't really make much difference to her at all.

Mother and Mrs McCullen, however, were relentless. They drummed life into the baby's tiny body as though they could will her into animation by submission to routine. While Mrs McCullen rested, Mother would wash and change Phoebe, barking orders sharply at Amelia and me.

'Fetch this, Amelia. Hold that, Caroline. Hurry now, Amelia. Do stop dawdling, Caroline.'

William stayed downstairs in the sitting-room during these proceedings, gazing glumly out of the grubby windows into the empty street. Clearly both Mrs McCullen and Mother had decided that babies were strictly a female zone.

And then Amelia and I would be allowed to watch as Mrs McCullen fed Phoebe. She cradled the baby with enormous tenderness. No necessity for Mother to remind her to support the tiny head. Phoebe fed, not greedily or even hungrily, but obediently and lethargically; when she lost the nipple, which occurred frequently, she made no attempt to find it again, but lay there without movement until Mrs McCullen thrust it again between Phoebe's pale lips.

How those breasts both fascinated and revulsed me! I couldn't remember having ever seen the breasts of a grown woman before, and these enormous shaking mounds, pale lolling mountains swollen with milk, and with dark and livid areolae around huge and crinkled nipples, these were the stuff of nightmares. I stared at them with horror and amazement until Amelia nudged me. I blushed then, embarrassed at my

172

behaviour, but could not help shooting covert glances at Mother's chest. Was this what lay beneath that primly frilled and ironed blouse? Was this what Amelia and, worse, I myself, would one day develop? It seemed a horrific, fantastic idea to me, and, unable to keep my gaze averted for long, I stared again at those enormous breasts.

'Have you seen your ma's bosoms?' I asked William when we were alone together, blushing both at the impertinence of the question and at the awful word that I had to say out loud. I was fearful of what William might reply.

'No,' replied William. 'Of course not. At least, not since I was a baby, but I can't remember that.' And then it was his turn to question me. 'Did you see Phoebe?' he would ask. 'What do you think is the matter with her? Do you think she's getting worse? Do you think she'll end up like Mr Ambrose's sister?' But I was a hopeless provider of either information or opinion. I could only shrug helplessly and suggest that he ask Amelia or, better still, Mother.

After some persuasion from William, with a half-hearted murmur of support from me, Amelia agreed to ask Mother what it was that was wrong with little Phoebe.

It was one of those occasions when we had been bathing the baby, Mother directing operations as usual and herself undertaking the most skilful duties, while Amelia and I fetched and carried and held as instructed. All the while Mrs McCullen watched us from where she half lay, half sat, propped up on the pillows of her bed, the buttons of her broderie anglaise nightdress already undone and the pale mounds of her breasts peeking forth in preparation for the feed.

Back in our own home, Amelia broached the subject carefully. It was unusual for my bold sister to bother with caution.

'Mother,' she began, and then, a little more loudly, 'Mother?'

'Yes dear?'

'Was there a . . . a problem, when Phoebe was born?'

'What sort of problem, Amelia?' Mother was frowning a little now and her lips were pursed.

'Oh, I don't know,' Amelia replied, shrugging her shoulders as though she didn't care. 'A difficulty, I suppose.'

She looked away from Mother and twisted her fingers together in her lap. Mother stared hard at her averted face.

'What do you mean, Amelia?' Mother asked. 'And look at me while you are speaking to me.'

So Amelia looked towards her, tilting her chin towards the angle of defiance and determination that was usually reserved for her more ferocious arguments with William.

'Phoebe,' said Amelia, her voice quick and furtive, despite the tilted chin. 'What's wrong with her, Mother? She's not normal, is she? Even Caroline is able to see that. Did she get dropped or stuck or something? Is she going to end up like poor old Dotty Ambrose?'

Mother's face was an outraged mixture of incredulity and anger. These two emotions suffused her whole being, from the glare of her eyes and the set of her lips to the jut of her shoulders and the belligerent thrust of her neck. Those emotions, instead of her usual logic, were behind her reply.

'Amelia West,' she stormed, and her voice, although raised, was cold. 'I am surprised at you and I am ashamed of you. Dotty Ambrose, indeed! Phoebe dropped! Should you dare to even mention such a thought to me again, I promise you I'll give you such a hiding that you will never, ever forget it.'

She paused briefly. Then her look sharpened and her voice rose again. 'Have you mentioned this nonsense to Mrs McCullen?' she asked, and Amelia, subdued, perhaps even slighty scared, for Mother's rage was a fearful thing, shook her head. Her lower lip trembled although I could see her teeth biting hard on it, trying to control it.

'Well,' continued Mother. 'Don't you ever even dream about it, because if I find that you have been spreading your nasty, low-minded, cruel little thoughts about the McCullen household, then you will be sorrier than you can possibly imagine.' Mother's eyes glittered menacingly, and Amelia cowered back in her seat with tears welling up in her eyes behind her spectacles.

If I had been braver and cleverer, I might have spoken up then and told Mother that Amelia's nasty, low-minded, cruel little thoughts had actually originated with William, in the McCullen household. But I was much too afraid to speak out amidst such tides of fury. And then Mother rounded upon me.

'And don't you think that you're excluded from this either, Caroline West,' she snapped. Although her voice was quieter now, it seemed to have lost none of its original rage. 'If I find out that one tiny weeny peep of this nonsense has got back to Mrs McCullen, then both of you, yes, you, Caroline, as well as Amelia, are for the high jump.'

Tears sprang up in my eyes too, hot and insistent, for it was horrible, terrible to have Mother so angry with us.

'It must be bedtime now for the two of you,' Mother continued firmly, sounding calmer. 'Stop snivelling now, Amelia. You're old enough to know better. And Caroline, I don't want you to start boo-hooing either. I think it would be best if we all tried to forget this conversation ever happened. I'm sure that my girls are wise enough to agree with me.'

Although cups of tea and hot buttered teacakes had been planned for the evening, Amelia and I nodded mutely and, with our eyes still shining damp, went quietly upstairs to bed.

That evening was never again mentioned by any of us, not Mother, nor Amelia nor me. Similarly, the topic of Phoebe McCullen's mental and physical state was never again raised for discussion with Mother. But amongst the children, Amelia, William and me, Phoebe's health became an ever-present subject, like a constantly nagging worry, or an ominous threat which would not leave us alone. Mother's response to Amelia's questions had managed to augment our doubts rather than vanquish them.

The following day was a school day, for the autumn term had not long begun, and William was waiting for Amelia and me outside Worthingtons. He immediately demanded as to what verdict Mother had meted out for his baby sister. I waited for Amelia to describe Mother's tremendous fury. I wondered whether she would mention our own welling tears and the early bed without supper. But she said nothing of these things. Instead she looked very gravely at William, her bespectacled eyes assuming an owl-like seriousness. Her piping voice dropped to a low and rather rasping whisper.

'She didn't get dropped, anyway,' Amelia said. 'She must have got stuck.'

There was a pause. I felt that we must look like conspirators, huddled together outside the little news-agents, William and I craning forward to hear Amelia's throaty whisper.

'Don't mention it to anyone at all,' Amelia continued. 'Least of all Mother or your ma. You know what they're like.'

William nodded his head slowly, and took off his cap. He ruffled his fingers through his hair so that it assumed even more chaotic angles.

'Stuck!' he repeated in a low, slightly awed voice. 'That's just exactly what I thought must have happened. Yes, you're right Amelia, we mustn't tell anyone at all.'

William made us take a vow of silence on Phoebe's diagnosed 'stuckness', and, although I didn't understand, I vowed anyway. I didn't want to have to ask them to explain. Stuck! Stuck? In my mind's eye I saw Phoebe's tiny hands clawing feebly, and yet with a desperate wildness, at the entrance to a tunnel, dark and deep and forbidding. I heard her voice too, high, fluting, an imaginary voice, calling out for assistance. 'Help me! Help me!' she cried. 'I'm stuck! I'm stuck!'

Stuck? What did it mean? I remembered that Amelia had asked Mother if Phoebe had got stuck. And what had she replied? She had not admitted to this stuckness, but she had not denied it either. Instead her fury had broken about us like a storm. Surely Mother would have told Amelia, in her characteristically clear and certain terms, if Amelia's theory had been wrong; besides, everybody knew that Amelia and William were cleverer by far than me. Although I didn't understand, and I could not comprehend Mother's rage, it did seem to be the only explanation. Phoebe had got stuck.

Phoebe McCullen, tiny, fragile mixture of pale skin and delicate bones, seemed to dominate our lives that winter. It was her, not school, around which everything revolved, and while I was content for this to be so, Amelia and William were not. They acted increasingly as though they resented Phoebe's small but powerful intrusion into our lives. While I still assisted Mrs McCullen and, less often now, Mother – for she had marking and lesson preparation to fill her evenings – with the repetitive and never-ending tasks that Phoebe's inactive existence generated, Amelia participated less and less frequently. When she could be persuaded to help, she did so with an obvious lack of enthusiasm. She became surly and unco-operative around Phoebe's crib and she scowled down at the baby's pinched and waxy face as though she were somehow culpable of a lowly and despicable crime. Guilty, perhaps, of being stuck?

Rather than fetch and hold and carry, Amelia would remain downstairs in the McCullens' sitting-room with William. They stared out of the windows together, glowering at the reliable presence of our own home across the street. They spoke to each other in guarded whispers, as though harbouring their voices, grudging their use for unimportant purposes. Or they would cross Tredannick Close and go into our house, where they would sit on the rug in front of the living-room fire, a mean wisp of a fire often, for coal was dear and the weather not unduly cold. Amelia would sprawl on the rug, her gawky limbs spread here and there, but William would scrunch himself up into an angular ball, and here they would do their schoolwork. Claudia, who felt that the living-room was her own particular territory and did not wish to relinquish her post at the fireside, disliked this change in her routine.

During this time, I noticed that Amelia started gnawing on her fingertips. She didn't chew her nails, but instead worried at the little flags of skin that surrounded them, biting at them until they were red and raw and sometimes tiny bobbles of blood appeared, as though from pinpricks.

If I thought that I was alone in noticing these changes in Amelia's behaviour, previously so vivacious and optimistic, I was wrong. Once Mother and I met Mr Quigley, the optician, in the street and when he asked after Amelia, Mother gave a rueful smile.

'Amelia?' she said, and she touched Mr Quigley's arm confidingly. 'I'm afraid that she's reached that bolshie age, Geoffrey.'

On another occasion I overheard Mother talking to Mrs McCullen. I had with time and experience gradually been entrusted with ever more important, although simple, tasks for Phoebe. I was sprinkling talcum powder from the big purple tin over her wrinkled bottom and paunchy stomach, patting it into the folds and creases of her pale skin as Mother had shown me. Mother had become more stoical since our chance encounter with Geoffrey Quigley, although her reasoning had not changed.

'It's her age,' I heard Mother saying. 'You know what

it's like. And she's never been the easiest of children, not like Caroline.'

I analysed that last remark carefully and slowly. I looked into Phoebe's blank blue gaze as I considered Mother's words and tried, unsuccessfully, to make Phoebe smile. To my surprise I found that, perhaps for the first time ever, certainly the first time within my hearing, I was being compared favourably to Amelia.

Perhaps it was that comparison, which flattered me beyond expectation, that prevented me from bursting out to Mother with what I considered had caused the change in Amelia's behaviour.

'It's not her age,' I would have explained. 'It's little Phoebe. It's all because she got stuck. They think that she would be better off dead.'

If Amelia had not been an easy child, Phoebe was not an easy baby. Sometimes I felt bound to agree with the thoughts of William and Amelia, and surely, on rare occasions at least, Mother must have done so too.

Phoebe was, without doubt, a sickly baby. In the McCullens' home, always slightly damp and chilly and with a creeping tide of green-black mould on the bathroom walls, she seemed to be susceptible to every possible infection, despite all the trouble we took to guard her against them. She even managed to acquire a few infections exclusive to herself, for nobody else had them, and we wondered how the germs had managed to seek her out and creep into her frail and vulnerable body.

When she was ill, which was frequently, she would lose her silent passivity and become fretful. With fretfulness her face would become even more pinched and ugly than before. Her cries were thin and piteous wails of discontent, and, although they were not particularly loud, they were grating and insistent and quite impossible to ignore. Her little hands would bunch themselves into querulous fists which, when unfurled, would be found to have palms beaded with sweat. A huge globule of frothy spittle would drool from the corner of her mouth, leaving damp patches on her clothes and bedding, and her chin and neck would develop patches of rough red skin if the dribble was not mopped up sufficiently quickly.

In early November there was a virus rife in Truro that the adults called Mongolian flu, although I thought it a little unfair to blame it on Mongolia which was hundreds of miles away; even further away than Stonehaven. Everybody seemed to come down with it, all the teachers at my school including Miss Cutting, and even Amelia managed to catch it and had to take a day off school. She was annoyed by this, for it broke a lifetime habit of sneering at other people who missed school due to illness, and she lay in bed shivering and sneezing and unbearably irritable, despite the marvellous concoction of honey and lemon juice and brandy that Mother brewed up for her. William's nose became red and raw from almost constant use of his handkerchief, and Mother lost her voice for a full two days, and for the subsequent two days could only manage to speak in a hoarse and breathy whisper that seemed to come rasping up from the very bottom of her lungs.

But when Phoebe caught the Mongolian flu, life became grim and urgent. The world was a place of anxious adult whispers and long unsmiling adult faces; there were the quick and troubled footsteps of adult alarm. Dr Donnelly came twice to the McCullens' house with his black bag of medical magic. His arrival was heralded by ever more anxious whispers and serious faces.

He was, however, a comforting and sensible doctor. He had a brisk but steady tread and when he saw me, either swinging on the McCullens' gate or perching on our garden wall, he would nod and give me a cheery wave.

'Well, you're looking the bee's knees, anyway,' he would say. 'Did you enjoy your visit to the farm in the summer?' He would give me a lop-sided wink then, and he wouldn't wait to hear my answer.

During Phoebe's illness Amelia and William became, not exactly cheerful, but they expressed a lively interest that had been hidden beneath their dour expressions for months. They followed Dr Donnelly's entry, and subsequent retreat, into the McCullens' house with eager eyes from behind the straggle of spider plants in our living-room window. Later they would quiz me with an animated energy.

'Is she going to get better?' Amelia and William would ask simultaneously, but I had always been a useless informant. I could only shrug my shoulders in helpless ignorance.

After Dr Donnelly had paid his visit, I would be requisitioned by Mother to return to Phoebe's realm of dominance and assist with ministrating to her needs. Dr Donnelly was always at pains to point out that Mrs McCullen was being unduly wearied by her daughter and that she should accept whatever help was available. When I saw her after these visits by the doctor, I could understand his concern, for her face would be deeply etched with worry and the exhaustion of sleepless nights, her eyes lost again in cavernous sockets, so deep that they threw their own dark shadows.

Often Mrs McCullen's anxiety and tiredness would precipitate a migraine, and she would be obliged to lie by herself in a shaded room with a glass of cool water by her side and a damp cloth draped across her forehead. On these occasions, William, tiptoeing and gentle, would come to help. He would creep silently into his mother's room, his shoes left in an untidy heap outside her door, and, holding one of her thin fingers between his clumsy schoolboy hands, with their blotches of ink and broken, grime-encrusted nails, he would sing soft lullabies to her.

William displayed a remarkable maturity, that adults remarked upon with awe, when his mother succumbed to her weariness. He could be as gentle as a parent, as affectionate as a husband or a lover. He seemed, however, unable to overcome the disdain with which he regarded his pitiful sister. He ignored little Phoebe almost entirely, abandoning her to the ministrations of Mother and myself. When Mrs McCullen asked after the baby, the delight of her shrivelled life for whom she longed and fretted, he would hunch his shoulders and look away and refuse to speak.

Gradually, as a lizard in the sun discards its dulled skin, Phoebe shook off the Mongolian flu. But, when Dr Donnelly had pronounced her quite cured, she was not, as I had hoped, sparkling and new and vibrant. She remained a small and wretched infant with an inclination towards lethargy and whimpering, the latter seeming to be entirely without purpose or reason. Despite defeating the flu which, so Dr Donnelly told us, had claimed the lives of four babies and two elderly gentlemen in the city hospital alone, Phoebe was still a sickly baby and throughout the winter months her chest continued to heave and rattle with harsh, phlegmy coughs.

Mrs McCullen and Mother were, of course, over-joyed at Phoebe's recovery and if Amelia and William were disappointed that she had not succumbed, then they were neither foolish nor cruel enough to express their thoughts aloud. Instead they maintained a lofty and distant silence and rarely spoke of her at all.

And I? I felt torn between my loyalty, albeit from habit, to Amelia and William, and my loyalty to life itself. I could accept that what they had said to me must surely be right: that Phoebe McCullen had got stuck; that perhaps it would have been better if she had never been born at all. But here she was. I marvelled at the minute fragility of her fingers and toes. I was fascinated by the ugliness of her pinched and ancient face and the emptiness of the stare from her small blue eyes. These features of her became both familiar and dear to me and I could not wish them away. Her round belly was warm and white as I washed it tenderly and gently rubbed in the talcum powder, and her flailing limbs were helpless and innocent. I felt a warmth towards this useless creature that I was quite unable to express.

And all the while that little Phoebe, so novel and exciting in August like a new toy or game, was growing and ailing, ailing more and yet still growing despite this, gaining ounces, the bald dome of her head becoming slowly covered with a thin sheen of silvery hair, time went racing past.

I was still in Mrs Bolivar's class at school and as well as reading, more fluently now, grasping ever more complex words, I could also, after a fashion, write. With slow, painfully formed letters I could scribe out whole sentences of prose, copying carefully from the cards that Mrs Bolivar provided, and despairing of ever managing to compose lines of writing of my very own.

Amelia and William had both progressed forward a year at their respective schools, and they sneered now at the timid newcomers as though they themselves had never been in such a lowly position.

If my aspiration was to write from my own imagination a whole phrase of words, my letters looping together in an elegant copperplate rather than stumbling crookedly across the page, then the plans of Amelia and William blazed far beyond mine. Their schemes disappeared over the horizon into the frightening enormity of the future which I could barely imagine.

Amelia had mapped out a wild and hectic life for herself. She was to be a doctor, preferably a surgeon performing operations of tremendous skill. She was to be an archaeologist, working by choice among the Pyramids under a blazing Egyptian sun. She was to be a jockey with her own stables, champing with sleek and prancing thoroughbreds of proud Arabic stock; she would race at Taunton and at Cheltenham and she would win the Grand National at least once. Her final employment, having wearied of the others, would be as prime minister, but with which political party she was loth to disclose.

William said that he wanted to go into the Church, but I believe that was only to provoke Amelia.

'What! Like the Reverend Peploe?' she had scoffed in response. 'Yuk! He stinks of wet dogs. He can't even talk to Caroline without stuttering.'

'Well, at least I've already got a deranged sister like Penelope Peploe,' William replied bitterly, making a wry shape with his mouth.

This autumn term was different in other ways too. There were no bullies waiting for me outside Worthingtons, nor was there to be any participation by any of us in the Christmas Nativity plays; Mr McCullen's surprise appearance the previous year had made the very idea of them seem sour. Mrs Bolivar tried her best to persuade me, even offering me the chance of improving my role to that of the angel Gabriel. I would have wings then and words to say on stage, but, although I was tempted, I shook my head regretfully and looked down at the floor. Mr McCullen had spoiled the chance of any repeat performance for all of us. It would surely be a betrayal of William, of Mrs McCullen, even of little Phoebe, to accept the offer, and I had strong feelings of loyalty.

'But Caroline, you seemed so keen and enthusiastic last year,' said Mrs Bolivar with bewilderment, the cuffs of her mud-coloured cardigan waggling protestingly, and I could think of no adequate explanation or reply. Last year was centuries ago now. Last year a million things had not happened, Mr McCullen, Dorothea Ambrose, Phoebe McCullen. Last year these things, important as they were, had never even been thought of nor imagined. Everything was different this year.

So there were to be no more Nativity plays for me. Years and years later, I went to watch my own son, Billy, just six years old and shy and blonde, in his first

Nativity play, an insignificant angel like his mother and father before him. All through that performance I could feel the apprehension of looming fate, and I was haunted by the darkness of betrayal's guilt.

Christmas crept inexorably closer, and a heavy fog draped itself across Truro. No wind rustled the bare branches of the trees and all the birds were somnolent and muted. It was a lethargic sort of weather, uncaring and laden with doom; it felt like the false quiet before the storm. Everyone, especially Claudia the cat, appeared to be on edge and nervous. Claudia sharpened her claws on the base of Mother's sewing machine and bounded around the living-room on well-sprung paws, flicking her tail from side to side. All the world seemed ready and waiting for something, some huge calamity, to happen. But nothing was about to happen. Nothing at all, apart from Christmas of course.

On Christmas Day the fog had lifted and the sky was high and huge and blue, almost as though spring had crept up upon us early. Phoebe was left in the care of Mother, while William and Mrs McCullen went to the morning service. As the bells of all the churches and, of course, the cathedral, rang out across Truro, Mother and Amelia and I prepared the lunch. When our duties were done, we sat in the living-room beneath the carousel of streamers.

'This is what it should have been like last year as well,' I whispered to Amelia. But Amelia arched her eyebrows at me and looked pointedly across the room to where Mother clucked and cooed over Phoebe's crib.

'Really, Caroline?' she said in a voice of ice. 'I can't say that I agree with you.'

During Christmas lunch, Phoebe started to cry. Mrs McCullen, leaving her food cooling on her plate, reported from the crib-side that Phoebe had been sick.

There was a trail of vomit on Phoebe's clothes and bedding, and some of it clung like gruel to Mrs

McCullen's shoulder when she lifted the baby up to her.

'Poor little poppet,' Mother exclaimed and rushed over to help, while we three children sat uncomfortably at the table and watched the gravy slowly congealing on our mothers' plates.

After lunch was over and Amelia and I had cleared the plates from the table, Mother said that she was going to stay at home with Mrs McCullen and Phoebe rather than walk up the hill and down to the valley to visit Father's grave. I felt buffeted by disappointment then; Mother was abandoning the traditions and the rituals of our Christmas Day, betraying not only us, but our father, her husband, also. And all for the sake of an ugly and querulous baby. That surely could not be right.

Mother must have noticed my stricken face, for she smiled and kissed me tenderly at the front door.

'Life goes on, Caroline my love,' she said.

Mother gave Amelia the usual box of fairings as a gift for us to deliver to Mr Ambrose.

'We don't have to go and see him, do we?' Amelia asked petulantly, but she took the box anyway. I was frightened that another ritual was about to be brutally and heartlessly axed, another man betrayed. I spoke up quickly, anxiety ringing through my voice as clearly as the church bells had rung through the Christmas morning.

'Of course we've got to see Mr Ambrose,' I said. 'He'll be expecting us today.'

'Mother's not been to see Mr Ambrose since Dotty's funeral, have you Mother?' continued Amelia in her hardest voice and without acknowledging my words. 'Even though she promised to.'

'That's quite enough, Amelia,' Mother replied, her voice level but angry. 'It is still quite possible for me to send you to bed early without any supper even though it is Christmas.' She paused. 'I have been much too busy for visiting, as well you know. However, I will be going up to Alfred Ambrose's home before the New Year. You may criticize me then, Amelia, if I fail to keep my word.' And although she did fail to keep her word, none of us, not even Amelia, criticized her for doing so.

The narrow road down towards the valley was straight in some parts and in other parts winding and convoluted as a snake should be.

In the straight sections the hedges on either side of the road were low and brambly, and the grass verges were wide enough for a pedestrian to walk along easily without worrying that he or she might slip into the scummy darkness of the ditch. Over the hedges ploughed fields could be seen, bare and brown, or fields of silvered grass with cows whose snorting, stamping breaths created clouds of vapour.

At the bends in the road – there were two sharp ones and several softer, gentler curves – the verges narrowed, becoming no more than an inch or so wide at the sharper bends, and there were copses of tall straight beech trees whose branches splayed across the breadth of the road. In the summer these bends became green and shady tunnels, but in the winter they were cold and frosty and the bare limbs of the trees against the sky were like arms stretched out in supplication.

It was at the first sharp bend that we met three men in long dark coats and suede gloves. This was surprising: the road was usually empty, and besides it was Christmas Day.

'Happy Christmas,' Amelia piped up, her good humour happily restored by the bright sky. Her cheeks were flushed from the walk and she smiled her sunniest smile. But the three men regarded us gravely, even rather severely; it was obvious that they were waiting for something or someone, and in the straightness of their backs and the steadiness of their eyes was the look of officialdom. One of the men asked us, addressing his question to William rather than Amelia or me, where we were going. But it was Amelia who answered, explaining about our traditional walk to Father's grave on Christmas Day.

'And Mr Ambrose,' I chimed in, still worrying that he might be forgotten or neglected. 'Mother gave Amelia a box of fairings to give him,' I continued. 'Didn't she, Amelia?'

But at the mention of Mr Ambrose's name the faces of the three men became graver. They glanced quickly at one another, rapid, covert glances, that seemed to be both asking and answering unknown questions.

They were policemen; the car came to pick them up as we stood there talking. The driver looked as sombre as the three men who spoke to us. Behind the police car came a van containing the remains of Mr Ambrose's motorbike, and following the van was an ambulance carrying the remains of Alfred himself.

'He must have been going at some speed,' one of the policemen said. 'And with a drink or two inside him as well.' Alfred must have skidded, rolled, and the bike had exploded. Both bike and driver had been ignominiously and smokily scattered about the narrow lane.

'Was he doing a ton, sir?' William asked politely, shyly. The policeman who had been speaking blinked heavy eyelids over his steady grey policeman's eyes.

'I beg your pardon, young man?'

'I said,' repeated William, his voice a little louder and firmer, 'was he doing a ton? Sir?'

The man grinned briefly, but his eyes did not lose their gravity.

'On that old thing? He was going fast, no doubt about that, but you can't reach a ton on a machine of that age. Just not possible, son.'

The three policemen climbed into the car, tipped us slow smiles, and drove away. All three vehicles, the car first, then the van and finally the ambulance, moved rapidly down the lane away from us and towards Truro. I thought that their pace was too fast; it did not seem to me respectful to race along like that. It was as though they were in a hurry. But they probably *were* in a hurry; they would have had to forgo their Christmas lunches because of Alfred Ambrose.

We continued as far as Father's grave anyway; it seemed rather small and silent beneath the blue immensity of the sky. Then we turned and went back along the road to Truro, nibbling on the fairings, the box of which Amelia had, perhaps a little disrespect-fully, opened already. After all, Alfred wouldn't be wanting them now.

We were quiet as we walked, subdued by the grim-ness of the news that we had for Mother, and all of us, I suppose, thinking about Alfred. Perhaps Amelia was thinking of her earlier scorn of the man, her unwilling-ness to visit him. Perhaps she regretted her unkind words now. Perhaps William was thinking of the afternoons that he and Mr Ambrose had spent together discussing the beauty of his fatal machine. I was thinking of the mugs of milk and the slices, thick and generous, of bread and honey. I was thinking of his cheery greeting, 'Look who it isn't'. I was thinking of the feel of his lap beneath my bottom, the hard knobbliness of his knees. I was wondering who would dig the graves in the graveyard now. Who would dig the grave for Alfred Ambrose?

The site of the accident was obvious. We had seen it as we walked towards the graveyard after the police-men had left us. It was just before the second corner, at the end of a longish straight section of road. Some of the bushes on the hedgerow had been scorched and blackened. Amelia had sighed and William had stooped and touched the edge of a long black skid mark. His fingers had rubbed gently at the edge of one of the angry gouges in the road surface. None of us had spoken.

On the way back we paused again. The radiant sky above our heads seemed mocking and cruel. There was a light freshness in the air and a crispness in the

189

breeze; this was a day for being alive and rejoicing. This was not a day for dying.

'The motorbike will be completely smashed up.' William's voice interrupted my thoughts about the injustice of dying when the world was fresh and new and beautiful.

'So will Alfred Ambrose,' said Amelia, taking another fairing from the box and biting into it delicately. 'Do you think that he did it on purpose? It's exactly a year since Dotty's death.'

William didn't answer. He had seen something on the opposite verge, and he crossed the road quickly and picked it up. It was a piece of metal, perhaps a little under a foot in length, black in colour and slightly curved. William rubbed at it with his handkerchief. He spat on his handkerchief and rubbed again. The handkerchief went black and the piece of metal glittered chrome. It was scratched and slightly twisted and still black at the edges from the smoke, but both Amelia and I recognized it when William held it up to us. It was the chrome badge, torn from the tank of the motorbike. 'Triumph' it proclaimed in gothic lettering.

'Poor Triumph Tiger,' murmured William, and I was not really sure if he meant the motorbike or Alfred Ambrose.

190

Chapter Fifteen

In the days following Christmas and Alfred's untimely death, my sleep became repeatedly perturbed by uncomfortable visions and images, too hazy and indeterminate to be called nightmares, too bleak and troubling to be called dreams. These images came lunging and wallowing up from the twilight edges of my sleep and mocked my efforts to escape them. Huge turkey-like birds appeared in these visions, with ugly wobbling wattles, scaly, scrabbling toes and shrill demanding voices. Perhaps these creatures were my subconscious portrayal of the townsfolk of Truro, for they, with their gobble-gobble chatter and beady, questing eyes, distressed me even more than the death of Alfred.

It was not so much the things that they said about the Ambroses which upset me, for I had already heard, many years previously, the rumours of how Alfred had himself murdered his sister's child, stifling its laboured breaths with his own hands. It was the way that they spoke which upset me so, their voices and faces eager, curious and quite maliciously gleeful.

I walked into town with Mother to do the shopping, and people, respectable middle-aged ladies with over-powdered faces and cameo brooches pinned on the lapels of their heavy winter coats and wealthy-looking gentlemen with double chins and over-hearty laughs, stopped Mother on the pavement to speak with her. They asked her what she knew of Alfred's death and they put forward their own unkind theories about how Dorothea and Alfred had lived their now completed lives.

'They say that he not only killed that innocent baby, but Dotty as well,' these people declared. 'They say that he's done away with his own self now; he couldn't bear to live with himself after he killed poor Dotty and he turned to drink.' And the faces of the speakers would be grinning with the self-satisfaction of their own hideous beliefs.

'They say that the father of Dotty's baby was Alfred Ambrose himself,' the townsfolk reported to Mother. 'Her own brother! Can you believe it? It shouldn't be allowed.'

The latter, in particular, became a favourite cry which accosted us about the city's cobbled streets, and I was proud that Mother did not join in with her friends and acquaintances, but instead pursed her lips quite crossly.

'There's really no evidence for any of these silly tales,' she would respond to the smug faces, and their eyes, shining with greed for agreement, verification, provision of evidence and further unkind stories, would dim with disappointment. 'And besides, I would rather that these matters were not discussed in front of my daughter.'

The respectable ladies and gentlemen of Truro would appear surprised then, even mortified, and they would take a couple of steps backwards, apologizing profusely. At this point the men would laugh their too-hearty laughs and the ladies would adjust their brooches and cluck and coo and say how much I'd grown, then they would consult their watches and scurry away, their heads bowed with the weight of transient shame. Despite their averted faces, their eyes would dart hither and thither, searching for some other acquaintance, without accompanying daughter, to accost: someone to reinforce their beliefs in their own smug superiority and the dilapidated evil of the Ambroses' pitiful lives, and, most probably, to comment upon the foolishness of those atheist Wests.

And yet the embarrassment of these townsfolk when

Mother mentioned my presence seemed real enough: mouths dropped open, hands flew up to stifle gasps, and pinkness flushed across cheeks and necks. But surely they must have seen me standing there, waiting patiently beside Mother in my bright red winter coat. Perhaps they thought that I was too stupid to understand. I was clumsy and slow after all, almost simple, rather like poor Dorothea had been.

It seemed to me that the death of Alfred marked the end of an era. Amelia, however, would argue that the era that I spoke of had ended already. It ended with the death of Dorothea and it was precisely that, the ending of an era, which had resulted in Alfred's own death. Maybe Amelia was, as usual, correct, but either way a visit to Father's grave would never ever be the same again.

No more calling at the Ambroses' cottage; no more 'look who it isn't' served up with bread and honey. Amelia seemed philosophical, even blasé, about this change, but I hated it. I hated the way that time moved on so heartlessly, mowing down the people and things that I loved. I wanted my life to stay the same for ever and I cast my eye protectively and anxiously about me.

'Don't change,' I pleaded silently to Mother, Amelia, William, Mrs McCullen, Phoebe, Mrs Bolivar, even Miss Cutting. 'Don't die, don't grow up, don't change. Why don't we stay this way for ever?'

A stone had not yet been erected over Dorothea Ambrose's grave. The rose bush, Pink Cloud I remembered it was called, that Alfred had planted was carefully uprooted, Alfred's remains, rather charred I imagined, were interred beside those of his sister, and the bush replanted above them. Two, or maybe three, years later, Mother organized a collection to pay for a stone to be inscribed for them. Strangely it was the smug and gleeful gossips, perhaps because they could see their own destinies creeping inexorably towards them, who were the most generous. The inscription read:

'Alfred and Dorothea Ambrose: a devoted brother and sister'.

The little cottage did not stand empty for long. By March a new sexton had been installed and, as a matter of course, he took over the Ambroses' old home. His name was Robert Giles, and he could not have been more than thirty-five. He was tall and thin and awkward and he wore his hair, bouncing chestnut curls, rather long.

Robert Giles was engaged to one of the local farmer's daughters, Maggie Pentecost, pretty despite her fat ankles. They were, by all accounts, a kind and charming couple and Robert worked hard in the graveyard, maintaining it to Alfred's standard. He was particularly conscientious about keeping Dorothea and Alfred's joint grave well tended, the rose pruned neatly and the weeds evicted. Maggie Pentecost, whom Amelia unkindly accused of being soppy and senti-mental, often brought a posy of flowers for the grave of Dorothea's unnamed baby. But despite all this, I resented seeing Robert and Maggie there. I resented seeing Robert's tired and ancient springer spaniel flopped in a heap of brown and white fur on the front step of the Ambroses' cottage. It would always be the Ambroses' cottage to me. Any attempt at replacement seemed a heartless and disrespectful act.

At the end of March when the gusty grey clouds which, since Christmas, had flung drizzle at Truro with an almost vindictive malice were beginning to disperse, the weather softening into the gentle green gauze of spring, I began to think of the Pollards' farm.

'I wonder if there'll be any changes in Diggory or Annie or the Pollards' farm when we go there in the spring,' I mused after supper one evening.

'Are we going to the Pollards' farm in the spring?' interrupted Amelia. 'Oh goody! I didn't know that. Does William know?'

But Mother's voice was clear and resolute.

'Of course we're not going to the Pollards' farm in

the spring, children. Annie and Diggory are much too busy then to be tripping over us. We'll be going in the summer, just as we always do.'

I looked across the table at her in horrified amazement and then, after a pause which could only have lasted seconds although, in the urgency of the moment it seemed like centuries, I said, 'But you promised!'

I knew, of course, that adults do frequently tend to forget those things which are of little importance or value to themselves, but never before had Mother forgotten a promise.

'Did I really?' she asked, her voice vague. 'Well, that must have been because I thought that your trip there in the summer would be cancelled last year, but it wasn't, in the end. I especially arranged for you and Amelia to go there by yourselves. There's no necessity now for an earlier trip than usual.'

Such an explanation, rational though it seemed, had little effect on me.

'You promised,' I repeated. 'You *promised*.' I could feel my lips trembling and the insistent prickling of disappointed tears. 'I told Annie that we were going to go back in the spring and I've been so looking forward to it,' I said, my voice wavering uncertainly. 'I've been so looking forward to seeing all those baby animals that you promised.'

I burst into tears after that, crying with such abandon that my voice was choked and my shoulders shook convulsively, almost as though I was fevered. Perhaps this reminded Mother of what had happened the last time my anticipated trip to the farm had been all but denied me, for she sighed.

'Really, Caroline,' she murmured, 'surely you understand that as you and Amelia went to the Pollards' farm in the summer . . .' Her voice trailed off into silence. Possibly she recognized that these fast-flowing tears of mine were not just born of childish disappointment, but also of the other mixed emotions which had been bottled away inside me, and had taken this opportunity of the cork being slackened to bubble forth.

'It's been a difficult winter for all of us,' Mother said softly, apparently speaking more to herself than to either Amelia or me. 'Perhaps I could write to Annie and Diggory and see if it might just be possible . . .'

We travelled down to Hayle on the train. Just as on our last visit to the Pollards' farm with the McCullens, William and Mrs McCullen were attired in their Sunday best and their luggage was squeezed into the two Gladstone bags, more dilapidated and elderly than ever. But there was a major difference in this trip. This time Phoebe McCullen was with us too.

Little Phoebe appeared not to enjoy the train journey and she contrived to spoil it for the rest of us by maintaining a near-constant wail. No other travellers were either brave or foolish or deaf enough to come and share our compartment.

Mother and Mrs McCullen fussed and fretted over the crying infant as though their lives depended upon it. Mrs McCullen fed her, Mother checked that her nappy was clean and dry, both of them burped her over their shoulders and joggled her up and down on their knees. They lay her down, they sat her up, they scolded her and they sang to her. But nothing would silence that wail.

'She's teething,' Mrs McCullen explained more than once.

'That's terribly painful,' Mother confirmed. 'When Amelia was teething I couldn't get her to sleep for nights on end.'

But knowing the reason for this persistent nagging, grizzling noise emanating without let-up from Phoebe's little body did not make it any less un-pleasant or any more bearable. William and Amelia looked at each other, private exchanges of both query and reply, reminding me of the glances that the three policemen who had told us of Alfred Ambrose's death had given each other. It was an uncomfortable reminder and I shuddered and looked away.

Annie, meeting us off the train in the salt, sweet air of Hayle, was immediately, and to the minds of Amelia, William and me, amazingly, entranced by the sight of little Phoebe.

'What an angel! What a little love!' she cooed, and, almost snatching the child from her mother's protective arms, she went dancing up the station platform with her while we, standing foolishly amidst our luggage, stared after her. She showed off Phoebe to strangers waiting to board the train from Penzance and she accosted the station officials as well, who seemed only too pleased to pause in their various duties and smile down at the baby's wan and tear-stained face. And Phoebe, perhaps as amazed as us at this exuberant welcome, or perhaps merely exhausted by her endless tears, ceased her crying, blinked her red-rimmed eyes and fell asleep.

The Pollards' farm in spring seemed to be wonderfully and delightfully alive to me. The promised baby animals really existed and I felt that I could watch them for hours. The knock-kneed clumsiness of the calves, their ears flapping like slackened sails and their eyes big, brown, mournful pools fringed with luxuriantly curling lashes. The lambs, their tails spinning wildly as they fed, bounded with such a zest for life that it was almost contagious, and I could feel my face smiling as I watched them. One of the farm dogs had had puppies, and these fat, glossy creatures with eyes of startling blue were so plaintively charming that even Diggory admitted he was loth to get rid of them. Of all the young animals that I had seen, human babies were, without doubt, the least appealing. But perhaps it was just that Phoebe was a poor example.

The first day at the farm was grey and rather cold, with a salt-laden wind blowing in from the sea, but we didn't care. Amelia, William and I spent the day about the farmyard, hanging over the wooden palings in the barns, watching the animals and breathing in the warm dusty richness of straw and cows.

'Calves are so much cuter than babies,' Amelia sighed softly, voicing my own thoughts. I would never have dared to say such a thing, however, even though Mrs McCullen and Mother and Annie were well out of earshot, fussing over Phoebe in the farmhouse kitchen. Amelia's words seemed unkind and although in my heart I agreed with them, I wanted to disagree and defend little Phoebe from Amelia's heartless honesty. But of course I was too much of a coward to contradict her. I remained silent and later, so very soon afterwards, I bitterly regretted my reticence, apportioning to myself some of the blame for what happened next.

The following day was one of those true, blue days of a Cornish spring. The wind had dropped to the faintest murmur during the night and the sky we awoke to was cloudless and enormous. It was suffused with purity and lightness, and the sun beat down with warmth and strength. Everything was beautiful, wonderful and alive. We had not had such sparkling weather since Christmas Day. Now, everyone seemed to respond to the day as though it had been ordained for them alone. Everyone, that is, apart from Phoebe McCullen.

She had been fractious and complaining all night; presumably her teeth were still bothering her. Even in the bedroom that Amelia and I shared, up under the eaves of the farmhouse, Phoebe's cries had drifted up intermittently throughout the night. We could still hear a thin, exhausting cry as Amelia, for once eager to be up, the sky and the sunshine beckoning to her enticingly, climbed out of bed.

'Stupid, ugly, howling, idiot baby,' Amelia grunted, but she said it cheerfully enough. It was the sort of weather when it seemed impossible to be anything other than cheerful.

We had Annie's homemade pasties for lunch that day; how well I remember enjoying them. It is as though every succulent mouthful has been printed indelibly upon my memory. We sat out in the kitchen garden to eat, for Annie said that it was a crying shame to be inside in such glorious weather.

Perhaps that lunch is scorched all the more into my memory by a memento, for Annie persuaded Johnny the farm hand to take a photograph of us with a camera that her father had given her and Diggory for Christmas.

I have a copy of that photograph that Annie gave me years later, and I carry it almost everywhere with me in a pocketbook in my handbag. It reminds me of so many good things; it reminds me of so many terrible possibilities. It is a photograph of Eden before the snake, but of course we know that the snake was there in the Garden of Eden long before he spoke to Eve. I know that Annie gave Amelia a copy of that photograph too, but I have never seen it in her possession; not in her smart flat in Highgate, nor in her intimidating office off St James's Square, nor in her house on the Isle of Wight, her retreat from London and work. Perhaps she carries it in her handbag too; I have never dared to look.

It is a black and white photograph, slightly blurred, and there, in the top right-hand corner, is a smudge which must be Johnny's finger, so he also contrived, albeit unintentionally, to feature in it. I examine the photograph so frequently that its edges have become quite dog-eared, and there is a crease down the centre of it for which my son Billy is responsible. But the faces of everybody at that spring sun lunch of pasties are still clear and easily discernible; not quite everybody, of course. The face of little Phoebe McCullen cannot be seen at all.

In the foreground of the picture sit Amelia, William and I on a wooden bench. William sits between us and he is scowling somewhat at the camera. His left leg is a complete blur, so I imagine that he must have been swinging it. Indeed, I can almost hear the regular creaking of the bench as he does so. He is in his shorts and his other leg looks wintry-pale and thin, like a sickly and etiolated plant. His hair is awry as usual and in both hands he is grasping his pasty, as yet untouched, as though afraid that someone is about to try and snatch it from him.

Amelia and I have not begun our pasties, either. They lie beside us, one on each end of the wooden bench, and we are both smiling. Amelia's mouth is curved up into a triumphant grin and the sun is glinting off her spectacles, while my smile is lop-sided and diffident and I seem to be looking over the photographer's right shoulder at something behind him.

Mother and Annie are on the left-hand side of the photograph, sitting on straight-backed kitchen chairs with their hands folded demurely in their laps. Their pasties are lying on a plate on the grass at their feet, and they too are smiling. Annie's smile is perhaps a little strained and pouting, as though she might be instructing Johnny on the correct use of her camera, but Mother's smile is bright and natural and I think that she looks quite beautiful.

In front of Mother and Annie, Diggory perches on a low wooden stool. He has his heavy work boots on which make his feet look disproportionately large, and his face is shaded by a flat cap, the peak pulled down over his forehead. The lower half of his face is almost entirely obscured by his pasty, from which he has just taken such an enormous bite that his cheeks bulge. Despite the age and the inadequacies of the snapshot, I am sure that I can still detect the elfin twinkle in his eyes.

On the other side of the photograph, the right-hand side, against a backdrop of spring daffodils, sits Mrs McCullen. She is in a heavy easy chair, well bolstered with cushions, which Diggory has carried out to the kitchen garden for her. However, most of the chair and most of her body are not visible, for both are obscured behind a pram. This is low and fat and black, squat like a toad, and its canopy is fringed with small shiny black beads strung on to silk, giving it the appearance of an oriental lampshade or the sort of evening shawl that wealthy widows wear to the opera or to dinner parties. The pram had been borrowed from a friend of Annie's and despite its age, which was considerable, it was both clean and serviceable.

Mrs McCullen's face, peeking from behind the pram, seems very pale beside its blackness and the darkness of her own hair. It is a slightly lined and weary face, for Phoebe's wailing throughout the night had left her tired. Nevertheless she is smiling, and there is something almost coy about the way her lips curve upwards, as though she and the photographer, at whom she seems to be looking directly, share some secret. Also she has raised one hand, her right hand, as if in greeting, although it could be a plea for omission or restraint.

It is impossible to discern whether the pram has a baby in it or not. Phoebe, lying within, probably still crying plaintively, is invisible.

Such was our lunchtime setting, and if I describe it in minuscule detail it is not merely because I have a photograph to prompt my memory, but because each moment of that lunch and afternoon is stamped into my mind: it is a sequence of events which I can neither forget nor ignore.

After the meal Diggory and Johnny had work to do about the farm and quickly excused themselves, while the rest of us lingered on over tea and Annie's cherry cake in the midday sunshine. Finally even Phoebe succumbed to the warmth and tranquillity, ceased her whining and fell asleep. Perhaps if she'd stayed awake, or perhaps if she hadn't worn out Mrs McCullen with her night-time crying, things might have been different. Perhaps, perhaps, perhaps . . .

As it was, when Annie suggested that we join her in a trip down to Gwithian village where she had promised to visit two aged and infirm ladies, only Mother and I agreed.

Mrs McCullen pleaded tiredness and the makings of a headache; she would rather doze in the kitchen garden, she told us, in this comfortable chair, with Phoebe sleeping peacefully, she hoped, in the pram beside her.

William and Amelia made disgruntled faces at the mention of visiting the old ladies.

'We were hoping to go to the cliff tops today,' William said.

'William has brought his paints,' Amelia added, by way of explanation. 'He wanted to paint a seascape, and I thought that he could have me sitting in the foreground, like a mermaid.'

'But do mermaids wear spectacles?' William enquired mischievously.

'And how about you, Caroline?' Annie asked. 'What do you want to do? Doze or paint or come with me? Or something else?'

'I'll come with you if I may, Annie,' I replied. It wasn't the old ladies or Gwithian village that attracted me, but the stretch of silver sand dunes which separated the village from the broad stretch of beach behind it. When Annie confirmed that the cottage of the two old ladies, Miss Felicity the elder and Miss Victoria the younger, did indeed back straight on to the dunes and that I would be free to go and play on them ('Why ever not, Caroline child?' she asked, smiling gaily), then I knew for certain that that was what I wished to do.

So, despite my trying to persuade Amelia and William that they would be missing a treat by not accompanying us, it was only Annie, Mother and I who went down to Gwithian.

Annie carried a basket, covered neatly with a clean white and red cloth, that contained not only a slab of her delicious cherry cake but also half a dozen eggs, freshly gathered from the barn and still smelling mustily of chicken feathers and straw, a small round pat of butter and a corked bottle of milk.

'Why Annie, you've become quite a little saint,' Mother declared teasingly, and Annie laughed and blushed prettily.

'We have so much food here at the farm,' she shrugged.

The thatched cottage of Miss Felicity and Miss Victoria, the former propped up on the sticks which enabled her to walk, the latter almost blind, and both of them obstinately deaf, was small and poky inside. Despite the bright spring weather, a feeling of decrepitude and decay clung about it like a bad smell. On the sitting-room windowsill was a jar of daffodils, the flowers petrified and bleached, the stems gradually disintegrating into the half-inch of scummy water still in the jar. Beside this were three dead flies, lying on their backs with their legs curled up amongst a scatter of fluff and dust: the patina of the disabled and the elderly.

Nevertheless, both the old ladies were delighted to see us. They greeted Annie with such grateful enthusiasm that it seemed as though she really were a saint, and they marvelled over me as though a child were a strange and quite wonderful phenomenon. But there was neither regret nor envy in their admiration of my youth: they had been there themselves and they knew that for me too it could one day end in dependence and infirmity.

Mother and Annie busied themselves about the cottage of Miss Felicity and Miss Victoria, Mother beating the dust out of an array of rugs, cushions, curtains and coverlets on the garden wall whilst Annie scrubbed and dusted and polished and generally put to rights inside. I walked along the narrow shaded path by the edge of the house, stepping carefully over the lost white bones of a dead bird, into the back garden.

Here it was wild with nettles and sorrel. Two climbing roses spread long thorny briars along the wall and the flowering blackcurrants had grown into exuberantly branching bushes. In the centre of one of these a thrush was sitting on its nest. But the back garden, for all its vigour and sunny freshness, could not hold me. I slipped through the gate and out on to the dunes.

Oh, that afternoon of spring freedom! It still sings brightly in my memory, despite the darkness which so soon succeeded it. Up there on the dunes I pulled off my shoes and socks and felt the fine silver sand, as soft and cool as silk beneath the glinting heat of the surface layer, pushing up between my toes. I bent down and lifted a handful of it, holding it high above my head and letting it trickle slowly but unstoppably through my fingers, as beautiful and transient as a dream.

I looked southward towards the blue and dancing sea, and then, quite suddenly, as though to surprise myself, looked away again and ran down the steep concave sides of a dune, a shallow bite in a hill topped with waving marram grass. As I ran I shouted and laughed out loud. It was a pure and wild exultation in both my youth and my freedom, and although I felt that Amelia and William were foolish to have missed the opportunity to be here with me and that they might regret it later, I was glad to be alone. I lay at the bottom of the sand dune where I had flopped after my wild descent, my socks and shoes abandoned at the top amongst the gently susurrating grass, and I stared up at the huge eternal sky. Above me a single gull was gliding through the air, pure and white against the blueness, graceful and apparently effortless, alone and free. I waved both my hands and my bare feet up at it.

'Hello, seagull!' I shouted up into the sky. 'Do you see me, seagull? Do you see that I can fly too?'

I scrambled back up the dune. It was tiring work which made me hot and sweaty and my calf muscles ached a little, but I knew that the effort was worth it for the pure joy of the descent. I paused briefly at the top, just long enough to look again at the sun sparkling on the sea. Then I turned and ran down again. With my arms flapping and the rush of my descent in my ears, it really did feel as though it could be flight.

We were back at the farm before five, and the beautiful spring day, that day of youth and freedom and flight, was cooling now, beginning to cast the long deep shadows of evening.

Mrs McCullen and Diggory met us at the farmyard gate and I shall never be able to forget the looks that were cast across those two faces, previously so dissimilar. No words of mine could adequately describe those two pairs of eyes, those two mouths, the set of the contours of their strained, pale faces. Fear, or perhaps an emotion closer to naked terror than simple fright, looked out of their eyes. And hope was there too, a desperate hope, however, a hope that anticipated hopelessness and was more of a pleading for mercy. Then there was the numbness of incredulity and also a bewilderment, the sort of bewilderment that made their faces crumple like pocket handkerchiefs. Phoebe McCullen had disappeared.

The story was simple. After Annie, Mother and I had left for our outing to Gwithian, Amelia and William had gone into the house to gather together their requirements for the afternoon: a rug, William's paints and sketchpad, a bottle of lemonade. They had come and said goodbye to Mrs McCullen, still sitting in the easy chair with Phoebe asleep in her pram, and then set off out of the farmyard towards the cliffs. With nobody near, Diggory busy about the farm, and Phoebe quiescent, Mrs McCullen had leaned back comfortably in the herb-scented warmth of the kitchen garden, and, already exhausted by a night of the baby's fretting, had fallen into the easy embrace of a deep sleep.

If Phoebe had awoken then and cried, surely Mrs McCullen would have awoken too. But Phoebe did not stir, and together mother and daughter slumbered on.

When Mrs McCullen did finally awake, perhaps after an hour, perhaps earlier, perhaps later, there was silence from the pram, and she assumed that little Phoebe, also exhausted from her querulous night, still slept.

Somewhat refreshed, Mrs McCullen only dozed lightly now, waking, sleeping, waking and sliding once again into the pearly-soft edges of sleep. From lowered eyelids she watched the birds around her, the blackbird bouncing along the edges of the garden bed, the thrush beating a tattoo with a hapless snail on a glinting block of granite. Basking in the sunlit warmth, she felt the true, deep satisfaction of peace. She kept saying to herself that soon, soon she must wake Phoebe; if the baby slept for too long now she would surely not sleep later, and besides she would wake up hungry and irritable. But the honeyed peace seduced Mrs McCullen and she remained dozing in her chair.

Diggory came into the kitchen garden, his boots clattering on the flagstones, and he stretched his back and sighed. Two of the calves were scouring now and it would surely spread to the others. He asked Mrs McCullen if she would care for a cup of tea; but she would not trouble a man with such a task, especially a man with the worries of livestock on his mind.

'I'll make you a cup of tea, Diggory,' Mrs McCullen suggested. 'And surely Johnny would take one too? But first I must wake Phoebe and feed her, otherwise she's sure to cry.'

Diggory smiled his agreement and thanks.

'I'll get your little girl out of the pram for you,' he offered, crossing from where he leant against the sun-warmed kitchen wall to the squat black pram, no more than three or four feet from Mrs McCullen. Diggory's voice, usually low, calm, self-assured, softly Cornish, sounded surprised and high and scared then.

'But Mrs McCullen,' he had said, 'Phoebe's not in here. The pram is empty.'

Although Phoebe could not, of course, get out of the

206

pram by herself, could not walk, or even stand, they searched for her in all the most likely, and unlikely, places. They searched not only the kitchen garden, but the farmhouse, the farmyard and all the barns and sheds. They asked Johnny if he knew of Phoebe's whereabouts. They asked if he had touched or seen her, and Johnny stopped repairing the fence around the paddock and helped them search. They summoned Old Roderick, Diggory's ancient friend and mentor who helped out on the farm at busy times, from his ramshackle cottage three fields down, but although he scratched his head and thought, he could not help either. No sign of little Phoebe McCullen was found and nobody knew where to look.

'I know,' Diggory had said. 'Annie must have taken her along to Gwithian to see Miss Victoria and Miss Felicity. You know how old ladies dote on babies.' But Phoebe was not, of course, with us.

The five of us stood in silent perplexity. 'I know,' Mother said brightly. 'Amelia and William will have taken her on their sketching outing to the cliff top.' My heart sank a little when she said this, so hopefully, so reassuringly. I was afraid that she might be right and the thought gave me little comfort.

William and Amelia returned less than half an hour after us. They had both caught the sun on their faces: their cheeks were flushed pink and their eyes blazed with sea-air vitality. William carried a large bag over his shoulder and Mother snatched it from him, as though it might contain his little sister, and emptied it on the floor of the farmhouse hall. The contents of the bag fell out in a disorderly jumble: paints, sketchbook, brushes, an empty bottle which had contained lemonade, the tartan rug and . . . one knitted baby's bootee. Mother seized this like a trophy.

'Where did you get this from?' she shouted, shaking it wildly in front of Amelia's and William's startled faces, and they cowered away from her as though she had gone mad.

'I don't know,' William replied hesitantly. 'It's one of Phoebe's bootees. Perhaps it was wrapped up in the rug.'

'Yes, William's right,' agreed Amelia. 'I saw it wrapped up in the rug when we took it out on the cliff.' Amelia's voice was breathily nervous.

'On the cliff . . .' began Mother, her voice slow, too slow, too terrifying.

'Yes,' said Amelia. 'On the cliff.' There was a brief pause. 'But what's wrong with you all?' she asked with fear in her voice. 'What's happened? Why are you looking at us like that?'

Before Mother could answer, Amelia, cool-headed, sensible Amelia, had burst into tears. Annie put her arms around her and looked reprovingly at Mother. 'Don't,' she said. 'Don't even think about it. They wouldn't have hurt a hair of that poor baby, I'm sure.'

Some policemen came to the farm and an elderly, silver-haired doctor who gave Mrs McCullen a sedative and said she should go to bed. The policemen were tall and serious, just like the ones we'd met on the road to Father's grave. The tallest, most serious officer took notes in a book with a dark blue cover, but Amelia and William and I weren't questioned. We were sent up to bed and told by Mother, in a harsh and worried whisper, to be good.

'What did you and William do with Phoebe?' I whispered across the bedroom to Amelia, a motionless mound in the bed next to mine. The darkness made me braver than I had thought possible, but still my heart beat uncomfortably in my chest as though my ribs were constricting it, and my hands, damp with sweat, were bunched into tight fists.

'We never did anything with Phoebe,' Amelia replied and, despite the smallness of the bedroom, her voice seemed lost and tiny and fragile. There was a pause, and the previous night this pause would have been filled by Phoebe's peevish wailing. This night,

208

the silence was as heavy and complete as an accusation.

Amelia spoke again, and now her voice was sure and firm. It had refound its accustomed confident ring. 'We never did anything with Phoebe,' Amelia repeated. 'We never touched Phoebe at all, Caroline. Make sure you don't forget that.'

The policemen interviewed two groups of gypsies, one camped near St Erth and one near Marazion. At one point they thought they had discovered something which would bring delight and relief to Mrs McCullen, for they heard dismal crying coming from inside a caravan that the gypsies claimed was empty. The policemen forced an entry, but all that they found was a cardboard box containing three kittens, nothing more than skin and bone, mewling piteously against their starvation.

The policemen interviewed landowners, farmers and villagers from miles around. They checked hotels and inns for possible abductors, and they posted notices in police stations across the county and had them printed in the newspapers. But no sign of Phoebe was found, and the faces of Diggory, of Annie, of Mother, of Mrs McCullen were graver and older than I had ever seen them.

It was about a week later that the crew of a St Ives fishing smack, the *Molly Jane*, caught the body of a child, no more than a baby, in its nets. It was a girl, less than a year old the policemen reckoned, but probably older than six months. Any positive identification was impossible, for the little body was naked and the face disfigured beyond recognition. From the wounds on her face and other injuries on her body, it was assumed that the child had probably fallen from a great height before ending up in the sea.

The body was buried, without name and without mourners, in a discreet corner of a cemetery just outside St Ives. Although the policemen never admitted it, I am sure that they thought she was Phoebe, for their searches tailed off soon afterwards.

'We can't do any more,' they told the adults. 'We've done everything we can. You've got to try and go on with your lives. You've got to try and forget about little Phoebe McCullen.'

Chapter Sixteen

It was strange and rather horrible how easy it was, once back in our own home in Tredannick Close, to allow our lives to slip back into the regular groove that gave them the semblance, at least, of normality. But there were, nevertheless, still differences. It seemed to me that the disappearance of little Phoebe McCullen had robbed Amelia and me, and William also, of whatever was left of the easy acceptances of our childhood. The attitude of Mother towards us also changed. She began giving me more responsibility and sometimes, just occasionally, she snapped at Amelia in a way that she had never done before. Sometimes I saw her watching Amelia consideringly and I would shudder and look away, unwilling to try and contemplate what her thoughts might be.

Mrs McCullen and William did not stay in Truro for long. They moved quietly back up to those distant parts from which they had originally come, returning voluntarily to Stonehaven, to the nervous hands and the hard, hurting fists of Mr McCullen. When they left, Mother nodded to herself.

'I think it's for the best,' she said. 'Don't you, Amelia?' But Amelia only grunted in reply.

After the McCullens had gone, the house across the street looked forlorn and sad for a while, lonely in its emptiness, but not for long. A young newly-married couple, Mr and Mrs Rawlinson, moved in. They replaced the sagging wooden gate with one of wrought iron painted shiny black and, at weekends, Mr Rawlinson would drape his jacket over it as he dug the garden, industriously planting rows of leeks and carrots and other staid and sensible vegetables. Life moved on.

Life moved on and Amelia took and passed exams with ever-increasing skill. As she progressed up the high school her grades and percentages rose with her, and she became quiet and studious. Her new spectacles from Mr Quigley were owly-round and intellectual, and the lenses seemed to accentuate the intelligent glitter of her eyes. She went up to Cambridge to read law and when she came home in the vacations of her first year she brought a case of thick and tedious books with her each time. She would sit in the living-room and read them avidly rather than talk with Mother and me. Her visits to Tredannick Close thereafter became more and more sporadic and Mother and I, although maybe slightly offended, understood. The temptation to return to us in Truro was not as enticing as those things which kept her up in Cambridge; we simply could not compete.

Amelia did brilliantly at Cambridge, and she moved up the ranks of the legal profession with a certainty that surprised nobody, least of all herself. Before long she had her own practice in London, based in a plush suite of offices off St James's Square. She took on celebrated cases of the famous and the infamous, and when I once visited her at her work I was intimidated by the high, ornately corniced ceilings, the uncomfortable leather button-backed chairs, and by her personal assistant, a young man with a moustache and a silk bow tie called Timothy Monkton-Harris.

Amelia took to championing particular causes: the rights of women, abortion, education. Her name appeared with increasing frequency in the more serious-minded newspapers and she was invited by all kinds of interested bodies to speak, debate, or to join their ranks in some elevated honorary position. She bought her large centrally-heated flat in Highgate, not far from Parliament Hill, and then she purchased her retreat, a fully modernized cottage on the Isle of Wight.

212

She was well-respected, wealthy and aloof. At one point, the gossip columns became mildly interested in her and tried, unsuccessfully, to interview mother and me. They described Amelia as brilliant and ruthless, and they asked unpleasantly why she had never married.

Meanwhile, in Cornwall, Mother had remarried. Just as Amelia had predicted, all those long years before, she succumbed to the bright eyes, large nose and booming laugh of Geoffrey Quigley the optician. The house in Tredannick Close was sold and she moved into his considerably smarter residence on Lemon Street. I was glad that she was happy, and I was glad to share my wonderful mother with Mr Quigley and his three children, one of whom, the son – for the pretty daughters had long since married – still lived with his father despite being quite grown-up and working in the bank.

And I? I, always the antithesis of Amelia, took up employment in a milliner's small establishment in Truro, serving behind the counter and pinning the gauze, netting and artificial flowers on to the stupendous, flamboyant creations of my employer. The milliner was located not far from the shop of Mr Mayberry the fishmonger and, in time, I met Harold, Mr Mayberry's son, who now worked for his father. He was my twin angel from the Nativity-play chorus of my youth, second row from the back, fourth from the left.

Our courtship was a matter of months and our wedding was small and quiet. Mother, Mr Quigley, Mr Mayberry, Amelia, Annie and Diggory were our only guests. To Amelia's disgust, and presumably Mother's also, although she never admitted to it, the Mayberrys were Christians. Eventually I felt that I understood Harold's belief; I respected his faith and wanted to share it. It was a lifeline during grief, a ray of hope during the darkness of despair. I wished that I had known and understood earlier, and, at the first opportunity, I was baptized and joined the Church. But still I was too afraid of Amelia's disparagement to tell her of my conversion, my infidelity to our once-shared hate of the cathedral. When my son Billy was born, I didn't invite Amelia to his christening.

Billy grew up and left home. He went to New Zealand to seek his fortune. The years passed. Harold became ill and died, and although I was sad, I was also glad when he was dead for his last months had been full of pain and misery. Some two or three months after Harold's death, Mr Quigley collapsed and died in the street near the cathedral, not far from where Father had died so many years before. I moved in with Mother then, and cared for her through her brief, sickly period of elderly widowhood, cheated out of not one husband, but two, and petulantly irritable that her favourite daughter, the brilliant Amelia, was far away. She became what is popularly termed senile, and had long conversations with herself about how selfishly and inconsiderately Amelia was behaving. Occasionally, when she was at her most restless, she would talk of babies and bootees, cliff tops and death, murder and, more often, guilt. I held her hands as she raved and tried to soothe her. She spoke to my father too, and Mr Quigley, and it was less than a year after the latter's death that she died, apparently without pain, in her sleep.

Amelia came to Cornwall for the funeral and she suggested to me that I should move up to London. She told me that she would buy me a small flat, quite close to her own home, and she would, as she put it, 'be able to keep an eye on me'.

'Surely that's Billy's duty,' I protested. 'He is my only son after all.' But Amelia only laughed.

'Come now, Caroline, he's on the other side of the world, and besides, he's young. You can't want to drag him prematurely into middle age, can you? And where would you prefer to move to? London or New Zealand?'

So I moved up to London and Amelia installed me in

a compact flat in Tufnell Park. She did, as she had said she would, keep an eye on me, calling in on me regularly on Sunday evenings (and I wondered if she could detect the taint of Christian ignorance, smelling it on my breath like alcohol, for I attended my local church every Sunday morning), telephoning me at least once during the week and often inviting me along to her dinner parties.

I avoided these occasions if I could, for they were formal and smart affairs, and Amelia's guests were intelligent and viciously witty. They terrified me with their sarcasm and their refined politeness, and I used to cower in Amelia's kitchen. This refuge was itself terrifying, all shining and clean and bristling with the latest technical gadgetry, and the glittering array of glass and chinaware was of the best and most expensive. Nevertheless, hiding in the kitchen was better than having to demonstrate my foolishness and inadequacy at the dinner table.

And the McCullens? After they had left Truro for Stonehaven it appeared that they had, more or less, vanished from our lives. But when Amelia came to Truro for my wedding to Harold, she showed me a clipping from a colour supplement from one of the quality Sunday newspapers. The journalist described the life of a William McCullen who had founded a retreat, something like a sanctuary, for young offenders normally incarcerated in institutions. The retreat was based on a small windswept island off the north-west coast of Scotland that this William McCullen owned. It offered, so the article said, a chance for peace, recuperation and reflection for the troubled and guilty soul.

'Surely that can't be *our* William McCullen,' I had said with awe and Amelia had smiled, a knowing and slightly sardonic smile.

'Turn over,' she suggested. On the next page was his photograph, red hair all awry, bright eyes sparkling with intelligent merriment.

And then, and it had been at the least mentioned in nearly all the papers, William McCullen had died. He had killed himself. From the highest cliff on his island retreat, his refuge for peace, recuperation and reflection for the troubled and guilty soul, he had hurled himself, completely naked despite the time of year, into the cold Scottish sea. And not one paper that I saw offered an explanation.

It was Amelia's idea that we attend the funeral for William – it was to be in his birthplace – and we travelled up on the train via Glasgow. We arrived in Stonehaven in the late evening and took a taxi to the hotel overlooking the sea, where Amelia had made our reservations.

Stonehaven was cold and rainy that November night, with a brisk wind blowing in off the sea. The following day dawned grey and chilly, although the rain had stopped, and even from our hotel we could hear the noise of the waves on the beach, grinding the pebbles together. It was a hard and unforgiving sound, and despite my Damart underwear I shivered. Even as a child gazing at Stonehaven in the atlas, Amelia pointing it out to me as she sprawled on the rug on the living-room floor, I had thought that the sea around Stonehaven looked particularly cold and forbidding. No polar bears, however: even I knew that now.

Amelia and I took a brisk walk on the beach that morning, wrapped up in our coats and scarves. Amelia was unusually silent and withdrawn, as though her enveloping clothes kept her in isolation, but she paused once and listened briefly to the suck and roar of the sea on the stones.

'That sounds like the McCullens' voices,' I thought I heard her murmur.

Just one row of buildings separated the sea front at Stonehaven from the main street, and after our beach walk we wandered back through the town. It seemed curiously old-fashioned to me, and it reminded me of my childhood. We stopped in a timeless teashop, ourselves the only customers, and had milky tea and homemade Empire biscuits.

The funeral service for William took place that afternoon, and the church was crowded. Many of the congregation looked no more than teenagers; they had a nervously defiant air, and I wondered if these were the young offenders that William had made his life's work. While this contingent stood in grim and silent rows, the older mourners held muttered conversations.

'Tragic,' I head them saying. 'Such a waste. So tragic.'

The minister spoke of William at length and his voice was full and sincere. He described William as a truly forgiving man with enormous kindness of spirit, as an exemplary Christian visionary whose gifts to the world had touched the hearts and souls of thousands. Out of the corner of my eye I saw Amelia, standing stiffly beside me, frowning at this description. Was this William? William McCullen? The William McCullen of our childhood?

'Who knows,' the minister intoned, 'what drove William McCullen to this last sad and desperate act? Only God will know the answer and only God can provide the forgiveness for which we and William now seek. Let us pray.'

As I bent my head, I saw that Amelia, staring ahead, refusing to follow ignorant Christian instructions, had stopped frowning. Her lips had twitched up into a grim smile, as though the minister had made some private, ironic joke.

William's body was buried in the graveyard of St Mary of the Storms, less than a mile up the coast from Stonehaven. It perched on a cliff top; the endless grey sea, shining with November chill, lay below. Inside the stolid walls of the graveyard was the ruin of a chapel or a church, and all around ancient weathered tomb- stones tilted at hectic angles.

The few more recent graves were towards the

seaward side. William's coffin was lowered into a grave not far from that of his mother and father, who, so it seemed from their shared stone, had died within days of each other some three years previously. Amelia saw me looking towards their memorial.

'A road accident,' she hissed. 'Mr McCullen lingered on for a day or two in hospital.' It didn't cross my mind to ask her how she knew.

Afterwards the mourners straggled in a slow black line up the slope towards the car park of the nearby golf course. There was the sound of an iron hitting hard against a ball, and I felt annoyed. It seemed so irreverent to be playing golf on this cold, November, funerary day.

Amelia lingered for a while beside William's grave, and I stood beside her quietly.

'I wanted to show you something,' she said, 'now that all the others have gone,' and she gestured towards where the last mourners were disappearing on to the road. Then she walked towards the wall which lay behind the McCullens' burial plots, and I followed. There was a rectangle of clean white marble set into the wall. Amelia looked from me to this plaque and then to me again, and I read the engraved words aloud, my voice slow and careful.

'*In memory of my sister, Phoebe Alexandra Louise McCullen, who tragically died before I ever knew her*', the first line read. There was a gap before the next two lines and I paused briefly and licked my lips. They had become dry and cracked in the cold salty air.

'*Like as the waves make towards the pebbled shore,*
So do our minutes hasten to their end.'

I had not read these words for so long that seeing them now sent my mind spinning backwards in time. I could see Mother's shining eyes and hear the delighted claps and cheers of Annie, Amelia and William. I paused again after these two lines, once so familiar to me, and I could feel that my eyes were awash with tears of unwilling realization. I blinked them away.

218

There was another gap on the plaque before the final line. I read it slowly and tremulously.

'Suffer the little children to come unto me.'

Amelia and I walked back towards Stonehaven along the coast path. We stopped at one point and rested on a bench that overlooked the sea. The bench was cold and it was made of thin pieces of metal. It reminded me of a skeleton.

'I wonder what they will choose to write on William's headstone,' I said, breaking the silence which had fallen between us since I had read out the memorial plaque to Phoebe McCullen.

'I've spoken to the executors of his will,' Amelia replied, 'and I think that they will take up my suggestion.

William McCullen, born in Stonehaven; lived in truth; died in innocence.'

My mind went whirling backwards again, and I pressed my back against the hardness of the seat to stop myself feeling dizzy. I could barely hear what Amelia said next; she spoke more to the sea before us and to herself than to me.

'He did live in truth,' she said. 'He did die in innocence.'

Postscript

Annie and Diggory Pollard died together in a fire as old, old people. Diggory was ninety-eight, Annie was ninety-six, and the fire had engulfed the retirement home in which they lived. Four other old people died in the same blaze. I went to the funeral of Annie and Diggory in Cornwall, the cremation of what hadn't already been cremated, but Amelia refused to come with me. She said that she was much too busy, and besides, after William's burial in Stonehaven she'd had enough of funerals for a while. Perhaps they reminded her of her own mortality.

After the funeral I went down to St Ives. The narrow winding streets were full of holiday-makers: children carrying garish buckets and spades, fat middle-aged couples with Birmingham accents licking ice-cream cones as they strolled; strident over-confident teen-agers in Bermuda shorts, calling out to each other and pushing aggressively as they headed down towards the harbour. But I was going beyond the town, beyond the glare and blare of the amusement arcades and the ghetto blasters.

The cemetery was quiet and a little run-down. An elderly lady, who was sitting enjoying the sun in her nearby garden, told me that nobody had been buried there for fifteen years.

'They all get cremated these days,' she said. 'Cheaper, I suppose, and perhaps they don't like the idea of being eaten by worms.' She was a sprightly old lady with a twinkle in her eye. 'I don't mind either way,' she said. 'Once you're dead, you're dead. No need to be sentimental about an old corpse.'

She told me about a couple, perhaps a man and wife, who had been the last ones to have any work carried out in the graveyard. Ten years ago they had erected a white marble tombstone over a small and long-neglected grave. My heart quickened as she spoke and I wanted to hear more, to have confirmed what I was sure I already knew.

'What did they look like?' I asked her.

'A funny couple,' she said vaguely. 'It was a few years back now, mind. But I remember them because the lady at least didn't look at all like the sentimental type.'

I went into the cemetery then and although I had never been there before, for none of us had been to the funeral of that baby girl trawled from the sea in the nets of the *Molly Jane*, I knew exactly what I was looking for. A little grave in the most shady, forgotten corner of the graveyard.

Although the small white marble stone was much newer than the grave it was already overgrown, lost amongst long grass and brambles. I had to bend and pull up handfuls of weeds before I was able to read the three lines of words that I already knew I would find engraved there.

'Like as the waves make towards the pebbled shore,
So do our minutes hasten to their end'

read the first two lines, and then there was a gap. And then that final line. The line that was now so familiar to me.

'Suffer the little children to come unto me.'

THE END

Shining Agnes
by Sara Banerji

'A delightful tale . . . blackly comic'
Philippa Logan, *Oxford Times*

In a once great, now falling, mansion live an aristocratic
family: Alice, huge, sad and longing for love; her
paralysed mother who is subject to wild and eccentric
enthusiasms; and the foster child Agnes, whose desire to
be an actress sets in motion a train of bizarre and
horrifying events.

Then love comes to Alice in the form of the beautiful but
furtive Vincent who has moved in next door. But does he
want Alice for herself or for the treasure that she digs from
the rubble of her tumbled home? And how does he view
Alice's obsession with compost, the making of which she
compares to the growth of spirituality and the purging
away of sin?

Black comedy lurks beneath the surface of this gloriously
imaginative new novel from the author of
Cobwebwalking, The Wedding of Jayanthi Mandel and
The Tea-Planter's Daughter.

'A novel as robust and muscular as Alice herself, and as
rich, dark and fertile as her compost'
Christopher Potter, *The Listener*

'Banerji's writing has the darkness of Muriel Spark and
the grace of Alice Thomas Ellis'
Clare Boylan, *Sunday Times*

0 552 99459 6

BLACK SWAN

Zig Zag
by Lucy Robertson

As teenagers, Zag and her adored older brother, Ziggy, visit Kenya to spend a few months as guests of Ziggy's friend Marsdon. Marsdon's parents own a tea plantation, and Zag and Ziggy find themselves part of a colonial expatriate élite. Zag, whose austere upbringing by her repressive guardian, Aunt Bernice, has led her to believe she is plain and inadequate, finds comfort in the kitchen with the native servants, while Ziggy, her golden hero, falls under the spell of beautiful Arabella, a fellow guest.

Zag's tentative efforts to make friends across the great divide of class and race lead to scandal and a kind of exile on the coast at Malindi – where it is Ziggy's turn to step beyond the pale . . .

Lucy Robertson's darkly funny story of love in all its guises has a devastating twist in its tail. A gimlet-eyed observer of the results of kicked-over traces, she is a new writer of exceptional, and exciting, ability.

'I liked Lucy Robertson's sparkling writing, and the witty originality and dry observation of the characters in ZIG ZAG appealed to me greatly'
Sara Banerji

'A remarkable talent . . . I admired the exuberance of her style'
Hilary Mantel

0 552 99483 9

BLACK SWAN

A SELECTED LIST OF OTHER BLACK SWAN TITLES

☐	99198 8	THE HOUSE OF THE SPIRITS	Isabel Allende	£6.99
☐	99313 1	OF LOVE AND SHADOWS	Isabel Allende	£5.99
☐	99248 8	THE DONE THING	Patricia Angadi	£4.99
☐	99201 1	THE GOVERNESS	Patricia Angadi	£3.99
☐	99385 9	SINS OF THE MOTHERS	Patricia Angadi	£3.99
☐	99489 8	TURNING THE TURTLE	Patricia Angadi	£5.99
☐	99459 6	SHINING AGNES	Sara Banerji	£4.99
☐	99498 7	ABSOLUTE HUSH	Sara Banerji	£4.99
☐	99537 1	GUPPIES FOR TEA	Marika Cobbold	£4.99
☐	99508 8	FIREDRAKE'S EYE	Patricia Finney	£5.99
☐	99558 4	THERE'S ROSEMARY, THERE'S RUE	Lady Fortescue	£5.99
☐	99557 6	SUNSET HOUSE	Lady Fortescue	£5.99
☐	99488 X	SUGAR CAGE	Connie May Fowler	£5.99
☐	99467 7	MONSIEUR DE BRILLANCOURT	Clare Harkness	£4.99
☐	99387 5	TIME OF GRACE	Clare Harkness	£4.99
☐	99447 2	MAMMY'S BOY	Domini Highsmith	£5.99
☐	99480 4	MAMA	Terry McMillan	£5.99
☐	99449 9	DISAPPEARING ACTS	Terry McMillan	£5.99
☐	99481 2	SIDE BY SIDE	Isabel Miller	£4.99
☐	99483 9	ZIG ZAG	Lucy Robertson	£4.99
☐	99506 1	BETWEEN FRIENDS	Kathleen Rowntree	£5.99
☐	99414 6	FLIES	Sadie Smith	£4.99
☐	99439 1	DOSH	Sadie Smith	£4.99
☐	99529 0	OUT OF THE SHADOWS	Titia Sutherland	£5.99
☐	99460 X	THE FIFTH SUMMER	Titia Sutherland	£5.99
☐	99494 4	THE CHOIR	Joanna Trollope	£5.99
☐	99410 3	A VILLAGE AFFAIR	Joanna Trollope	£5.99
☐	99442 1	A PASSIONATE MAN	Joanna Trollope	£5.99
☐	99470 7	THE RECTOR'S WIFE	Joanna Trollope	£5.99
☐	99492 8	THE MEN AND THE GIRLS	Joanna Trollope	£5.99
☐	99082 5	JUMPING THE QUEUE	Mary Wesley	£4.99
☐	99210 0	HARNESSING PEACOCKS	Mary Wesley	£5.99
☐	99304 2	NOT THAT SORT OF GIRL	Mary Wesley	£5.99
☐	99355 7	SECOND FIDDLE	Mary Wesley	£5.99
☐	99393 X	A SENSIBLE LIFE	Mary Wesley	£5.99
☐	99258 5	THE VACILLATIONS OF POPPY CAREW	Mary Wesley	£5.99
☐	99126 0	THE CAMOMILE LAWN	Mary Wesley	£5.99
☐	99495 2	A DUBIOUS LEGACY	Mary Wesley	£5.99